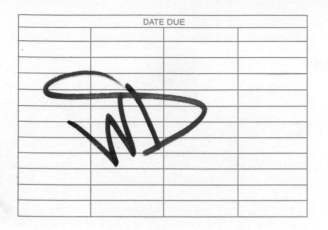

Jason & Kyra

DANA DAVIDSON

JUMP AT THE SUN

HYPERION PAPERBACKS
NEW YORK

First Hyperion Paperback edition, 2005
3 5 7 9 10 8 6 4 2

Printed in the United States of America
ISBN 0-7868-3653-9
Library of Congress Cataloging-in-Publication Data on file.

Visit www.hyperionteens.com

To every reader
who opens the cover
and turns the pages,
thank you

1

The late-model black Volvo pulled up in front of Cross High School. Its leather interior was carefully maintained and had the warm, pleasant scent of the expensive oil used to treat it. The street was packed with other parents' cars depositing their children in front of the school and students crossing Second Avenue toward the school's main entrance. Jason shifted his backpack from the floor of the car to his lap, preparing to leave the vehicle.

"Don't come home with any crap, either, Jay," said Michael Vincent to his sixteen-year-old son. The senior systems analyst for a small but wealthy engineering firm, Mr. Vincent was dressed in a beautifully tailored charcoal-gray suit. He was the only black male in upper management. That, plus the pressure of the job, kept him working long and late hours frequently. His handsome face was entirely composed, and his eyes followed the flow of traffic and teenagers in front of his car.

Jason sat looking straight ahead, his jaw tight. The familiar hot, churning anger began filling the pit of his stomach.

"Did you hear me? Answer me when I speak! Don't come home with any crap, Jay."

"I won't," Jason said. He turned then, and looked into his father's eyes, so much like his own.

"Well, what are you waiting on?" Mr. Vincent asked nonchalantly. Just then Jason wanted to walk out of the car and never return. Ever.

Jason shoved out of the car, lifted his bag onto his shoulder, and joined the flow of Cross High students heading in for the first day of school. The warm late August morning air hit his face, and he took one deep breath, trying to fan his father's words and manner from his mind.

"Crap" to Jason's father was any request or complaint that interfered with his comfort. This time the "crap" was Jason's inquiry into when he'd be able to pick up his car. It had been in the shop for a week now. Michael Vincent had assured his son a week ago that if Jason paid for the bulk of the repairs himself, $200, he would cover the rest, $75. Mr. Vincent felt it imperative that Jason learned to make his own way. Of course, Mr. Vincent had been in a better mood then. Now Jason was out $200 and had no ride. He'd have to put up with his father's changing moods first thing in the morning, indefinitely.

Badass start to the day, he thought.

"What's up, Jay?" someone said from behind him. It was Greg Hoover, Jason's best friend and the center guard on the Cross basketball team. At six feet four and 200 pounds, and with the grace and speed of a gazelle, Greg was a serious force on the court.

"What's up, Greg?" Jason said, giving him a play. Jason tried to push thoughts of his father from his mind as he greeted his friend. Mind over matter, he reminded himself. "You ready for this?" Jason asked, referring to the new school year.

"Hell no, man. I'm still feeling this summer vacation. I've been working forty hours a week for my uncle's landscaping company. The money was so good! I hate to give that up."

"I hear you. I called myself making a little something up at Carla's CDs."

"A little something! Please! Jay, I'm not even hearing that. You were making much money up there. All the honeys coming up to Carla's CDs just to get up in your face? And you were commission and hourly? Please, I know you were getting paid! Ain't that many CDs and cassettes in the world, but that place stayed packed when you worked," Greg countered, grinning at his teammate and friend.

Jason just smiled, and he and Greg moved on through the halls. At six feet even, well muscled, with broad shoulders, a tapered waist, and long, strong legs, Jason could easily turn heads. Added to that, his face was traffic-stoppin' fine. He and Greg went up two flights of stairs to their lockers on the third floor, front hall of the school.

When Jason cleared the last steps to the third floor he looked up and saw his girlfriend, Lisa, standing near their lockers along with her best friend, Jackie. Lisa was, quite simply, gorgeous. Her skin was golden light brown, perfectly smooth and clear. She had large gray eyes, thin nose and lips, and naturally reddish-brown hair that she wore just past her shoulders. It was permed and cut into the latest sleek and shiny style. Plus, she knew how to dress to show off her curves. All the guys wanted her, and she knew it and liked it. She had a bit of a big head, but most would say that she wore even that well. Jason wasn't so sure. She and Jason had been together for nearly a year.

Lisa smiled when she saw Jason come up the stairs.

"Hey, Jason," she said.

"Hey, Lisa. What's up, Jackie? How you doing?" He took Lisa into his arms for a hug.

"Better now," she said, hugging him back. She felt soft and smelled lightly of something flowery and expensive. Greg and Jackie started talking to a few kids who stood nearby. "My mama is getting on my last damned nerve."

"Yeah?" Jason said as he let her go. He backed away from her and started twirling the combination of his lock. "What happened this time?" he asked, careful to keep the slight air of boredom out of his voice. Her mother owned a chain of nursery schools and her father was a financial consultant. Between the two of them they worked around 130 hours a week. That didn't leave much time for Lisa. So Lisa picked fights with them. Lisa and her parents always argued over the same three things: money, Lisa's grades, or Lisa's smart mouth. Sometimes that tripped Jason out— Lisa was always provoking her folks, while he tried to avoid fighting with his father.

"She knows that today is a half-day. She knows that we all go out and do something on a half-day. I ask her for twenty dollars and she acts like I'm asking for her damned left arm." And the answer, Bob? Jason thought sarcastically— money! Tell the man what he's won!

"So you're broke?" Jason asked.

"No," Lisa said, smirking at Jason. "I've got thirty dollars, I just wanted some more money."

"Well, I'm gonna go on to class. I'll meet you back here at noon," Jason said, trying to stifle his irritation.

"All right. When will your car be fixed?" Lisa asked.

"I don't know. I've got to go, Lisa. I'll see you," Jason said and moved on, glad to leave. On the one hand, he was into her. She could be funny, loyal, and sexy. On the other hand, she just got on his nerves sometimes with the way she antagonized her parents, blew off school, and could be a real snob when she wanted.

He walked around the corner of third floor and entered room 303, his homeroom. After fifteen minutes of filling out cards and speaking to his people, Jason was on his way. Like the rest of the Cross student body, today Jason would follow an abbreviated version of his schedule for the semester.

First hour was chemistry, straight-up boring. Second hour was French 5. Jason actually loved French, but he'd rather be shot than admit it to his crew. In French class he saw a few associates from his last two years of high school, and that was cool. Third hour was AP English. Mrs. Devon was known for being a real hard-ass. He walked into class about two minutes before the tardy bell and took a seat in the back. His friends had been ragging on him for bothering with an Advanced Placement English class. He just blew them off. He liked writing and thinking about novels and poems and discovering their themes. Even the boring ones had one or two points worth either considering or arguing against. He didn't even bother showing people his essays. He nearly always got A's.

The AP classes were usually small, and this one would apparently be no different. About fifteen students milled around, getting reacquainted. Most classes at Cross had thirty to thirty-three students. Jason knew most of the kids from seeing them in the hallway, and about half from previous honors English or French classes. He had just finished calling "What's up?" to everyone and settling into his seat when the bell rang.

"Well, let's get started," Mrs. Devon began.

Before Mrs. Devon got a chance to get into her little speech, the door to her classroom flew open, and Kyra Evans strode into class. She glanced around the room and smiled at a few people directly.

"How very generous of you to take the time to attend my class, Miss . . ." Mrs. Devon's voice dripped sarcasm. ". . . Kyra Evans." Mrs. Devon completed her sentence as Kyra handed her the hall pass she carried. Mrs. Devon peered at Kyra pointedly after she read her name.

"I'm sorry, I had a conference with Mr. Hillard." Kyra took a seat toward the front of the class. Jason watched as she sat down and folded her long, slender legs. Extremely faded, loose-fitting Levi's were held to her waist by a black leather belt. She wore a plain white T-shirt, with sleeves folded to expose well-toned brown arms. On her feet she wore a pair of expensive, earthy, black leather sandals. He was pretty certain that even in a school of twenty-eight hundred students, like Cross, no one else had a pair of shoes like those. They weren't exactly the *in* style.

Her features were lovely. Now, that wasn't a word that he'd usually think to use, and most definitely not one he'd say aloud. But it fit her, he decided. Her almond-shaped eyes were huge and dark brown, with thick, dark lashes framing them. Her cheekbones were high, her nose slim, and her lips looked soft. Her teeth were bright and even, and she had an easy smile. Her hair was long, thick, and wooly. She nearly always wore it in natural braids, no extensions, which lay between her shoulder blades. Shells and beads decorated only a few braids. Her hair was what pretty much everyone called nappy, but Jason suspected it was soft. He couldn't explain why, since it was nothing like anything he had been taught was beautiful, but he'd wanted to touch it since he first saw her in ninth grade.

She was on the fringes though, most definitely. It was a combination of things that put her there. It was her hair, her clothes, her brains, even the way that she carried herself. She had a lot of poise and confidence—not cockiness, but confidence. She was just a little *too* different. But what nailed the coffin shut was the fact that she obviously didn't care.

She turned slightly as she bent down to retrieve the spiral from her backpack. When she did he caught her eye and nodded. He'd meant to smile, but he hadn't done it. She nodded slightly in return.

The rest of the class passed uneventfully. Mrs. Devon passed out the class syllabus, embarrassed a couple of people, took attendance, had the students complete class registration forms, and dismissed the class after the bell.

Before noon the school day was over. Jason met his crew outside the school in the student parking lot. Half a dozen vehicles had their windows wide open and their music blaring. Students milled around talking to one another, and a warm August sun shone in the clear blue sky. Lisa stood beside Jason with Jackie on her other side. A jam was playing on the radio, and Lisa and Jackie bobbed their heads in time to the beat. Lisa came around and stood in front of Jason. Her head still bobbing to the bass, she gently swayed from side to side as she put her arms around his waist. She tilted her head backward, and Jason could tell by her eyes and lips that she wanted a kiss. Hell, she bugged him sometimes, but he cared for her, and he for sure wanted her.

He kissed her softly and briefly. As he lifted his head and opened his eyes he saw Kyra Evans directly ahead of him in the parking lot. She didn't notice him. She was circling around her car and pulling her keys out of a side pocket of her backpack. She was laughing at something her friend, a girl, was saying. He recognized her friend as a star on the track team. Jason was caught by how relaxed and genuinely happy Kyra seemed to be.

He wanted to be that happy.

"Well, let's get on up outta here," Greg said, interrupting Jason's thoughts. Greg and Tommie, a middle-distance runner on the Cross track team, stood beside Greg's gray Ford Escort.

"Where to?" Jackie wanted to know.

"Let's hit The Biz," Tommie said. "I'm hungry."

"All right," Jackie said. "Let's go." She climbed into the backseat of Lisa's car and Jason climbed into the passenger seat. He tossed one more glance Kyra's way and let her slip from his mind. Lisa rolled down the automatic windows, turned on her music, and eased out of the parking lot into Second Avenue traffic. Ten short minutes later they were pulling up in front of The Biz.

The Biz was the popular after-school, after-party meeting place for Cross students. The food was delicious, and the latest sounds played nonstop on the jukebox. Lieutenant Harold Simpson owned it, a former officer in the Vietnam war. At fifty-two he was a tall, erect, and handsome dark-skinned man. He was generally pleasant but tolerated no mess in his shop.

Jason and his friends took a booth fairly near the door. As expected, the place was jumping on the first day back to school. Neon lights proclaimed RIBS, BURGERS, CHILI FRIES, SANDWICHES, PIES, and COBBLERS. The booths had black-topped tables, some seats were done in turquoise, some in fire-engine red with matching checkered floor tiles.

"What are you getting?" Jackie asked Lisa.

"The usual," Lisa said without even looking at a menu.

"Me too," Jackie said. Jason and Greg rolled their eyes at one another. Jackie always did whatever Lisa did.

Ashley Gordon came over to take their order. She was a senior at Cross.

"Let me hear it," Ashley said pleasantly. She held her order pad and pen poised and ready.

"Hey, Ashley," Lisa began. "I'll have a large Sprite and a small tossed salad with ranch dressing."

"Me too," Jackie said.

"Let me get a vanilla milk shake, a basket of chili cheese fries, and a cheeseburger," Tommie said.

"What a pig," Jackie said, shoving Tommie playfully. "That basket of chili cheese fries could feed three people."

"What? I told you I was hungry," Tommie complained good-naturedly.

"How about you, gorgeous?" Ashley said to Jason with a friendly smile. Lisa didn't let it faze her too much. Girls were always flirting with Jason. She knew that. But Ashley had known Jason forever and thought of him as a brother. Besides, she had a boyfriend, the tight end on Cross's football team.

"Let me get a Vernor's with light ice, some fries, and some buffalo wings. A large order," Jason answered.

"What about you, big fella?" she asked Greg.

"I'll take a corned beef on rye with fries. Give me a large Sprite with that, too," Greg said.

Once Ashley walked away with their orders they settled comfortably into their half-circle booth. Jason stretched his arm around Lisa and gave her a quick kiss on the cheek. He felt pretty good. His father's words had been scratching at the back of his mind all day, but they were finally beginning to fade away. He was relaxed, with his friends, his girl, and in one of his favorite places.

They sat around talking until their orders arrived and then they dug in to their food.

"I'll tell you this," Greg said. "If they don't beat Ruether next week their confidence will be shot when they face them in the play-offs at the end of the season."

"You're right," Jason agreed. "Ruether's game is always tight. Let 'em get a win and their heads become so big you can't beat them later on."

"Except, there's no way that Cross will beat Ruether. The guys on their team are tanks—they gotta be, what, twenty years old?" Tommie joked. Everyone laughed.

"Where's your school spirit, man?" Jason said with a grin. "Of course they can beat Ruether, it's a matter of strategy, timing, brains. Now, you know our boys have got that."

"True that," Tommie smiled. His braces caught the sunlight and twinkled. "You going to the game?" he asked the group.

"Oh, yeah! It's gonna be hype," Lisa said.

"And it's gonna be at Ruether," Greg said with a tinge of gloom in his voice. The home field advantage was always an issue.

"That's why it's going to be hype! We love turning it out in someone else's backyard," Jackie said, giving Lisa a play.

"And you know that!" Lisa agreed with a smile. Lisa and her friends did not even go to the football games to focus on the game. Like many of the teens who showed up, male and female, they came to see and be seen.

"We'll check that out," Jason said, referring to the game. "The football team is good about showing up at our games when b-ball season tips off. You know I'm down with them," Jason said. They ate and talked until nearly two o'clock. "Well, I've got to get on up outta here." Jason rose as he spoke and laid money on the table for both his and Lisa's orders. Lisa never paid for any of the things they did together.

"All right then, check you later," Tommie said.

"Yeah, man, see you tomorrow," Greg said.

"All right," Jason responded. Jackie, Lisa, and Jason headed out.

Fifteen minutes later, Lisa was pulling up in front of Jason's home after dropping Jackie off only a few blocks away.

"Are you going to call me?" Lisa asked. She sat turned toward Jason, one hand on the steering wheel, the other on his thigh.

"Yes. You know that." Jason leaned over and gave her a long, lingering kiss. "You taste so good, girl," he said softly into her ear.

"You too," she murmured into his.

"I'll talk to you tonight." He climbed out of the car, lightly tossed his backpack onto his shoulder, and shut the door behind him.

2

Kyra pulled out into the Second Avenue traffic in front of Cross High School and made a left on Benedict Street. Her best friend, Renee Harris, sat beside her, strapped in by the seat belt that Kyra demanded everyone in her car wear. Renee popped in a CD, and she and Kyra slipped on their shades.

"Now, you said Angie, Crystal, and Portia are meeting us right away at Pizza Hut, right?" Kyra asked. Kyra had known Renee, Angela, and Portia since elementary school, and Crystal since middle school. They were her group, but Renee was her girl.

"Yeah." Renee bobbed her head to the music as she

looked out of her open window. "So this is it," Renee said.

"This is it! We're upperclassmen. Halfway done," Kyra said with a grin.

"Oh, yes!" Renee exclaimed. "This is a nice ride you got, girl," she said, admiring Kyra's new car.

"Thank you. When Daddy said that he and Mama were going to get me a car for junior year, I thought it would be something low-key, you know."

"I know," Renee said excitedly. "But you got a Jetta. A black Jetta at that! CD player, air—you got practically everything it comes with."

"Yeah," Kyra said, grinning over at Renee. That was one of the best things about their friendship. Each girl was genuinely happy for the other, whatever they got or accomplished.

"So are you going for the Hamilton Science Scholarship?" Renee asked her friend, flipping through the other CDs Kyra had in a case.

The Hamilton Science Scholarship was an extremely tough competition in which juniors and seniors across the state competed for more than $250,000 in scholarship money. Top prize was a $50,000 scholarship that could be applied at any university or college of the student's choosing; $5,000 scholarship prizes were awarded to the top twenty-five finishers. No junior had ever won the top prize in the history of the contest. Several, though, had been selected for the $5,000 scholarships and the even smaller savings bond prizes of $100 to $500 awarded to the bottom fifty awardees. Entrants invented and presented innovative science projects and were then subjected to rigorous interviews by science professors from the state's top university, college, and high-school science programs on the theory, math, and science behind their projects. It began at the school level, then the district and regional competitions, and ended with the final state-level competition in March. It was major stuff. Most serious competitors began their projects in the spring of the school year prior to their competing year. Kyra was, of course, a serious competitor and so had begun her project in April of tenth grade.

"Absolutely. Why?" Kyra asked. She drove carefully, keeping her eyes on the road, but glancing quickly over at Renee after that question.

"Oh, I'm just asking."

"It *is* open to juniors, Renee."

"I know, I know. It's just that only about a hundred or two hundred juniors ever enter, out of—what—fifteen hundred entrants?"

"Yes, that's true. But, so what?" Kyra countered with characteristic confidence. "Will it be hard? Yes. Will it take up mucho amounts of my time? Yes. It's already started to do that. I don't care. I want this. Do you know how excellent that will look on my college applications to say that I won a highly competitive and prestigious Hamilton Science Scholarship in the eleventh grade? Oh, yes! You'd better believe I'm entering this year."

"And you know what?" Renee looked at her friend thoughtfully and seriously.

"What?"

"You could win one. Hell, you could win the entire thing. You really could."

"Thanks, girl," Kyra said. They smiled at one another.

"So when does practice begin?" Kyra asked Renee.

"Next week," Renee said. "This off-season training is the worst." Renee was referring to her track practice. She was the city and regional champ in the half mile. At five-foot-six, she was a thin, delicate-looking running machine with the heart and will of a lion. She had missed winning the state meet by only 1.5 seconds.

She wore her black permed hair in a short layered cut. It suited her distinct, small, almost plain features perfectly. In fact, she might have been plain except for her megawatt smile and warm personality.

And it wasn't enough for Renee to be this supreme jock—no, she was smart on top of that. Cross, while a public school, was a college-prep high school. Its program was widely respected throughout the city, state, and nation. It had a reputation for turning out success story after success story in every academic field. The students were divided among curricula, which were similar to college majors. The top curriculum was Arts and Sciences, the program reserved for the those who tested in the top five percent of Cross's admittance exam. Renee and Kyra were both in this program. It was generally understood that a 3.0 or above in the Arts and Sciences curriculum meant even more than a higher GPA in a different major. Renee had a 3.4, Kyra a 4.0.

"So, you're running cross-country, right?" Kyra asked, surprised.

"God, I hate cross-country. Coach Glynn is after me to run it, though. I hate it!"

"But you know that you need to run it. It had a lot to do with how well you did last year. It'll make you strong."

"I know, I know," Renee said in mock exasperation. "It probably will."

They pulled up at Pizza Hut and went in to join their friends for lunch. Afterward, Kyra dropped Renee off and headed home.

"Anybody here?" Kyra called when she walked in. Kyra lived on a quiet, tree-lined street in Willow Village. The neighborhood was racially mixed and sat near the downtown area of the city. It was a historic district with huge houses set back from the street. Many houses had five or more bedrooms and spacious rooms throughout. Most houses in the small neighborhood had been built over eighty years ago; some were well over one hundred years old. The Evanses' home was a large brick Tudor with six bedrooms, a living room, a dining room, gourmet kitchen, family room, library, three floors, a full and finished basement, walk-in pantry, four and a half bathrooms, screened-in side porch, and a large covered back porch. A woman named Yvette Henderson came in four times a week to clean and do laundry.

No one answered her call, and she wasn't surprised. Her mother and father were, of course, at work. Her sister could be anywhere, including upstairs asleep, and her brother, Sadi, had left for Morehouse University, where he was a junior, last week.

She went into the pantry and helped herself to a couple of gingersnap cookies and poured herself some apple juice from the refrigerator. There was a note on the counter from her father, and Kyra picked it up to read at the island in the center of the kitchen. She straddled a stool and began munching on a cookie and reading.

Akila and Kyra,

I'll be home around 6, Mama will be home even later. Hold dinner for me. Ky, don't forget, it's your turn to cook. I hope your first day back to school was fine. Akila, pick up some milk and cereal from the store.

Daddy

In the Evans family everyone had at least one night a week to fix dinner. Kyra's was Thursday, Akila had Wednesday when she was here, and when her brother, Sadi, was home, he had Tuesday. Her mother cooked on Sundays, and her father on Fridays. Everyone was on their own on Saturday, and Sunday's huge meal served as leftovers on Monday. Now that Sadi and Akila were gone, Tuesday and Wednesday had become take-out and dine-out days.

Kyra finished her snack and went back to scan the refrigerator again. There was chicken thawed and fresh zucchini, and she knew that there was rice in the cabinet. That's dinner then, Kyra thought to herself, and left the kitchen.

She went upstairs to her bedroom and turned on her small music system. A popular R&B station was already set on the dial. Listening to the music as she kicked off her sandals, she heard the woman croon about a man so fine he took her breath away, and Jason Vincent popped into Kyra's head.

At first she asked herself why. But then she shrugged and said aloud "He *is* fine." But he's also an intellectual lightweight, and a spotlight-grabbing jock, she thought. Jason was practically the leader of the "it" crowd for their class at Cross. He had been since the ninth grade. Half the girls in school were dropping their number in his hand whenever they got a chance. He wore expensive designer clothes nearly every day. If anyone was giving a party, they wanted to be sure that Jason got a flier. He had been the ninth- and tenth-grade phenom on the basketball team, and was featured in both the school and city newspapers. He looked so good and always seemed to know the right thing to say, so that he hardly ever had to actually think, Kyra was sure. Advanced Placement classes were supposed to be for the best and brightest. They'll let anyone into AP English these days, she thought smugly.

She picked up the mystery novel she'd been reading the night before and Jason left her mind. An hour later she was still stretched across her bed, engrossed in the novel, when Akila came and stood inside her open doorway. Akila and Kyra looked a lot alike, but Akila's clothes were trendy and she wore her thick, medium-length hair permed. Her flat stomach was exposed in the space between a tiny butter-yellow cotton sweater and low-slung tight white jeans.

"What's up, Ky?" Akila greeted her sister pleasantly.

"You." Kyra sat up. "Did you get Daddy's note?"

"Yeah, I just came back from the store."

"What kind of cereal did you get?"

"Honeycombs and that all-natural oatie stuff they like." Akila wrinkled her nose.

"Cool. Where've you been today?"

"Target. Out trying to get the last few things I need before I head back to school."

"You were just at Target yesterday. Why don't you make a list and stop wasting gas?"

"Why don't you stop telling me what to do?" Akila said, obviously unperturbed by her sister's slightly bossy tone. "What are you cooking tonight?"

"Broiled chicken, zucchini, and rice. Maybe I'll pop some biscuits in the oven, too."

"That sounds all right. Don't put too much salt on the chicken this time," Akila warned, recalling Kyra's last chicken dinner.

"Uuuggh! Don't remind me," Kyra moaned. "I don't know what I was thinking about."

"How was school?" Akila came in and sat on Kyra's full-size bed, supporting her back against the wall.

"Fine—you know."

"Any cute little boys?" Akila asked. Since she'd left for

21

the University of Michigan, all high school boys were "little boys."

"Why—are you interested in high school boys again?"

"Of course not. That doesn't mean that some of them aren't good to look at, though. Anyway, asking you is perfectly safe since you never seem to notice boys."

"Actually, I did see one," Kyra said defensively.

"What?" Akila said sarcastically. "Sweet Ky noticed a boy?"

Kyra immediately regretted saying anything. Her sister loved to poke fun at the fact that Kyra always had her head in the books. The fact is, Kyra noticed boys as much as most girls her age, but they simply didn't seem to notice her at all. None of that was true for Akila. She loved boys and they loved her right back. If she wanted a date or a boyfriend, she always had one. She was pretty, and she had a way about her that boys had always liked. She didn't even try hard and they usually fell all over themselves trying to get her attention, phone number, or time. On top of all of that, she was fairly popular with the girls, too. Akila seemed to effortlessly select just the right clothes and do the latest dances, while at the same time making others feel comfortable. She wasn't phony, she was just naturally sociable.

"Forget it," Kyra said quickly. Once again the boy that came to mind was Jason Vincent. *What is up with me?* Kyra asked herself with some irritation.

"No, I'm just messing with you. I am curious, though. Who was he?" Akila's tone was serious now.

"A boy in my AP English class."

"God, a fine nerd? Tell me more."

"He's not a nerd. He's on the basketball team, in fact."

"I'm just teasing you, Ky." Akila rose and began leaving the room. "I'll check you later." Akila smiled at her younger sister as she left.

After Akila left her room, Kyra asked herself why Jason Vincent kept coming to mind. After a few moments of toying with the idea, she decided that it didn't deserve that much thought. She checked the clock on her wall and realized that she only had about forty minutes to spend working on her science project before she needed to start dinner. She got up from her bed and went downstairs to the home office to use the computer. In moments she was engrossed in her science project, and Jason and everything else was swept from her mind.

3

Jason and his father lived alone. His mother had died of cancer when he was three, and he hardly remembered her. That didn't stop him from missing her, or the idea of her, sometimes. They lived in a three-bedroom condominium, in a complex of identical condos. A service kept everyone's lawn mowed in the spring and summer, the leaves raked in the fall, and the snow shoveled in the winter. His father hired a woman, a nice lady named Mrs. Gillman, to clean the house and cook four dinners a week. She cooked big meals that allowed for leftovers, which he ate on her nights off. Jason had very few chores at home: the trash, his room, and his laundry. But Mrs. Gillman often did his laundry without asking, and she gave his room a thorough cleaning every other week. Jason wasn't really all that messy anyway. The house often looked as if no one lived there, as though it were simply a model of a beautiful modern condo.

It was quiet when he entered. Mrs. Gillman had already come and gone, leaving the house smelling sweet with lemon cake. He put his bag down on the bench in the entryway and headed directly upstairs. His room was the second door. The first was his father's, and they used the third bedroom as a computer room. In his room Jason peeled off his well-ironed T-shirt, navy jeans, and Nikes. He dressed in a pair of beat-up black sweat shorts, a black tank top, and his gym shoes for practicing.

He trooped over to the computer room and popped on the computer. He checked his E-mail. "You've got mail," the familiar female computer voice said. He opened the one from his father.

```
Jay,
     I've gone to Boston for work. I'll
be back Saturday afternoon.
     There's money in the usual place
for your car, gas, and incidentals.
     As always I'll call you at 9 p.m.
and 7 a.m. each night and day. Page
me if there's any problem. Stay off
the streets.
     Dad
```

Most teenagers would be glad to find out that they had the house to themselves for two nights and days. Not Jason. His father had been leaving him home alone for as much as three nights in a row since he was thirteen. What he would prefer, Jason thought, was a little more interest from his father. Hell, a lot more, Jason admitted to himself. Whenever his friends would say how excellent it must be to be home alone so often, Jason played it cool, as though he agreed. He took advantage of it sometimes and had someone over, but for the most part he didn't like it. It was lonely. And deep down inside Jason worried that his father simply didn't care that much about him.

Jason signed off and shut down the computer. He went to his room and opened up his old toy chest. It was small and wooden and sat at the end of his bed. Slipped into the back of the chest was an envelope. Inside the envelope was $125.

"How was your first day back to school?" he asked, feeling sorry for himself. It was something he never did in front of others, and rarely did privately. "Fine," he answered himself aloud.

He went downstairs and scooped his basketball up from the floor of the front-hall closet. A backboard and hoop were secured above the garage doors and Jason went outside to practice. Frustrated with the idea of being left home alone without warning, as usual, Jason began his practice. The practice was what it typically was for him, methodical and therapeutic. He shot a hundred free throws and did fifty layups from each side, a hundred total. Then he finished up with twenty-five jump shots. He took each shot carefully and precisely. He then moved on to dribbling drills, which lasted for more than twenty minutes. It was this sort of daily practice that gave him a ninety-two percent rate at the free-throw line and precision and confidence on the floor.

"Looking good, Jason," Mr. Welton called from across the street. Middle-aged and pleasant, Mr. Welton and his wife were enjoying their "empty nest." Their youngest child had graduated from college last year and was living on her own. Mr. Welton was just emerging from his garage. He used it as a small workshop and Jason could just make out the porch bench that Mr. Welton had begun a couple of weeks ago.

"Thanks, Mr. Welton. How's Mrs. Welton?"

"Oh, fine, fine. School started up today, right?"

"Yes, sir."

"How did that go?" Jason appreciated his asking.

"Just fine, sir. The first day is the easiest."

Mr. Welton chuckled at Jason's small joke. "You take care. Be sure to let me know when your season starts up."

"I will. Tell Mrs. Welton that I said hello. You take care, too."

"I'll tell her. See you later."

Jason went inside and locked the door behind him. He stripped off his shirt as he went up the stairs and headed for the bathroom. Once there he took off the rest of his clothes and took a shower. As he showered he admitted to himself that he was glad his father was gone tonight. Considering the mood his father was in this morning, there was a very good chance that he would have continued cutting into Jason when he got home.

After his shower he dressed and went downstairs to see what was in the refrigerator for dinner. He turned on some music to fill the quiet. Mrs. Gillman had left baked chicken, butter-and-herb seasoned noodles, and fresh green beans with almonds. Her delicious lemon cake sat on the counter covered in the glass cake dish.

He fixed his plate, and while it heated, the telephone rang.

"Hello," Jason said.

"I thought that you said you'd call me," Lisa complained.

"Hey, Lisa." He was paying more attention to his plate, which he was pulling out of the microwave.

"What have you been up to?" Her voice was more relaxed now.

"Practicing."

"What are you doing now?"

"I'm about to eat dinner."

"Do you want me to call you back?"

"I'll call you after I eat," he assured her.

"Is your father home?"

"No, he's going to be gone until Saturday." Jason stirred the noodles, releasing their fragrant heat. Then he sprinkled garlic salt and pepper on them.

"Do you want me to come over?"

Jason thought a moment. If Lisa came over they would

probably have sex. But he didn't feel like it right now. "No, not tonight. Can you come tomorrow after school?"

"Okay."

"I'll tell you what, though. I do need a lift to school in the morning. My father finally came up with the money for my ride, so we can go and pick it up after school, if you want to give me a lift to the shop." Jason turned off the music, moved to the family room, and settled in front of the TV.

"Sure. I'll talk to you later, okay?"

"Okay."

"Bye."

Jason ate his dinner in front of the TV while watching a football game. His boy Greg called, and they kicked it for a while about this and that. A girl he used to spend time with called and they talked for a minute. Then he called Lisa back.

All evening he talked to no one about anything that was important to him.

4

The first two weeks passed smoothly. Everyone got back into the groove of school and began dealing with the demands of going to Cross.

Kyra worked steadily on her science project after school, from three o'clock to nearly five o'clock, three days a week. She hung out at home or over at Renee's and did homework.

Jason started preseason conditioning with the basketball team. Like last year, he was starting in the point guard position. He did his homework, hung out with his crew, and spent some time alone with Lisa.

Then Mrs. Devon introduced the first research project for her class.

"Well, we might as well get started on the research portion of class. Over the next week you will be well advised to take copious notes. I will go over, in detail, exactly what will be expected from this first research paper, and then you will be given two weeks to turn in said paper. It will be a relatively short one." The class listened attentively. Mrs. Devon rarely went over anything twice.

"Now, because it's the first one and so early in the year, I always assign pairs of students to work on the paper together. That way you've got someone to fall back on, to assist you. I'll give you your partners today, and you can pick your topic from the board. I suggest that you exchange phone numbers and e-mail addresses with your partner and get right to work gathering information."

Mrs. Devon began calling off the pairs. "Patton and Washington, Adamson and Grover, Evans and Vincent . . ."

Kyra stopped listening. She glanced over her shoulder and found Jason looking at her. He sat as he did each day, his legs splayed wide open, his posture relaxed, yet erect. Today he wore a black T-shirt and prefaded blue jeans. The requisite overpriced name-brand gym shoes adorned his feet. Without even bothering to nod, Kyra turned back to glare at Mrs. Devon covertly.

I might as well be working alone, Kyra thought. Except that now I've got to pretend to pay attention to whatever his asinine ideas might be. Every day for two weeks he had sat almost entirely mute during class discussions. Kyra, of course, had participated avidly. When Mrs. Devon returned their first paper, a typewritten one-page analysis of a poem, he hadn't discussed or shared his grade as everyone else in the class had done. The lowest grades she'd seen had been C's. No one had higher than a B+. Kyra had assumed that Boy Beautiful's grade must have been lower than a C. Mrs. Devon was tough, and the seven students who'd gotten C's complained that they were the lowest grades they'd ever received.

Great! Kyra thought in exasperation.

Jason heard Mrs. Devon call their names and experienced an unexpected and mild frisson of pleasure. Almost to his surprise, he had come to look forward to third hour so that he could see and hear Kyra Evans. She was smart, extremely smart. And articulate, and she liked to hear herself talk. Just about everyone else liked to hear her talk too, though. She was earnest, thoughtful, energetic, and well-read. She admitted when she was wrong, and sometimes she made the class laugh with her wit. Then she would smile too, and he would get to see that smile. Sometimes, though not often and not for long, she would look right at him.

The thought of spending time with her alone made him want to smile. So when Kyra turned to him after hearing their names paired, he was just about to smile until he caught the look on her face. She looked . . . pissed. Pissed? He couldn't fathom why. But he was pretty sure that he was right and that she did look upset.

"Go ahead and spend a little time with your partners; exchange numbers and e-mail addresses, if you have them, and select a topic from the board," Mrs. Devon instructed.

Jason rose and went over to Kyra. She hadn't moved from her seat.

"Hi," Jason said a bit warily. He wasn't sure whether her mood was directed at him or not.

"Hi," she said uninterestedly. She was looking up at him from her seat. He took the empty seat next to her. Its occupant had gone over to speak to his partner.

With him so near, and the warm, even gaze of his dark eyes on her, Kyra felt a bit embarrassed by her thoughts. She glanced down quickly, and when she looked up again, her look was more pleasant, if not friendly.

"Do you know which one you want to do?" he said, indicating the board by a glance in that direction.

"Number two looks good. How about you?" she asked, mainly out of a sense of politeness. She had every intention of choosing exactly the one she wanted.

"That's fine," Jason said. "You want to exchange numbers?"

"Sure." They traded spirals, each writing their number down in the other's notebook.

"Do you want to get started tonight?" Jason asked. He found himself hoping that she would say yes.

"Might as well," Kyra said, focusing on packing up her things.

"What's the best time to call?" he asked.

"Around eight."

"Okay, I'll call you then."

Later that day, between sixth and seventh hours, Jason and Greg stood in the third floor hall before the main staircase. They stood in the midst of a small group of kids, all talking and laughing among themselves. Jason was just looking over the head of one of the girls who was talking in front of him, when off to his left he saw Kyra approaching. She was alone and seemed preoccupied. She wore slim-fitting black jeans with a denim shirt tucked in at the waist. Her hair was in its characteristic braids and she wore black leather mules on her feet. Her black leather knapsack was on one shoulder. He took all of this in a glance. At the same time, he realized that it gave him a jolt of pleasure to see her.

"Check her out," Jason said to Greg.

"Who?" Greg asked, looking right past Kyra.

"Right there, blue top, black jeans," Jason nodded toward Kyra.

Greg followed Jason's eyes and description, and his eyes landed on Kyra. "Kyra Evans?"

"Yeah," Jason said, not taking his eyes off her. She didn't notice him in the crowded hallway. She continued on past him.

"Yeah, she's all right. She's cute. She needs to do something with that hair, though," Greg said. "Remember her sister, Jay? She was a junior when we came in as freshmen. Talk about fine; that girl had it going on!"

"Yeah, I remember," Jason said. And he did remember. Akila Evans had been one of the junior girls that all the fellas talked about. Of course, she wouldn't give a freshman the wrong time of day. And that was all right; they didn't expect her to.

"Why? You scopin' that?" Greg asked, referring to Kyra.

"Hell, man, I'm always scopin'," Jason said, giving his friend a play and a grin. He wasn't actually "always scopin'," but he knew the expected comment to give.

"True," Greg said, returning the grin, "but you're not always asking."

Jason simply shrugged and his friend let it drop. Greg knew that he could count on Jason on the basketball court, and more important, for anything he might need: support, money, an ear to bend, backup in a fight. Greg knew that he could tell Jay anything and it would never go any further than Jay. But Jason kept a lot of his thoughts to himself, and Greg knew better than to pry. Anytime that Jason had anything he wanted to say, he said it. Otherwise he kept it to himself. For instance, Jason had told Greg yes when Greg asked if he and Lisa were having sex. But Jay never mentioned it again, ever. That's just how he was: he didn't feel it necessary to brag about sleeping with one of the finest girls in a school of fine girls, and he didn't want people knowing his business.

Therefore, when Jason shrugged instead of answering, Greg knew not to press. But the fact that Jason bothered to mention Kyra Evans at all said something, so Greg made a mental note and tucked it away for future reference.

That night Jason's father was in a decent mood, and they ate Mrs. Gillman's dinner together while watching TV. His father asked about his day and Jason asked about his. They each kept their answers brief. After dinner, Jason cleared the table and put all of the dishes in the dishwasher. He had done the bulk of his homework before dinner and now at seven o'clock there was only his English assignment to work on.

He had been thinking on and off about the prospect of calling Kyra since he'd taken her number in third hour. He had sort of planned what it was he wanted to say. Then he felt foolish having done that. Why? he asked himself. Why do I care? She's my partner for a research paper, period. Lisa is my girlfriend. Lisa is good to me. Kyra's not my type, anyway.

He glanced at his watch again. 7:10. He hadn't been this anxious about calling a girl since he'd started talking to Lisa. Even then he wasn't quite like this. He'd known that Lisa liked him. She'd been dropping hints for weeks before he'd asked for her number. But not only did he not think Kyra was attracted to him, he had a bad feeling that she might not think well of him at all, although for the life of him he didn't know why. Besides which, all he was supposed to be concerned with in calling her was their research paper.

He lay across his bed and pictured her. He saw her walking toward him in the hallway as she did today. But this time she not only saw him, she spoke—she came over to him and touched his arm lightly.

He picked up the phone and dialed Lisa. He talked to her until just after eight, when he told her he had to go ahead and finish his homework.

"Have you done all your work?" he asked Lisa.

"Don't start with me, Jason," Lisa said in a bored voice. "Let's just say that I've done all that I'm going to do."

"Well, I'll see you tomorrow," Jason said, disappointed. Lisa talked as if she was all into him. But she wouldn't even work harder at school if he urged her to. So as far as he was concerned, she couldn't be all *that* much into him.

When he got off the phone with Lisa, he went over to his desk and got his English spiral and a pen. Sitting on his bed, the phone beside him, he opened the spiral to the page on which she'd written her phone number. He was aware of everything that he did, aware that each move brought him closer to calling her, talking to her. When he found the number, he allowed the spiral to rest on his legs and then he cleared his throat.

The phone rang three times.

"Hello," a man's voice said.

"Hello, may I speak to Kyra?"

"Who's calling?" the man asked.

"Jason. Jason Vincent."

"Just a moment, please," the man responded politely. It was quiet for a minute and then he heard her voice.

"Hello?"

"Hi, Kyra. It's me, Jason."

"Oh . . . hi, Jason."

"I'm calling about the homework," he began.

"Yes, I know. I've got my notes out. We can get started."

He hadn't quite expected her to get right to business like this. He figured that there would be some small talk. Every time a girl had asked if she could call about school, she'd used the opportunity to chitchat and try to get to know him. But apparently this was not Kyra's intent. All of his small plans were dashed, and he flipped his spiral to the pages that held his notes for the research paper.

"What I figured," Kyra began, her voice pleasant, yet all business, "is that we'd begin with . . ."

Jason listened to her go on and on with all of her plans for the paper. Not once did she ask if he had any ideas.

"So what do you think?" she finally asked.

"It sounds good. I did have a couple of ideas of my own, but yours sound good, too," he said. He waited to see if she would ask what his ideas were, but she didn't. He decided to let it slide for now.

"Can you meet at the university library this Saturday?" she asked.

"Yes. What time?"

"How about ten o'clock?"

"That's fine." They agreed to meet in the lobby of the library and said their good-byes.

Man, is she trippin', Jason thought when he got off the phone. She talked for, he checked his watch, fifteen minutes without needing a word from him. And I thought that I liked her for a second? he asked himself in disbelief. I don't think so!

Over the next couple of days in school, she did little more than say hello. Which, Jason admitted to himself, was all that she ever did. On Friday she came over to him at the end of class.

"So I'll see you tomorrow at ten, right?" she asked.

He was gathering his things up and he stopped to look at her. She was tall, around five seven, and he did not have to look as far down as he did with Lisa, who was five four.

"That's right. I'll see you in the lobby," he answered.

"Okay," she said, smiling as she turned to walk away. He smiled back. "Oh, here's my cell phone number. I'll be leaving the house around nine-thirty—call me if anything comes up and you can't make it."

"Sure," Jason said. She smiled at him again, and he, despite himself, warmed just a little bit inside.

5

Kyra backed into a parking space two blocks from the university library and stowed her keys in her backpack. At the end of class, the day before, when she'd glanced to the back of the classroom, she'd seen Jason talking to Mark Nettles. Jason was turned in profile to her. His features and his smile struck Kyra as he listened to something that Mark said. She took in the smooth, rich brown of his skin against his white Cross basketball T-shirt. She felt, then, an undeniable attraction to Jason, and that alarmed her. Because she knew that boys like Jason did not even see girls like her. But even more important, she couldn't see herself spending more than fifteen minutes with someone so . . . shallow.

She had made up her mind to have things perfectly organized so that they could complete their research as efficiently and quickly as possible. She had drawn up an outline, purchased one hundred large, colored index cards, and written out her preliminary ideas. She was not going to make the mistake of waiting until they got there to do everything.

The fact was, she didn't want to have to spend too much time with Jason Vincent. He was a part of the most popular group in school, which wasn't a crime. But they had an irritating habit of not seeing anybody that didn't look, dress, and act just like them. They rarely made eye contact with most students in the hall. It was as if no one existed, or mattered, except them and the chosen few that they deemed worthy of recognition. Kyra, for one, had never had an interest in being a part of their group, but simple courtesy only reflected good upbringing.

So with her mind made up, Kyra headed to meet Jason.

Jason was already in the lobby of the library. He had made up his mind that Miss Motor Mouth was not going to dominate the project. She would either share the load or he'd go off and do his own thing. He didn't know what her problem was, but he was determined that he was not going to allow it to become his.

When he saw her come in, he wasn't sure what it was—the different venue, the stretch of her long legs in stride, the bright red top that she had on against her warm brown skin—but his heart did a small double thud, and he knew that he wanted to kiss her or hold her, or have her look at him and really see him. Where's your resolve? he thought, taunting himself silently.

"Hi, Kyra."

"Hi, Jason." They walked together and found a group study room they liked. They took seats beside a window.

"How long can you stay?" she asked. She was already emptying the contents of her bag.

"As long as I like," Jason said.

"Me too, pretty much," Kyra said. If she was studying in a public place like this, her parents didn't tend to worry.

Jason watched as she set out her English spiral, a thin purple folder (which he later learned held a small stack of lined loose-leaf paper and some typed work), two blue pens, then a red, a purple, and a neon-blue pen. She then placed an orange and a yellow highlighter on the table, two sharpened pencils, a date book, and the books from class. She ended her unpacking by taking out the new index cards. He had been done once he pulled out his school book, spiral, and a couple of pens.

"You believe in coming prepared, don't you?" Jason asked as he gazed on her mass of supplies with a bemused look on his face.

A slow smile stretched across Kyra's face as she realized how this must look to him. "Yes. I do. And believe me, in the end, you'll thank me."

"I probably will." He smiled back at her.

She then pulled out her outline and typed notes. "Okay," Kyra began in her pleasant, let's-get-down-to-business voice, "here's where I am." She plunged into a description of what was before them.

The smile left Jason's face. He looked from her outline and notes to her face, and saw that she wasn't even looking at him; she was that intent upon the papers that she'd just pulled out.

"What's this?" The displeasure was evident in his voice. He couldn't believe that she'd gone ahead and done all of this without any input from him. Was this her research paper or theirs?

"An outline and some notes to get us started." Her voice automatically took on a defensive tone when she picked up on his.

"To get *us* started, or *you*?" He had folded his arms and sat back in his chair.

"Us. What's the problem?" Kyra couldn't believe this. She'd gone to the trouble of working late last night to pull this together, and he was complaining? It was beyond comprehension.

"The problem," Jason started, "is that I have some ideas—"

"Of course you do," Kyra said, cutting him off. "We'll get them in."

"They're not reflected in that outline because you didn't work with me on anything before you made it," Jason shot back. He could feel himself getting angry at her condescending tone of voice.

"No, but I thought it would be best if I got us started."

"Would you have done an outline without your

partner's input if you were working with Mark or Brandi?" Mark and Brandi were in the same honors curriculum that Kyra was in.

"Well, no . . ." Kyra said before she thought to stop herself.

"Why not?" Jason was angry now. Suddenly he saw exactly where she was going.

Kyra had the decency to look ashamed. She felt her neck and face heat up with her embarrassment.

"Why not?" he asked again. When she refused to answer, he spoke. "I'm not an idiot," Jason said quietly.

"I didn't say that you were an idiot!" Kyra said with unjustified indignation.

"No, but you think it," Jason responded.

"Look, I saw you over there when everyone got their first essay back. You wouldn't show anyone your paper, and everyone else was passing theirs around. You were sitting so quietly, I . . . I didn't want you to feel uncomfortable here. I've done research papers before. My brother and my sister had Mrs. Devon when they were at Cross. I thought I was helping." She floundered to a stop.

Jason gave her a hard look. He took a folder out of his backpack and from it he pulled his essay from Mrs. Devon's class. Silently he slid it across the table to Kyra and watched her look at it.

"*You* got the only 'A'?" Her voice was incredulous. "I'm sorry, I don't mean to say it like that, it's just that . . ."

"You thought I was some degree of an idiot," he finished for her.

Kyra stared across the table at Jason. She was so humiliated that she hardly knew what to say. She had insulted Jason's intelligence in her mind and actions since the moment she'd noticed him in AP English. She had behaved like an intellectual snob, and he knew it, and that made it all the worse.

"I'm sorry," she said simply. Jason looked at her and smiled, because he could tell she meant the two small words, and he could tell that she felt bad about the way she'd behaved.

"Forget it," he said easily. "You're a snob, though. You know that?" he teased, giving her one of his grins.

She nodded. "I'll do better, though, okay?"

"Forget it."

"Start again?" Kyra extended her hand for a shake.

Jason took her warm, slender hand in his, looked directly into her eyes, and shook hands. "Start again," he said.

From that point on they worked well together. Jason looked over Kyra's outline and liked a lot of what he saw. He flipped to some notes that he'd written in his spiral, and Kyra had to admit that she was impressed. They revised the outline, rather than throw it out entirely, and incorporated Jason's ideas plus some ideas that they came up with together. They sat side by side at computer terminals looking up their subject on the library's system and then the Internet. Two and a half hours after they'd arrived Jason wrote a sign that said THIS TABLE IS IN USE,

THANK YOU, placed it on their table, and they went off separately to find the resources that they'd located on the computer. They skimmed and read what material they could find and used the copiers to copy the things that looked useful.

At 2:30 Kyra looked across the table at Jason, who was industriously highlighting passages while reading through another page of copied material. She had to give it to him. Not only wasn't he a mental lightweight, when he got going he could work just as hard as she. But she needed to stop now.

"I'm hungry. Do you want to stop and get something to eat?" she asked.

"Yeah, that sounds good." He'd been hungry for an hour, but he was determined not to mention it, in case she thought he wasn't focused enough. They decided on the best place to go, somewhere within walking distance. They gathered up their things and headed into the September afternoon.

It was still warm, and the trees were lush with green leaves. The sky was a brilliant blue, decked with the occasional full white cloud. The university was a commuter school, the semester just beginning, and for those reasons this afternoon found the campus relatively empty. They walked side by side, pleasantly quiet. The sound of traffic was muted, for no roads passed through this portion of the campus.

"We're making pretty good progress," Jason said.

"Yes." They walked on. Jason wanted her to say more,

to hear her talk more, but he didn't press to initiate or drive a conversation. He felt . . . he paused to consider . . . comfortable.

"We'll probably get the research completed today if we stay a few more hours," she added.

"Yeah. Maybe we can figure out a schedule over lunch for getting the paper done by the due date. What is it, a little less than two weeks away?"

"That's right. Thursday after next."

They arrived at a popular tiny burger joint on campus and took a booth beside a window. They both grabbed menus and got right to the business of deciding what they wanted to order.

"What are you having?" Kyra asked, glancing up at Jason from her menu.

"I think I'll have a mushroom-and-Swiss burger and fries. How about you?"

"I'm having a strawberry milk shake, my favorite," she flashed him a smile, "and a mushroom-and-Swiss burger, too."

"A strawberry milk shake, huh?" He spoke as if giving the idea his deepest consideration. He twisted his gorgeous lips to the side for added effect. "Now that sounds like something worth having."

"It is," she said, her voice throaty and dramatic. "It's sweet, creamy, and delicious." The effect for Jason was thoroughly sexy. The best part for him was that Kyra had not realized how she sounded until after she'd spoken. She was obviously flustered now. His smile stretched, knowing and seductive across his handsome face, and to his delight, that only seemed to make her more nervous.

"Sweet, creamy, and delicious?" He kept his eyes pinned on hers as he spoke. "You're right, that is something I should have."

Kyra found herself unable to look away from his dark eyes until her eyes fell to his lips. Without thinking, he licked his lips quickly at just that moment, and involuntarily, her breath quickened slightly. What would it be like to kiss those lips? she wondered.

"Ready to order?" the waitress asked, breaking some of the developing tension at the table.

"Yes," Kyra said hurriedly.

"Fire away," the waitress joked dryly.

Kyra placed her order for the mushroom-and-Swiss burger with a strawberry milk shake, and Jason ordered the same. Kyra used the time to catch herself and find her bearings again. He is, she reasoned, a flirt. Everybody knew that, she reminded herself. He's just getting in a little practice with me.

"So," Jason began as he stretched and settled back.

"So."

"What does a baby genius talk about in between bustin' all A's?"

"Is that supposed to be a cute way of calling me a nerd?" Kyra's back literally stiffened in preparation for some wisecrack.

Jason looked a little surprised. "Do you think you're a nerd?" he asked her seriously.

"No, of course not. But I know that some people do."

"I don't. So what *do* you talk about in between bustin' all A's?" he asked again with a smile.

"I don't know. Whatever." Their milk shakes arrived, and Kyra took a long drink from her straw.

"Good?" Jason asked. The look in his eyes was flirtatious again.

"Try it and see," Kyra answered, doing a little flirting herself. She blushed and lowered her eyes as she drank from her own straw.

"It is good." Kyra just smiled at him. They relaxed and talked about Mrs. Devon and her class. They talked about a couple of movies that they'd both seen. They talked a bit about her classes and his basketball training.

"So do you have a boyfriend?" Jason asked. Although his voice sounded entirely relaxed and casual, he was hoping that her answer would be no. He wasn't sure why, since he couldn't really imagine anything happening between them. After all, he was with Lisa, and Kyra wasn't really his style, and he probably wasn't hers. Anybody could tell that, couldn't they?

"No."

"Why not?"

"You're getting kinda personal, aren't you? Why do you care?"

"I was just curious, that's all. I mean, you've got a lot going on, with school, you know. I just wondered if you made time for romance."

"Just because someone doesn't have a boyfriend doesn't

mean that they don't have time for romance." Kyra was beginning to feel a little uncomfortable with the direction of the conversation.

"Well, do you?"

"Do I what?"

"Have time for romance?"

Kyra could feel her face growing warm. Had he been able to read her thoughts about him in her face? Why was he asking her these types of questions? "Why do you ask?" she asked suspiciously.

"Just making conversation," Jason answered, not entirely honestly. All day half his mind had been on their research and the other half on the delicate smell of vanilla on her hair, or how soft the skin on her neck looked, or the way that she looked when she smiled or laughed.

"I have time for romance; I just don't have a romance."

"Oh." He wanted to ask why she didn't have a romance, but he felt that might be pushing it a bit.

"How long have you and Lisa been together?"

"Almost a year."

"I've never been with anybody that long. How is that?"

"It's cool." Kyra nodded at Jason's answer.

Just then the waitress placed the hot plates of food before them. As Jason looked over at Kyra he saw her lower her head silently and say grace. When she finished she looked up with a smile and a casual, "Let's chow."

The burgers were well seasoned and well done. They ate quietly for a couple of minutes.

"This is pretty good," Jason commented.

"Yeah, it's my favorite kind of burger. At home I usually make it with turkey and add some sautéed onions to it."

"That sounds good," Jason said. Kyra nodded. "So when do you want to get together to work on the actual paper?"

"Well, I think that we can finish taking all the notes we need today. And if you have time, we could do the outline today. At least some kind of outline."

"Yeah, that sounds tight. But we don't have to feel too pressed, we've got time."

"True, but I'd like to go ahead and knock it out as soon as possible. I'd like to finish a little ahead of schedule, if that's good for you. I've got a lot of stuff that I'm trying to keep up with in another class."

"Yeah? What's that?"

"Well, it's for science, but it's not exactly for my science class. I'm going to enter the Hamilton Science Scholarship contest this year. Work on that takes up a lot of my time."

"What's the Hamilton Science Scholarship?"

Kyra explained what the contest was about and described the project she intended to submit.

"Sounds pretty heavy," Jason said in an admiring tone. "Yeah, we can get the paper done as soon as possible if you want. I'm not stressed in any of my classes. Yet." They both smiled in understanding the fact that sometimes academic life at Cross High School could get seriously demanding.

"I know that we can't meet right after school. You've

got practice, and I've got to work on my project with Mr. Hillard. We could work over at my house," Kyra offered.

"Okay."

They took their time finishing lunch, talking back and forth about the research and the paper before them. By the time lunch was over they each felt fairly comfortable with the other. Back in the library they got right to work and, in a little less than three hours, they finished the research and compiled all of the notes that they felt they'd need for their paper. They took a break and called home to assure their parents that they were all right. Jason left his message on the answering machine. They spent the next hour thrashing out an outline. Afterward they stretched, talked for a while, packed up their materials, and headed out.

The day had turned to evening. The sun had begun its descent, and the air was still warm from the heat of the late summer day. The leaves above their heads murmured gently in the soft breeze, and the air was fragrant with the blooms that graced the college campus. Students strolled to and from their evening activities and studies, cars passed a block ahead on busy Third Ave. Somewhere, not far away, an outdoor musician strummed a guitar and sang a blues song. Kyra imagined people dropping coins and dollar bills into an open guitar case. Kyra and Jason walked slowly together, neither in any apparent hurry.

They arrived at Kyra's car first.

"Is Monday all right for you?" Jason asked.

"Yeah, that's good." They set a time for Jason to arrive at Kyra's house.

"Cool, I'll see you in class, then."

"Okay, I'll see you," Kyra said.

Jason waited for her to get safely into her car and start it up. As she pulled away from the curb she waved to him and he waved back. He headed off to his own car, just up that same block. As he walked he thought to himself. She's all right.

Later that evening Jason stood before his bedroom mirror fumbling with a tie. He wore a pair of cuffed black trousers of excellent quality and cut, a pale blue dress shirt, and a subtly patterned tie. Well, he would be wearing the tie, if he could get it on properly. His father glanced in as he walked by Jason's open door, heading to the bathroom. He wore a gray suit, tailored and tasteful, and, unlike Jason, his ensemble was complete with tie and jacket. Mr. Vincent said, "You wouldn't have so much trouble if you wore ties more often, boy." But his voice was pleasant, even a little teasing.

"Yeah, I know. But I don't have anywhere to wear them. I'm not a high-powered exec like some people I know," Jason teased back. His father smiled and came to stand before him. He deftly moved the tie, giving Jason verbal instructions as he worked, and in moments, the tie sat perfectly in place.

"Now you try it." Jason undid the tie, and his father watched and directed in an easy manner as his son carefully tied a perfect tie. "That's good." He turned and Jason followed his lead and they peered at their reflections in Jason's full-length mirror. "You sure are a good-looking young man," his father said with a proud grin. Jason just laughed and shook his head, for he looked very, very much like his father. Being all suited up like this made the resemblance especially thorough.

"You look all right yourself," Jason said. These were the times that he enjoyed being with his father. They weren't doing anything in particular, but they clicked. Times like these made Jason feel more whole.

"Well, we'd better get going. I don't want to be late." Jason was headed out to dinner with his father and his father's girlfriend, Rachel. He was so seldom included in their plans that he had been surprised by the invitation. His father explained that he just wanted the two most important people in his life to get to know each other a little better.

The dinner turned out to be pleasant. Rachel was gorgeous, with a pretty face and shapely body. She was about five years younger than his dad, and she seemed to have an easygoing personality. His father was certainly more relaxed around her. He talked a little more and even joked occasionally, and Jason felt fairly at ease dipping in and out of the conversation. On the way home that night, when Jason and his father were once again alone in the car, Jason said, "She's nice."

"Yes, very. Most of the time," and there was real warmth and pleasure in his voice. Jason liked that. He wanted his dad to be happy. First, because he was his father, second, because maybe he would have fewer mood swings if he were happier.

When they got home Mr. Vincent clicked on the TV to discover that the Lions football team was finishing up a close game. He and Jason took off their jackets and ties, got sodas from the fridge, kicked off their shoes, and watched the Lions pull off a hairy 14–12 victory. With that, the day ended as well as it had begun.

6

On Monday during lunch, Jason told Lisa that he'd be working over at Kyra's house that evening.

"Kyra who?" Lisa asked, interested.

"Evans."

"Oh," Lisa said, obviously losing interest quickly. "Ol' Miss Nappy Head." She and Jackie laughed at the little joke.

"Whatever," Jason said, finding that he was a little ticked off by Lisa's insulting remark. Kyra was good people, and Lisa didn't even know her. Jason allowed himself to realize that was exactly how Lisa could be: making judgments about people for superficial reasons. Lisa had decided that Kyra was of little interest because of her *hair*.

Jason pulled up in front of Kyra's home a couple of minutes before their appointed time. He took in the carefully maintained lawns that extended some distance from the curb. The street was quiet, and the large, imposing homes silently protected their inhabitants from the eyes and ears of passersby. Kyra's house was beautiful, with a deep porch that wrapped around three-fourths of the place. A tall iron gate blocked his easy entrance, and he got out of his car into the cool September twilight to ring the buzzer on that gate.

"Who is it?" Kyra asked.

Jason pressed the speaker button. "Jason."

"Just a moment," she answered. A quiet buzz notified him that he could try the door. Jason pulled the gate open and shut it tightly behind him. There was an answering click as the gate was relocked. He strolled up the walk, toting his school bag on his shoulder. Gracefully and easily, he climbed the stairs of the porch and the front door was pulled open before he had a chance to ring the buzzer at the door.

Before him stood a beautiful woman who looked very much like Kyra and her sister, Akila. She was slender, with the exact same complexion as Kyra, and with features of both of her daughters displayed on her face. She wore no makeup and her skin was lovely. She had on slim blue jeans and a red scoopneck sweater. A gold chain hung around her neck. Her hair hung to her chest in dark Nubian locks that curled slightly at their tips. She definitely looked too young to be the mother of three nearly grown children.

"Hello, Jason," Ms. Evans said with a smile. Jason stepped into the warm light of the foyer. Everything, even to his untrained eye, seemed of extremely fine quality.

"Hello, Mrs. Evans. I thought you were Kyra over the intercom."

"No," Ms. Evans said with a small laugh, "but she'll be down in a minute." As if on cue, Jason heard quiet footsteps on the wide staircase before him. Now, since Jason had assured himself that Kyra and he were only friends, new friends, there was little way to explain the quickening of his heart upon seeing her descend those stairs. She wore a thick oatmeal-colored V-neck sweater atop a pair of well-worn faded blue jeans. She wore her hair without braids this evening. It was pulled back into a loose ballerina knot. She wore the gold chain and bracelets that she always wore, all thinner versions of her mother's. The girl looked good, Jason admitted to himself.

"Hey, Jason," Kyra said. "Mama, this is Jason Vincent. Jason, my mother, Ms. Evans." Ms. Evans and Jason shook hands.

"Well, I'll let you two get to work," Ms. Evans said and left down the hallway.

"How're you doing?" Kyra asked.

"I'm straight," Jason answered. "How did you do on Mrs. Devon's pop quiz today?"

"Pretty good, ninety-six. How about you?"

"The same," Jason said with a smile.

"Come on, let's go get started, Lucky Boy," she said

with a smirk. She turned and began leading him down the right-hand-side hallway.

"Oh, I'm *lucky*, huh? What are you?" Jason kidded back.

"Smart, of course." Jason felt himself warmed by the sight of her smile and smiled himself at her slender, swaying back once she had turned away again.

They passed two rooms and came to the rear of the house to what was obviously used as a home office. One wall was a series of desks and tabletops. Two computers sat in the center of this line of surfaces, and cabinets and triple shelves were suspended from the wall above the desks and tabletops. Computer CDs were neatly shelved; reams of paper were carefully stacked. There were wooden cups holding pens, pencils, highlighters, markers, and paper clips. Dictionaries and thesauruses were visible. There were four office chairs and two comfortable chairs and a sofa for lounging and thinking. The rest of the room's decor and art, mostly in muted blues and greens, followed the same expensive, tasteful pattern of what he'd seen in the house.

At first Jason was going to pretend to be unimpressed. But after a few minutes of looking around the large office, coupled with the small portion of the house that he'd seen he had to say, "Your house is sweet."

"Thanks." Kyra's materials were spread around one of the computers, whose screen was bedecked with a geometric screen saver.

After getting himself settled on the floor Jason said, "Well, let's hit it." He didn't want to examine the feeling too much, but he was glad to be here with Kyra. After the conversation following their research for this paper, Jason felt as though he'd found a new friend.

"Sounds good."

The two worked well together. After an hour of going over the progress that each had made on their own, they began to knit their work together. After a while they felt that they had something worthy of putting on the computer and calling a rough draft.

"Let's take a break," Kyra said.

"Okay."

They left their work where it was and went out of the office. Kyra led him around to the kitchen. Jason was not surprised at how spacious it was, or at the large island in its center. Sleek, modern appliances and wood cabinets lined the walls.

"What would you like?" Kyra asked. "We've got juices, ice tea, water, popcorn, tortilla chips and salsa, fruit, cookies, and leftover dinner."

Jason grinned, "Whatever you're having will be fine."

Kyra pulled out a bag of chips, a carton of all-natural fruit juice, a jar of salsa, two glasses, one large bowl, and one small bowl. She poured chips into the large bowl and salsa into the small one. Jason poured juice into their glasses.

As they began eating Jason took his time looking around the expansive kitchen. "I've got to ask you, Kyra, because your house is incredible, what do your parents do?"

Jason's home was nothing to sneeze at, and several of the

kids he hung with had big houses, but he'd never been in one the size and quality of Kyra's. It wasn't just big and nicely decorated; everything in it looked like money.

Kyra looked slightly amused, but she didn't seem angry or put off, which Jason had worried a little that she might be. Most folks don't like to talk about money, even indirectly.

"Do you know Feathertone paper products?"

"Yes," he answered. Of course he did; their products could be on the shelves of nearly every grocery store, from Michigan to Florida.

"My great-grandfather founded that company, his daughter and her husband made it extremely profitable, and those are my mother's parents."

Jason stared at Kyra, stunned. Feathertone was a multi-million-dollar business.

"I didn't even know that it was black-owned."

"I guess a lot of people don't."

"I didn't know you were rich," Jason said before he could catch himself.

"Well, I'm not really. My mother and her family are," Kyra said with a playful smile. "Daddy is a pediatric surgeon, and Mama runs a couple of foundations and sits on the board of directors for a few places. My aunts and an uncle run Feathertone. I don't really talk about it. It changes people—that information. Most of the kids at Cross don't pay me any attention, and you know how some of them care about who's got this and who's got that. I don't need anybody pretending to be my friend because I've got money in my family." She spoke simply and frankly. Jason liked that about her.

"That's cool," Jason said.

"What time do you have to be home?"

"Whenever. My father's hanging out over at his girlfriend Rachel's tonight. He told me not to expect him until tomorrow."

"You've got a little break, then."

"Not really. He's gone five or six times a month for work. Then he spends the night at Rachel's sometimes. He doesn't get home until about nine most nights, anyway. He's been doing that since I was thirteen."

Kyra looked at him for a long moment and Jason looked up from where he'd been dipping his chip in spicy salsa. "That must be lonely," she said softly.

Jason stared back into her dark eyes. Everyone else who'd heard about his father's schedule had marveled at his freedom. They thought it the coolest setup a teenager could want. No one, until Kyra, had guessed the truth of his situation.

"It is, sometimes," he admitted. Kyra looked into his eyes and understood that his words were almost a confession.

"What happened to your mother?" she asked.

"She died when I was three. She had cancer."

"I'm sorry." Jason saw in eyes that she wasn't just saying what was expected. She was sincerely sorry for his loss. "Are you and your father close?"

"Not really," Jason hesitated, wanting to be careful

with his words. "My father can be sort of demanding at times."

Kyra looked at Jason's profile as he kept his eyes away from hers. She found him even more handsome suddenly. There was still his beautiful brown skin, expressive dark eyes, and heart-catching smile. But those were only the starting points now. Each time she talked to him she liked him more, found herself more attracted to him. Hearing about his home situation made her realize that everything was not perfect for the boy that everyone at Cross thought of as the perfect boy. She wanted to reach over and place her hand on his cheek. However, she reminded herself, he didn't need her comfort. He had a girlfriend and plenty of friends to provide that. She was his study partner. And that only until this paper was done. Suddenly the paper seemed too short.

He turned just then and looked directly into her eyes. He didn't smile and his stare was so probing and direct that it seemed to Kyra that he could read her thoughts. It felt to her that just by looking, he knew more about her than she cared to reveal. She opted to change the subject. "How has basketball practice been going?"

"Pretty good," he said and bit into a chip. Jason decided that he was grateful for the change in subject. Looking at Kyra, he realized that she truly listened to him. He felt that if he were not careful he would tell this bright, fine, direct girl his darkest thoughts. But what would someone like Kyra think of those? She had a mother and father at home, and a brother and sister in college. She had, as far as he could tell, a nearly perfect family life.

"Coach Grosse has us running a million drills and lifting weights right now. We won't start really playing for another couple of weeks."

"How long do you practice?"

"From three until around five-thirty most days. Sometimes longer."

"Sounds intense. Do you love it or just like it?"

"I love it. Even the training. I enjoy the discipline and meeting the challenges, going beyond the challenges sometimes."

"You're pretty good, huh?"

"You've never been to a game?"

"No, and don't sound so surprised," she remarked.

"I'm not."

She gave him a doubtful look. "Well, maybe a little," he admitted.

"Nope, never checked out a game," she confirmed.

"Why not?"

"Truthfully, I've never been interested."

"Oh." He didn't quite know what to think. At first he was a little bothered, but then he realized that it was nothing personal against him.

"Until now," she said, giving him a sidelong glance.

He smiled in return. "Why now?"

She only smiled. He did not need to hear her answer; he knew what it was. He felt himself grow warm and happy at this knowledge that Kyra would change her schedule, even a little, for him.

"So, do you miss your sister and brother when they're away at school?"

"Sure, but it's nice too, being an only child, sort of," she said.

"Oh, why is that?"

"I don't know, really. It's like . . . it's like there's a little less pressure."

"What kind of pressure?"

"Well, Sadi is this creative genius. He writes music, plays three instruments extremely well; he's even been recorded several times. And Akila is this beauty, and everywhere she goes she's like the 'it' girl. People don't just want to hang with Akila. They want to talk like her, dress like her, walk like her. Then it's like I'm the brain, and . . ." she allowed her thoughts to trail off.

"And what?" Jason prompted. Kyra only shrugged. When she didn't answer Jason tried completing the thought for her. "And you feel like your parents pressure you to get all A's and whatnot?"

"No, it's not as 'after-school-special' as that," she said with a small smile. "It's just that sometimes I get tired of being 'the brain.'" She rolled her eyes sarcastically as she said the phrase. "Sometimes I just want to *be*, you know?"

"Yeah, actually, I do."

"You know, it's almost as if my parents take it for granted that I'll get great grades and win scholastic awards and stuff," she said softly.

He looked at this girl who he had seen for two years.

This girl who he had, inexplicably, wondered what it would be like to kiss the very first time that he'd seen her. He had been curious about her, but not interested enough to bother to start a friendship. He looked at her and marveled at how much they had in common.

"I feel that way too, sometimes. It's like everyone expects me to excel in basketball, to talk a certain way, hang with certain people, and . . ." It was his turn to falter. He'd said more, much more, than he'd planned to say.

With the lull in the conversation Kyra noticed that they had mowed through their snack. "Do you want some more?" she asked, indicating the food on the island.

"No, thanks. You want to get back?"

She understood that he meant the paper, and she nodded, yes. They worked together to clear away their things and trooped back to the office.

At first, self-conscious after their personal confessions to one another, the two worked quietly for the next half hour, each keying half of the paper into the computer they sat before. Kyra got up and switched on the radio to the popular R&B station. Soon they relaxed and began chatting easily to one another as they worked. Jason cracked a joke on Kyra's singing, and that started a series of remarks from each that made them laugh. An hour passed and they found themselves finished typing the rough draft.

"Well, that's done," Jason said, stretching. Kyra watched his broad, lean, muscular chest expand beneath his evergreen sweater. He brought his arms down when his stretch was completed, glancing at the Tag watch on his exposed forearm. Kyra watched the stretch and pull of the muscles and tendons in that forearm and turned her eyes away.

"It's nearly nine o'clock," Jason commented. "I've still got a chemistry assignment to complete. I'd better go."

"All right. I'll walk you out."

Jason found himself a little disappointed that Kyra did not ask him to stay for a little while longer. But when he considered, he had to admit that there was no reason why she should.

Outside, the autumn evening had turned to night and they stood on Kyra's porch in the purple-black darkness. Jason's Cross letterman jacket was open to the cool breeze. Kyra had slipped her feet into a pair of unlaced gym shoes, and she stood with her arms folded against the chill.

Jason thought she might be cold. "Do you want to put on my jacket?" he asked.

"No, but thanks," she answered. They stood in a comfortable quiet.

"I can give you this draft tomorrow when I see you in class," Jason said. They had agreed to edit the rough draft separately.

"You don't have to be *that* pressed."

"It's no problem. I can do it in health class; we won't be doing anything in there tomorrow."

"All right, then." They talked as they looked into the night. The street was quiet, disturbed only by a car that drove through, and the lone bark of a distant dog.

"I'll see you tomorrow, then," he said as he shifted his

bag up on his shoulder. He did not want to go, but he could think of no reasonable way to prolong his stay.

"See you tomorrow," Kyra said. Jason headed down the walkway through the gate, and she stood watching until he got into his car. She turned to go into the house as his engine hummed to life.

7

The next day in school Jason found that his mood was up—way up. For a while he tried to deny the source of the feeling. But in the end he gave in and admitted to himself the truth. He couldn't wait to see Kyra. He only regretted that he wouldn't have any real time to talk to her in Mrs. Devon's class. The night before he had called Lisa and talked to her for only a few minutes. He hadn't had much to say to her. Greg had called and they kicked it for a half an hour, talking about the upcoming season, practice, and this girl that Greg had met at the mall. After he got off the phone Jason buckled down and got his chemistry homework out of the way, and then it was eleven o'clock.

He realized that he had been filling in the time until it was too late for him to make a fool of himself by calling Kyra. He most definitely wouldn't call her this late. All night, ever since he'd left her porch, she'd been on his mind. She was in the back of his thoughts as he talked to Lisa and Greg. She kept flitting across his mind's eye as he worked on his chemistry lesson. He pictured the cinnamon brown of her skin, the gentle curve of her neck as she bent over the paper they worked on, her smile in the kitchen, and the sway of her slender hips when she walked and moved. But what he most especially recalled was the look in her eyes when they'd spoken seriously in the kitchen. He had felt a connection to her then, a connection that he had not felt with anyone else, ever.

What he wanted, he admitted to himself, was to talk with her more and more. He wanted to hear her thoughts and tell her things about himself that weighed down on him sometimes, like anvils on his shoulders and chest. He wanted to kiss her soft lips and hold her in his arms, pressing her body against his.

But just as quickly as he admitted these thoughts, he chastised himself. He was sure that a smart, confident, together girl like Kyra would not want to be bothered with someone like him. Hell, he told himself, she'd be looking for her intellectual equal. He was pretty good in English and French, but a science and math whiz he was not. He got good grades, sure, but Kyra was taking AP courses in all of her major subjects, and she was taking two science courses at the university. Plus, he figured that he just wasn't her type. Despite her professions of wanting to "just be" sometimes, he'd never seen her hanging at The Biz. She admitted that she'd never been to a basketball game, and he doubted that she partied.

Still, he couldn't deny how he felt.

When the bell rang for third hour, Jason headed directly for Mrs. Devon's class. He couldn't believe his luck when he saw Kyra approaching from the opposite direction. He'd have a chance to talk to her for a minute before class. They met up outside the door of the classroom.

"Hey," she said with a smile.

"Hey," he said, smiling back. "What's up?"

"Nothing. Did you get a chance to read the paper?"

"Yeah, it's tight. I caught a few things here and there, mostly typos."

"Cool. I'll check it over tonight and we can go ahead and knock that second draft out," Kyra said. "We won't have to meet up to do that. One of us can just type it over with corrections we've made."

"All right." Kyra wasn't sure, but she thought that she saw disappointment flash across his face. But that couldn't be, could it?

They filed into class and took their seats. A couple of times during the hour Kyra found excuses to steal glances Jason's way. Both times he was looking at her. She didn't know what to make of it. She couldn't believe that Jason could actually be interested in her romantically. She was a nobody on the Cross social scale. She knew that, while maybe not everybody considered her a geek, she was certainly considered a brain. And let's face it, brains were not popular. Not to mention that Kyra knew that Lisa had her beat hands down in the looks department. Still, there was a little something in the way that Jason looked at her that she couldn't quite explain when she considered all of these facts.

As the day passed, Kyra found herself thinking of Jason more often than she should. She kept telling herself that her thoughts would do her no good, but she didn't seem capable of stopping them.

Finally two o'clock found her regular schedule over, and she was free to go to Mr. Hillard's, where she could work on her science contest project. This was Mr. Hillard's preparation period and he was frequently in and out of the room, leaving Kyra alone for stretches of time. She was working alone now, the room quiet and empty. She was just getting into her work when she heard a familiar voice behind her.

"What's up?" Jason said.

"Hey, Jason, what's up?" Surprise showed on her face. An immediate sensation of pleasure washed over her at seeing him unexpectedly.

"I was just going to my locker when I decided to stop in and visit you for a minute. I remembered that you told me you worked on your project here seventh and eighth hours," Jason said easily. The truth was that he'd gotten the pass specifically to get out and see her for even just a moment.

"Oh. What class are you in, or out of?" Kyra asked, glancing at the small pass in his hand.

"Ms. Wheatly's trig," he answered. He was looking at her project as he spoke and Kyra was looking at him. He looked gorgeous, as usual, another pair of loose-fitting jeans riding over his slim hips perfectly, and a soft gray wool polo shirt falling smoothly across his broad shoulders and chest. The top two buttons of his shirt were undone, exposing his strong neck and the top of his chest. When Kyra looked up from her brief inspection she was embarrassed to find Jason's eyes on her face, a tiny smile playing across his perfect lips.

"This looks good," he said, looking back down at her project again. "I mean, it looks really good."

So do you, Kyra thought. "Thanks," she said aloud.

"What's it about again?"

"I'm looking at how to isolate a particular hormone and determine its molecular structure, a hormone that might reduce the adverse effects of diabetes. I work here with Mr. Hillard, and also with professors who mentor me at Wayne State University. That gives me access to a much larger database and the higher-quality equipment I need to do my research."

"Like I said, it looks real good. I mean, I don't understand a lot of it, but it looks impressive," he said.

"Thanks, Jason," she said, unable to keep from smiling back. She could tell that he was serious and teasing her at the same time.

"I'd better get back," he said as he raised his pass slightly.

"I'll see you tomorrow." She felt foolishly glad inside.

"Yeah, check you later," Jason said in a falsely nonchalant tone.

That night Kyra sat in her room editing the rough draft of their paper. She took in the way that he wrote a tiny note in the margin. *This paragraph is weak*, it read. *Reread and try again.* It was obviously a note that he had written to himself. There was an arrow beneath the note, and Kyra flipped the paper over to find that he had indeed tried the paragraph again. It read much better after he'd redone it.

She thought of how he had shown up during seventh hour, and a smile spread across her face. She was glad that he had remembered her schedule and had bothered to stop in for a moment. But she was careful not to get too excited about it. She knew that Ms. Wheatly's class was near Mr. Hillard's.

She was done editing the rough draft and done with all of her homework for the night. There hadn't been much. She decided to move on to the second draft of their paper. Now she realized that she could just do this directly, but she wanted to hear Jason's voice, so she decided to call him and tell him that she would start the second draft tonight. As she dialed his number, she felt her stomach flutter in an unaccustomed manner.

"Hello?" a man's voice said across the line.

"Hi, may I speak to Jason?"

"Just a minute," Jason's father said. "Jason," he called out, his mouth away from the telephone.

She did not hear Jason's response, if he made any, but then there was his voice on the line, "Hello?" She heard the click as his father hung up his extension. His voice was deep and melodic, and Kyra felt the thumping of her heart inside her chest. She pictured his mouth close to the receiver.

"Hi, Jason."

"Who's this?" He did not sound particularly curious. Although he had a girlfriend, Kyra imagined that more than a few girls called Jason up. And, in fact, he wasn't curious or interested. Jason sat across the width of his bed, playing his PlayStation. He was relaxing with only a pair of shorts on and a tall cup of fruit punch nearby.

"Kyra," she answered.

"Kyra?" She thought that she detected a slight rise in his voice at the question.

"Yeah. Are you busy? I can talk to you tomorrow—"

"No," he said, cutting her off. "I'm not busy. What's up?" He placed the controls of the game aside.

"I just finished editing the rough draft and I was going to go ahead and type up the second draft. That is, if you didn't need to see the rough draft again?"

"Oh, yeah, that's cool." Is that what she called about? he wondered.

"Actually, it's looking so good, this next draft could be the last draft."

"That's straight."

"What were you up to?"

"I'm on my PlayStation, chillin'."

"Oh."

Oh, no, he thought, this was most definitely the lamest conversation that he'd had with a girl since he was twelve years old. The worst part of it was that he really wanted to keep Kyra on the phone.

"How was school?" he asked, hoping to get a conversation going.

"Pretty good. How was practice?"

"Hard, but good. Oh, yeah, did you hear about what happened up on six?" Cross High School had six floors, but students and staff had not used the much smaller sixth floor for a good ten years. Most of it was blocked off.

"No, what?"

"Couple of guys were caught up there smoking a joint."

"Who was it?"

"I don't know, but I heard that they were juniors."

"Do you smoke?" Kyra asked.

"Naw, it's bad for my game. Weed *and* cigarettes."

"Have you ever?"

"Yeah, a couple of times, back in the ninth grade," he admitted. "Have you?"

"No, never."

"Scared?" he asked with a smile in his voice that Kyra could detect over the phone.

"Not the way you mean. When I was little, maybe seven years old, my parents took me to see this exhibit down at the old police headquarters. There were these huge black and white, extremely graphic photos of addicts. Those images stuck, you know? They weirded me out. I don't *ever* want to go there."

"I hear you."

"It was so sad. Those people were out of their minds,

literally. There were people sitting in pools of their own urine, little kids staring at their doped-out parents. Too much."

"Yeah, it sounds like too much for a little kid."

"No, not the pictures," she said, sensing his meaning. "The addicts. What they gave up, what they went through. *That* was too much. No, my parents talked me through the whole thing, so that lowered my stress, if you know what I mean. But their little field trip had its effect on me. I don't ever want to lose control of my life like those people did."

She stopped talking for a moment and Jason visualized the photos that she described. But even more important, he saw a seven-year-old Kyra, young and small, walking between her two parents, holding their hands. He saw the love and fear and disgust in her eyes as she looked up at these two people who looked down at her with love, concern, and understanding.

"I hear that," Jason concurred. "I don't mess with the stuff now. I did it then, trying to be cool. But after I did it a couple of times and saw how stupid the other fellas would be after they got high or drunk, I was like, later for all that. That's not who I wanted to be."

"I agree. God, don't we sound like a couple of Goody Two-shoes," Kyra teased.

"Yeah, yeah, we do."

From there the conversation continued, relaxed, filled with humor and seriousness as they talked about teachers at Cross, students, and school policies that they felt were unfair. They talked of things on the news and on the Tom Joyner and Tavis Smiley radio shows.

"Is it really eleven-thirty?" Kyra asked, genuinely surprised. She had turned her lamp off earlier and had been lying across her bed talking in the dark for some time. Now she'd raised herself up and looked across her room at her alarm clock. She kept it there in order to force herself to get up when it rang, if only to shut it off.

"Yes."

"I don't believe we've been talking for over two hours."

"Yeah," Jason said simply, and enjoying every minute of it, he thought to himself.

"I better get off. I'm still not ready to get out of here on time in the morning." Jason could hear the regret in her voice.

"All right. I'll see you tomorrow, okay?"

"Yes, I'll see you tomorrow."

They said their good-byes, and Kyra hung up the telephone and lay still in the darkness of her bedroom. She replayed parts of their conversation again in her mind; she recalled the melodic quality of his voice, the richness of it over the telephone line and into her ear in the quiet of her room. She could still hear his low laughter at something that she'd said, and the thought made her smile. Kyra rolled over onto her stomach and sighed. What are you doing, girl? she asked herself. It would be, she assured herself, very stupid to fall for the most popular boy in school in the first place, worse since he was going with one of the most popular and attractive girls in the school. Despite her own warning, she kept thinking of Jason as she headed into her bathroom.

For his part, Jason got off the telephone troubled and glad at the same time. He was troubled because he could sense feelings growing inside of him for Kyra that might not be kosher for a brother with a girlfriend. But at the same time, he was glad because of the way that he felt after talking to Kyra. He felt good all over. He could have talked to her all night. His father rarely bothered him about the amount of time that he spent on the telephone as long as his grades were above the 3.0 mark, which they always were. If Kyra hadn't said that she had to get off the phone, he would still be talking to her. He had known exactly what time it was all along, and he couldn't have cared less.

They hadn't spoken much about themselves after the discussion turned from their views on drugs, but he had learned more and more about Kyra as they talked about everything else. He had learned a little of what made her laugh, what she thought about this and about that. They had flirted, just a little, but mostly they had talked as friends. He had enjoyed that. He needed that. He and his friends did not really talk about things that mattered much. They discussed the social happenings at Cross, and almost exclusively about their circle of friends and associates, at that.

But tonight when he'd spoken with Kyra, he felt comfortable going as deeply into a matter as he wanted. When he'd turned the conversation to something that he'd heard on the national news about the Middle East, she'd moved into the conversation easily and knowledgeably. That led into another serious discussion about how the black community spends its money. They agreed on some matters and argued good-naturedly about others. She refused to relinquish her position to please him, as so many girls he'd talked to would do. He argued just as forcefully as she, and relished the few times when she conceded that he'd made good points.

The two hours that he'd spent on the telephone with Kyra had slipped by so easily. Now, just off the phone with her, he thought about what the conversation might signify. It was possible that the two of them could end up as friends. He could tell already, that if things progressed, it could be the richest and fullest friendship that he'd ever had. That was if he didn't jack it up by trying to throw some romantic crap up in there. She liked him, he could tell, but as a friend. That would be enough, because it was so much more than what he had with anyone else.

8

"Let's just go to The Biz and get something to eat," Renee said. Kyra had stayed late after school in order to give Renee a lift home. She'd used the extra time to get homework done and read some of a novel. Renee had come out of the girls' locker room clean and tired. The first thing that she had said was that she was hungry.

"All right," Kyra agreed. The Biz was busy, and music thudded through the air. Kyra and Renee looked around for a place to sit, but every seat seemed to be taken. They took a few more steps inside and continued to look around. That's when Kyra saw Jason sitting at a booth near the rear of the restaurant. He was talking to someone, but the booth concealed who it was. Jason looked up and saw Kyra then, as though he'd felt her eyes on him. He waved them over.

"Look," Kyra said, nudging Renee, "there's Jason." Renee saw him waving, and the two headed over.

"What's up?" Jason greeted them.

"What's up?" said the other person in the booth. It was Greg.

"Hey," Renee said. "We're trying to find someplace to sit, but this place is packed."

"Sit with us," Greg said.

"Yeah," Jason motioned. "Come on, Kyra." He scooted over to make room for her and Greg slid over for Renee.

"Thanks," Kyra said.

"So I hear you got AP English with Old Boy here," Greg said to Kyra.

"Yeah," Kyra said.

"Is he any good?" Greg wanted to know.

"Oh, yeah. We're working on a research paper together. Jason's good. He can really write."

"Cool. What have you been up to, Renee?" Greg asked.

"This and that, you know. School, practice, the usual," Renee said.

"I hear that," Greg said.

"What about you?" Renee asked Greg.

As those two began to converse, Jason took the opportunity to look at Kyra. She was looking across the table at Renee and Greg as they spoke to one another. Her fingers played casually with a paper-covered straw. "How have you been?" Jason asked. He kept his voice low, trying not to interrupt Greg and Renee's conversation.

"Fine," Kyra turned to look at him as she spoke. She had never been quite this near him. His eyes were very dark and his lashes and brows framed them perfectly. She couldn't see any way to improve upon his eyes. Her eyes dropped involuntarily to his mouth. Or his lips, she thought. "How about you?" she asked.

"Real good," Jason said. "I'm a little surprised to see you here."

"Yeah, Renee was hungry. This is where she wanted to come."

"Oh." Jason signaled the waitress.

"Hey, what's up?" the waitress said. "I see you-all have some guests. What'll it be, ladies?"

"BLT on wheat and a lemonade," Renee said.

"Regular fries and a lemonade," Kyra said.

"I got it. It'll be a few minutes," the waitress said and left.

"So who are you going to the homecoming dance with, Kyra?" Greg said.

Kyra looked and felt slightly embarrassed. "No one."

"That's cool. A lot of people are going in groups," Greg said.

"No. I mean, I'm not going."

"Why not?"

"I don't know. I don't have a date and I never really considered going. I'm not that interested," Kyra said.

"Aaaw, you should go," Greg said. "Shouldn't she go, Jay?"

"Yeah," Jason said looking at Kyra. Most definitely.

"That's what I keep telling her," Renee said. "But she won't listen to me."

Kyra grimaced at Renee and shook her head slightly. They should all find something else to talk about, she thought.

"I know that you can take a break from your science project and all of your homework for one night, Kyra," Jason said. Kyra looked over at Jason and smiled. He was teasing her.

"I guess you're taking a break from all of your practice and studies to go, huh?" she asked Jason.

"Yeah, a brother's gotta take a break sometime," Jason said with a smile.

"I hear that," Kyra said.

Renee and Greg looked on and watched the quiet way that Jason and Kyra spoke to one another, almost as if, in a room full of people, they were alone. Renee and Greg looked at one another, then back at Kyra and Jason.

What do we have here? Greg thought.

9

"Hello," Kyra said into her telephone receiver.

"May I speak to Kyra?"

"You're speaking to her," Kyra said. She was braiding her hair in small plaits. She was nearly finished.

"What's up?" Jason asked.

"Jason?"

"Yeah. What are you up to?"

"Braiding my hair."

"Oh, yeah? Are you gonna be a while?" She had a lot of hair, so it probably took forever, he reasoned.

"I'm almost finished."

"What are you doing after that?"

"I guess I'll walk my dog, Killer."

"Do you want some company?" he asked impulsively.

"Sure," Kyra said. Oh, God, she thought. "How about you come over in a half an hour?"

"Cool, I'll be there."

Kyra hung up and grinned. What'll we talk about? she wondered. "Forget that," she said aloud. "I have to hurry up and finish my hair." She quickly braided the last five long braids and changed out of her grubbiest sweats into some nicer ones. While she checked herself in the mirror the doorbell rang. "I've got it," she called out. She hurried down the stairs to get to the intercom by the door.

"Who is it?" she said into the intercom.

"Jason."

She pressed the buzzer and looked through the peephole so that she could watch undetected as he came up her walkway. Good lord, he looks good, she couldn't help thinking. He knocked on the door and she opened it.

"What's up?" he greeted her.

"What's up? After I got off the phone my mother told me that she'd already taken Killer for a walk, so it's just you and me."

"Okay. You ready?"

Kyra pulled a denim jacket from the hall closet and put it on. "All set."

They headed into the sunny Saturday afternoon. While some of the trees still held green leaves, many had already completed their turn to yellow or red or brown. The temperature was a mild fifty-three degrees, and no wind stirred. The sky was a pale blue, almost white, and it held no clouds in its vast embrace. They walked together, wordlessly and entirely comfortably. Kyra did not know why she felt so relaxed with this boy she was only beginning to know, but she did. Jason thought much the same thing, and it made him sigh with satisfaction. They walked for some time in this quiet.

"It's nice out," Kyra said.

"Yes."

"Do you take a lot of walks?"

"I was just thinking that I don't know the last time that I took a walk. I drive everywhere."

"Yeah. If it weren't for Killer I probably wouldn't take many either." They walked a few paces silently, then Kyra said "What kinds of things do you and Lisa do together?"

Jason looked over at her, but she looked back with only a look of relaxed expectation. "We go to the malls, we go to the movies, to parties, to games. You know, the regular stuff." She nodded. "What did you and your last boyfriend do together?"

"I've never really had a boyfriend, exactly. I was talking to this boy early in the summer, but we didn't really go together. I guess we did pretty much the same stuff Lisa and you did. We didn't go to any parties or games, though."

They walked on for a little while before Kyra spoke again. "So you and Lisa are pretty tight, huh?"

Jason looked over at her again, but this time she was looking down as she walked. Her braids swung forward, blocking his view of her face. "Yeah, I guess."

"Do you-all talk a lot?"

"What do you mean?"

Kyra looked at him then and Jason tried to read her eyes. He couldn't. "Do you-all have deep discussions? You know, like about life, school, the future, your families, stuff like that."

"Why?"

"I don't know. I guess I'm just curious." She looked directly at him as she spoke, and this time he was sure that he saw more than curiosity there.

"No, not really. I mean we talk about that kind of stuff, I guess. But we don't have *deep* discussions and whatnot."

"Oh."

"To tell you the truth, some of the talks you and I have had have been deeper than anything that I've had with Lisa."

"Oh." This time, though, when she spoke the word, she tingled inside just a little. She looked over at him and found him staring at her. His eyes were serious and quiet and she felt that she wanted to take his hand in hers.

"How is your science project coming?"

"It's coming along well. Mr. Hillard is really pleased. I've had a few problems, but that's to be expected."

"Explain it to me."

"The problems or the project?"

"The project. You can explain the problems to me some other time." She smiled at the implication that their conversations would continue and develop. She told him in simple, clear terms what her hypothesis was, the methodology of the series of experiments, the research behind it, and why she was interested in this type of experimentation in the first place. It was complicated. She left a lot out.

"That's impressive," Jason said.

"Thanks," she said with a smile. She was proud of her experiment. She'd thought of it on her own after doing some research. It was the kind of project that could do a lot to prepare her for the field of medical research, which is what she planned to do as a career.

"What do you want to do when you grow up, Jason?"

"I don't even know."

"For real?"

"For real," he assured her. "What about you?"

"Something in medical research. I'm not sure what. I want to help find a cure for cancer or AIDS or sickle-cell anemia or something."

"You'll probably do it, too. You're smart as hell."

"You're pretty smart, too."

"Not as smart as you."

"Yeah, you are. There's all kinds of smart. You're smart with writing and social stuff. You're very smart, Jason. Plus, you get good grades." Jason looked pleased.

"I hope you come to the homecoming dance."

"I don't go to a lot of parties."

"You should come. Maybe we can have a dance together."

Kyra smiled and decided to change the subject. "So is the team going to have a good season?"

"I hope so. I think so. We seem ready to play hard. I know I am."

"That's good." They walked on for a while in quiet. "It's nice out."

Jason smiled at her. "You said that already."

"Oh," Kyra said, embarrassed.

"But it is nice. It's nice enough to say it twice."

Kyra looked over at him, her embarrassment wiped away by his statement. If she wasn't careful, she could really like this boy.

10

"Jason," Mr. Vincent called as he entered the house. Jason had heard his father pull into the garage, but he'd remained where he was playing his PlayStation in the den.

"Back here!" Jason called. He kept playing.

"What are you doing?" his father said, entering the room and looking things over. "What the hell are you doing up in here?"

Here we go, Jason thought. "Playing some games."

"That's all you've got to do, huh? Sit around all night playing games! Where the hell is your homework?"

"I finished it already," Jason said. His insides knotted up as he smelled the alcohol on his father's breath and heard the familiar cadence of his time-to-pick-a-fight voice. That's how it went; things would be fine for stretches of time, and then *boom*, his father turned nasty.

"I didn't ask your stupid behind *what* you did, did I?"

Jason just looked at his father.

"Answer me!"

"No."

"No, *what*, boy?"

"No, sir," Jason said grudgingly. Jason despised the demands to call his father "sir" when his father was purposefully humiliating him.

"So I'm going to ask you one *more* time. Where is your homework?"

"It's upstairs."

"Go get it. Now!" Jason marched up the stairs and retrieved his homework from the desk in his room. All the way there and all the way back he hummed the chorus of a song that meant nothing to him under his breath. He was trying not to think. Jason came back and handed his father a spiral and a small stack of loose-leaf papers. His father began to read it over, but his concentration was obviously impaired by his drinking.

"This junk doesn't even make any sense! What in the hell are they teaching up there at that school?" He tossed the papers onto the low table before him.

Jason just looked at his father, waiting, gauging his father's condition and how long this session of trash Jason might last.

"Not much, I can tell you that," his father continued. "I can hardly make out a damn thing you wrote. On the other hand, you're so dumb that even the best school can't help you that much. Can it? Can it?"

"No."

"No, *what*, damn it!"

"No, sir."

"Don't let me have to tell you one more time, Jay! Understand me?"

"Yes, sir."

Mr. Vincent plopped himself down on the couch and stared at his son with glazed, angry eyes. Jason remained standing where he was when he'd handed his father his homework.

"You know," his father started up again, his speech slurred slightly by his intoxication. "You make me so sick! You know why?"

"Why, sir?" Jason whispered.

"There you stand, with your weak self, staring at me. Why are you always staring at me when I'm trying to talk to you? I'm trying to teach you something, boy. You're never going to amount to anything. You ain't got no heart. You've never had to struggle for a damn thing, not a damn thing. I hand you everything."

Jason simply looked at his father. All the familiar hurt and anger rose up against his will. And though he told himself time and time again not to let his father's words get to him, they did. God, how they did! But, I never ask you for anything, Dad, not a thing. I don't ask you to come to my games anymore. I don't ask you to listen to me, I don't ask you to come to teacher's conferences, I don't ask what you think about a girl I like, I don't ask you for a damn thing! Do I? Jason thought in a silent rage. Do I? No, *sir*!

"You're too damn lazy, that's the problem," his father continued. "You think you're something special because of that basketball, don't you? Well, you're not! Hell, I played ball in high school. Football. Now that's a man's ball game! You learn to take some punches, you learn to give 'em. You gotta have balls to play football, Jay! Not like basketball, where you get to cry 'foul' the minute anyone bumps into your sorry ass!" Jason's father heaved himself up off of the couch in two cumbersome tries. "I'm sick of looking at you!" He left the room and went upstairs to his bedroom, slamming the door loudly.

Jason let out a huge breath that he hadn't even realized he was holding. He spun around and pounded the pillow on the couch over and over until he felt just a little of his rage seep out of him. When he was done he plopped down on the couch, exhausted. He was nearly as tired after these sessions with his father as he was after a good workout on the court. His mind raced with all of the things he wanted to shout back at this man he both loved and hated. Every remark he thought of was cutting enough to make his father fall apart and cry, to beg his son for forgiveness.

Jason turned off the game, then the TV and, finally, the lamp. He sat in the darkness brooding. He felt entirely alone. He wished that there were someone he could call, someone to make him feel better. Lisa would just frustrate him further, and he didn't feel like talking to Greg. He got up from the couch and walked as quietly as he could to his room. He retrieved his book bag from his room and went back downstairs. His father, when drunk, fell asleep quickly and deeply. Jason figured he wouldn't have to hear his mouth again tonight.

Jason switched a lamp on when he got back to the family room. He took his five-subject spiral out of his bag and flipped to the English section. He kept flipping through the pages until he found it: "Kyra Evans 555-0020." He dialed the number before he gave it too much thought. While it was ringing he allowed himself to consider—What'll I say?

"Hello?" a woman's voice said.

"Hello," Jason coughed to clear his voice. "Hello, may I speak to Kyra?"

"This is she." Kyra was lying across her bed reading *Vibe* magazine. The cordless phone had been lying on the bed next to her.

"Hi, it's Jason."

"Jason?"

"Jason Vincent."

"I know who you are, I'm just a little surprised to hear from you."

"Why? We've talked before, right?"

"Yeah. What are you up to?" she asked.

"Nothing much, you know, chillin'." He cleared his throat again.

"So . . ."

"So, how are your classes going?"

"Good. I mean, my grades are good. Some of the classes could be better."

"What do you mean?"

"Well, Mr. Jackson can't teach, for one thing. All he does is put page numbers from the history textbook on the board and say, 'Read that, do the questions at the end.' Sometimes he doesn't even *say* it, he just *writes* it on the board!" She laughed at her own joke, and Jason had to chuckle. Of course, she was right. Everybody knew what a bad teacher Jackson was.

"Okay, that's one. You said some of your classes."

"Well, I'm taking an art appreciation class. But I don't really appreciate it."

"That's horrible," Jason laughed. "But you don't really appreciate it." He shook his head.

"What about you, how is school going for you?"

"About the same as for you."

"Go on."

"Well, math always did get on my nerves—too many numbers."

"Too many numbers, yeah, that's about as bad as my jokes."

"Worse."

"You're right, worse." They paused for a minute. "So, you sounded sort of down when you called."

"I did?" He was surprised that she picked up on that.

"Yes, you did. What's the matter?"

"Nothing."

"Now, don't say 'nothing.' Say you don't want to talk

about it, or tell me about it, but don't say 'nothing.' I hate it when people do that."

"Now you hate me?"

"No, I said I hate when people *do* that, not the people, not you."

"Oh, I was just checking."

"Well, you've checked, now answer the question. What's the matter?"

Jason flicked the lamp off, shrouding himself in darkness. "What's the matter . . . what's the matter." Jason sighed. "I got into it with my father. Well, actually, he got into with me. That's usually the way it goes."

"Usually?"

"Yeah, he'll get a buzz on and kinda gives me all this noise," he said, drastically underplaying it all.

"I see."

"You do, huh?"

"I think so. I want to." Jason heard the sincerity in her voice and almost wanted to tell her. But why would she want to take on somebody with all his problems? Her parents seemed so cool, so great; she wouldn't even know what to do with somebody who had a nutjob like his father for a parent.

"Yeah, well, it's . . . it's a headache when it happens. But it doesn't last too long, so I guess it's all right."

"Oh." She wanted to say more, but she didn't know what more to say. She detected some hidden hurt in his voice, but she could also tell that he didn't want to talk about it. "I'm glad you called."

"Me too."

"I don't get to talk about school enough."

Jason chuckled. "You make the worst jokes."

"You laugh every time, though."

"True, that. I have to stop encouraging you."

Kyra laughed at that. "Let's play twenty questions."

"How do you play?"

"To tell the truth, I don't really know. But the way I want to play it is where we ask each other ten questions and you have to answer honestly."

"I thought it was called twenty questions."

"It is. I don't want to be on the phone with you *all* night."

Jason laughed. "Okay. Let's play." Jason felt his mood shifting and lifting. He wasn't exactly sure why he'd called this girl, but he knew that he was glad he had. He felt kind of excited. What would she ask him? What would he ask her? "You go first."

"What's you're favorite color?" He liked her voice. It was rich, sort of mature.

"That's easy. Blue."

"Everybody and their aunt Mabel picks blue, Jason. I figured you for someone more original."

"You can't help what you like."

"You got that right. Your turn."

"Who's your favorite singer?"

"Hey, you were supposed to ask me my favorite color."

"Why?"

"Because I asked you your favorite color."

"We're not playing follow the leader, are we? We're supposed to be playing the reduced-calorie twenty questions game, ten questions." Jason grinned into the darkness.

"Fine," Kyra pouted playfully. "I have more than one favorite singer, though."

"Okay, tell me all of them."

"India Arie, Jill Scott, Charlotte Church, and my mom and dad play this woman named Shirley Horn—her stuff is cool, too."

"I only know two of those."

"Which two?"

"India Arie and Jill Scott."

"You should listen to the other ones sometimes. They're excellent."

"I bet I don't know anybody with their CDs."

"You know me."

"You're right. I know you. Can I come over and listen to them sometime?"

Kyra swallowed. "Yes." She cleared her throat.

"Your turn, Kyra."

She liked the way he said her name. "What's one of the best things that ever happened to you?"

"Winning the city championship game last year and being picked MVP. You do know what that means, don't you?"

"Ha, ha, ha, not funny."

"What's the scariest thing that ever happened to you?"

"That's a good one. Let me think," Kyra said. "Dang! I

can't think of anything. I mean, other than some horror flick."

"No, that doesn't count. That didn't happen to you. And you have to answer. I don't care if you have to think."

"Okay." Kyra thought for a bit more and Jason said nothing. He flipped the television remote in the palms of his hands, over, then over, and then over again. "This didn't exactly happen to me, but in a way it did. A few years ago my brother had an asthma attack and my parents had to call an ambulance and they rushed him to the hospital. I thought he might die, we all did. I didn't want to lose my big brother."

"That must have been scary."

"It was. I hardly even think about it now, though. But sometimes, if we get a phone call late at night, I worry that it might be about my brother. I have to stop doing that."

"Yeah, you've got to stay positive."

"I know. Okay, my turn. What's the most painful thing that ever happened to you."

"Whoa! Don't you want to start kinda slow?"

"You started it. You're the one who did that 'scariest thing' thing."

"All right, fair is fair." Jason debated with himself whether to be honest or to lie. He could just tell her something mildly painful; he didn't need to tell her the most painful thing. She wouldn't know the difference. For reasons he wasn't sure of, Jason told her the truth. Maybe it was the fact that when he spoke, she really seemed to be listening, like when she picked up on his mood when he first got on the phone. Maybe it was the fact that as he sat here talking to her in the dark, he was beginning to admit to himself that he wanted Kyra for more than a friend. "The most painful thing that ever happened to me was when my father told me that I was the reason my mother died."

Kyra sat in stunned silence.

"How could he say something like that to you? You didn't believe him, did you?"

"I was six years old. I believed every word."

An anger toward his father and utter empathy for Jason leaped into Kyra's heart. What kind of man would say something like that to his own child? His own *six-year-old* child at that? Kyra began to figure that if Mr. Vincent would say that to a six-year-old, then what Jason called "getting into it" was probably pretty nasty.

"Do you believe it now?"

"Is this one of your ten questions?"

"Yes."

"A little." Kyra sat quietly thinking about what he'd told her.

"Don't. Not even a little. Your mother wouldn't want you to think anything like that." Jason breathed deeply and felt his chest expand, then he exhaled just as deeply and quietly. He felt as though words were caught in his throat. He'd always wanted to hear that. Why should it matter so much that this girl said it to him?

"She wouldn't, huh?" His voice sounded doubtful.

"No, Jason," Kyra spoke quietly into his darkness. "No,

she'd want you to know that you were the best thing that ever happened to her. The best thing, Jason."

"You know what?"

"What?"

"You're all right, Kyra Evans."

"Yeah, I'm all right" she said in a joking voice. "So are you."

"My turn, right?"

"Right."

He decided to shift gears. "Are you a virgin?"

"I'm not answering that! That's none of your business."

"None of what we're saying is the other person's business, is it? We've been telling it anyway, haven't we?"

Kyra didn't answer his questions. Am I a virgin? Shoot! Now what have I gotten myself into? What was he up to asking me that, anyway. Why should he care? "Yes."

"I see," he said knowingly.

"What do you see?"

"I just see."

"Are you a virgin?" She figured she already knew the answer to that.

"No. My turn. Why are you still a virgin?"

"Because I don't want to have sex yet."

"But why?"

"Because."

"Because why, Kyra?"

"Because I'm not ready yet. Because I don't want to get some disease or get pregnant. Because I'm going to do it with someone I love the first time and I don't love anybody. I mean, I don't love any boy right now. That good enough?"

"Yes. That's good enough."

"Are you glad that you had sex?"

Jason laughed softly. "Oh, yeah!" Kyra blushed on her end of the line.

"Why?" she asked him.

"Do you really want to know?" he asked, lowering his voice. It took on a deeper tenor.

"Yes." Kyra unconsciously lowered her voice as well.

"Because it feels so good."

Kyra blushed even more. "Yeah?"

"Yeah. Haven't you ever wondered?"

"Of course, just not enough to try it."

"Too bad."

"No, it's not. Sex isn't going anywhere."

Jason had to laugh. "You're right. It's not going anywhere."

"I better go, its pretty late."

"All right. I'll see you tomorrow. Okay?"

"All right. Bye."

"Bye, Kyra."

After they'd hung up Kyra rolled over onto her back and smiled. Jason Vincent called me. But as a friend, she counseled herself. Still, he'd called, even as a friend.

She couldn't wait to see him tomorrow. As a friend.

11

The next day in school Jason arrived early, and instead of going straight to his locker where Lisa, Greg, and everyone else would be looking for him, he headed for Kyra's locker. In class he'd asked where her locker was: second floor, back hall. She was there, ramming books into her locker, when he rounded the corner and headed her way. She didn't notice him or anyone else walking by. Her girl Renee was at her locker right next door, and they were talking while they got their backpacks ready for the morning classes.

"Hey, Kyra," he greeted her. "What's up?" he said, nodding at Renee.

"Hey, Jason," Kyra said, surprised.

"What's up?" Renee returned, looking Jason up and down on the sly.

"What are you doing over this way?" Kyra queried as she slipped a couple of folders into her bag. She spoke to him from her kneeling position. Once her folders were in her bag, she stood up and left the heavy backpack on the floor.

"I'm just coming in. I was headed for my locker and I thought I'd stop by here for a sec," he said casually. He felt anything but casual inside.

"Oh, you remember Renee, right?"

"Sure, what's up?"

Kyra took in the black three-quarter-length leather jacket that he wore today. It fit perfectly across his broad shoulders and chest. Underneath, he wore a black sweater and black jeans with a black leather belt. The effect of all that perfectly fitted black attire, along with his gorgeous brown skin, black hair, and chocolate eyes, was perfection. At that moment Kyra knew what it was to be physically drawn to someone. It wasn't just the clothes, though. It was the way he stood, smiled, spoke. It was the rich, unexpectedly deep timbre of his voice. It was the fact that he always seemed so poised, confident, and comfortable. The fact that his black-on-black outfit accentuated his physical presence only added to his allure.

Jason turned to find Kyra staring at him, and something inside him caught and warmed. Something in her eyes, nothing that he could pinpoint, told him that she noticed him, in that way. He saw it just for an instant, and then her eyes were simply friendly again. It happened so fleetingly that he wasn't quite sure that he'd seen it.

"You got that paper?" he asked lamely, unable to think of much else to talk about with Renee standing there.

"Oh, yes, it's here. I guess we can turn in this final draft now," Kyra said. The first bell rang as she finished speaking. That left them five minutes to get to first hour.

"Well, I'd better go," Jason said. "I'll see you in Mrs. Devon's."

"Okay," said Kyra.

"Check you later, Renee," Jason called.

"Yeah, check you," Renee said. Kyra got busy looking through her already organized backpack. "So-o-o-o," Renee began in an exaggerated fashion, carefully eyeing her best friend. "What have we here, Miss Thang?" Renee asked, her voice rich with curiosity.

"What?" Kyra asked as she looked up from her backpack. "*What?*" she asked again when Renee did not respond.

"Yeah, 'What?'" Renee said sarcastically, not fooled for a moment by Kyra's feigned ignorance. "What's up with Mr. Gorgeous popping up at your locker this morning? That's what, Kyra."

"Oh, you heard him, he was just heading to his locker," Kyra said, placing her backpack on her shoulder again.

"Don't give me some mess like that, Ky! His locker is on the third floor, front hall. Everybody in Cross knows that. He would only end up back here if he was headed here, and you know it! So don't even try to play me," Renee said in a teasing, yet determined, voice.

Kyra was trying to be careful not to squirm under Renee's scrutiny. Kyra hadn't told Renee about the phone calls and the walk that she and Jason had shared. She was afraid that if she told her friend about it, it would all come off sounding like more than it really was. Kyra didn't want to have anyone, not even her best friend, spoil her feelings by warning her against the relationship. She wasn't ready to hear someone else say what she already suspected: a girl can't be just friends with Jason Vincent without falling for him, and that she'd only be hurt in the end. She knew she'd have to face those facts soon enough. So she said, "Well, that's what he said. If it's something else, I don't know, I can't read his mind."

"Yeah, right, play it that way," Renee said, unperturbed. Renee knew that when she was ready, Kyra would open up. She could wait. You may not be able to read his mind, Renee thought, but there's no mistaking what his eyes say. "I'll see you at lunch."

"Okay."

They headed off in different directions. Renee left, wondering what Mr. Joe Cool had in mind for her friend, hoping that it wasn't something that would hurt her.

Kyra was bubbling over inside with the delicious feelings that Jason's unexpected visit had awakened within her. Of course, Renee was entirely correct about the fact that Jason's visit was planned on his part.

Kyra had already come to that conclusion.

12

Over the next month Kyra and Jason's friendship grew and deepened. They called one another, not every day, but every other day. But they both wanted to call every day. They didn't say it to one another; they hardly even admitted it to themselves. They talked about nearly everything, and told one another things that they'd never told anyone else. They talked of everything except their feelings for one another. Jason even told her much of the true nature of his relationship with his father. Much of it, but not all.

Kyra told Renee how often she and Jason spoke. Renee told her girl to be careful. Jason told Greg that he thought Kyra Evans was pretty cool and that they'd had a chance to talk a few times. Greg simply nodded and wondered.

They were both careful to arrive at Mrs. Devon's class a little early to talk for a minute or so before class. Twice, while waiting for Renee to finish at track practice, Kyra had gone to the gym and watched Jason practice with the basketball team. She stood near the door for only a few minutes. He waved and smiled at her each time, and thought about her after she turned and left. Jason made his way to Mr. Hillard's class three more times during seventh hour as Kyra worked on her science project. He came over to her house for a walk on two cool October Saturday afternoons. Afterward he stayed for a soda and talked with Kyra and her parents in the kitchen.

Renee finally talked Kyra into attending the homecoming dance, just five days before the event. With so little time, they raced around trying to find just the right dress and accessories. Though she spoke to him regularly, Kyra didn't tell Jason she was going to the dance.

Their conversations were always nonromantic. Entirely. They were both careful of that. Very careful. But that was the problem. They should not have had to be careful at all.

13

Lisa had assured Jason that she would rather be caught dead than arrive at the homecoming dance before ten o'clock. So they arrived at ten minutes after ten and planted themselves in the midst of their crew. Jason stood around, half listening to what was being said, his mind distracted. All night he'd been thinking about Kyra. At dinner with Lisa, Greg, and Jackie, his thoughts had strayed to Kyra again and again. Even when Lisa and he had pulled over to mess around on Belle Isle, Jason found his thoughts drawn to Kyra. He had felt bad, thinking about Kyra while kissing Lisa. But wasn't able to stop so he'd made himself stop messing around with Lisa.

The homecoming dance was held at the elegant Roostertail. An entire wall of windows faced the black ribbon of the Detroit River. The lights of Ontario twinkled in the near distance, and a few boats floated lazily on the cool water. A DJ was hyping the room up with the latest beat, the bass rhythms dominating. The girls were dressed like women, in the latest style of slim and sleek long dresses with high slits and deep cleavage. Many of them had their hair piled high in sophisticated French rolls, while others wore smooth, shiny styles that lay against their necks or backs. The guys were dressed in dark suits with ties, and a few wore tuxedos. The dance floor was packed, but plenty of people sat at tables, or stood around talking to one another and watching the dancers.

Jason hit the dance floor with Lisa and then with Jackie for one song. He was a good dancer, and moved easily and gracefully with the rhythm of the music. He and Jackie rejoined the group at the end of a song, and Jackie slipped right back into the conversation that Lisa and some of the kids were having.

Jason scanned the room over Lisa's head, not even pretending to listen to the conversations in front of him anymore. He was irritated by the thought that it would be too late to call Kyra by the time he got home. He hadn't talked to her all day.

Jason turned casually to scan the room on his left, having finished looking to his right, and stopped short. His heart thumped a little harder, and before he could stop himself, a grin spread across his face. He wiped it away quickly and continued to stare. For there, seated in profile to him, all alone, was Kyra. Jason could not believe it. For just an instant he wondered if wanting to see or hear her so badly was making him imagine her here now. But no, there she was, very real, and reaching up to gently scratch her shoulder as she sat watching others dance. The people across the wide circular table from her talked among themselves. While cups and coats sat upon the table and chairs around Kyra, no one sat near her.

Her slender body was sheathed in a long silky dress of a rich wine color. It was far more provocative than anything Jason would have imagined her wearing, but still more modest than what most of the other girls wore. Her braids were pulled up and twisted into a simple style that left the long slender curve of her neck bare.

As he watched her, he wanted, badly, to be over there with her, and as if on cue, the first slow song since his arrival began to play.

"I'll be right back," Jason whispered into Lisa's ear.

"Okay," she answered distractedly. She didn't even look to see where he was headed.

Kyra did not see Jason approaching her. He came up behind her and bent to whisper into her ear, "May I have this dance?"

Kyra turned as though he had not surprised her at all. And, in fact, he hadn't. She had been waiting for him since her arrival at nine-thirty. She smiled without saying a word as she turned and looked into his dark, smiling eyes. His hand was extended, and silently, she placed her hand in his. He led her out onto the dance floor and did what he finally admitted to himself he had wanted to do for weeks now: hold her near. The couples around them were pressed closely, their bodies grinding provocatively, with eyes closed or peering into the distance. Jason held them apart from one another, but their eyes were locked. He was aware of the beating of his heart, the feel of her hand in his. He felt the pulse of her nearness and the warmth of her large eyes on him, and he felt good all over.

"You look beautiful," he said. He had never meant it more.

"You look beautiful too, Jason." She said it so simply that he knew that there was no coyness about it at all. No girl had ever said that he looked beautiful.

"I've been thinking about you all night, Kyra."

"I've been thinking about you, too." You're why I'm here, she thought.

She looked at him, her eyes full of questions and a growing heat.

Jason could feel a tightening in his stomach, and realized that he was actually nervous. He always knew exactly what to say to a girl. Furthermore, he was always pretty sure of a favorable reaction to whatever charming thing he said. He wasn't conceited about it, he just knew this from experience. He was always straightforward with girls, honest. They liked that. So many boys tried to come at them with a line, but not him. But he was a bit unsure, dancing with Kyra in his arms. She was unlike any girl he had encountered before. She was more confident, better read, more experienced in some ways, more innocent in others.

"I'm surprised to see you here. I thought that you weren't coming," he said.

"Renee talked me into it."

"Remind me to thank Renee." Kyra felt her insides melting under the warmth of his gaze and was not surprised at all when he drew her in closer. Their bodies just barely touched, each intensely aware of the other. Jason closed his eyes as he drew Kyra in closer still and allowed himself the luxury of breathing in the gentle vanilla fragrance of her hair. His left hand rested above the small of her back, and he felt his groin tighten with her rhythmic sway. She was soft and firm at the same time, and he longed to be alone with her and experience the feel of her privately.

For her part, Kyra danced with her eyes closed as well. She enjoyed the feel of his warm, smooth palm cupped around her hand. She held his shoulder, and was very aware of the feel of his well-developed muscles moving beneath her hand. He looked amazing, in a suit of charcoal gray, a pressed white shirt, and a blue tie. The suit made him look so mature and sophisticated.

Neither of them spoke, and the words of a popular R&B artist floated around them, between them, inside of them, speaking of the sweetness of a woman's desire to be with the man she loved.

"Hey, who's that with Jason?" Jackie asked, leaning in and whispering into Lisa's ear. Jackie knew exactly who it was.

114

"Where?" Lisa asked, attempting to follow Jackie's gaze.

"Right there," Jackie said, indicating Jason and Kyra on the dance floor.

Lisa had to scan the area that Jackie pointed to for several seconds before she spied Jason and Kyra. The dance floor was semidark and crowded. "Oh, that's just Kyra," Lisa answered dismissively.

"You don't sound too worried," Jackie remarked. Jackie took note of the way the two dancers kept their eyes on one another.

"I'm not," Lisa said confidently and with a certain amount of disdain in her voice at the very idea. "Believe me, Jackie, the day that I have to be worried about the likes of Kyra Evans will be the exact day that hell freezes over!" With that little witticism, Lisa turned smugly around to talk with their friends, not even bothering to look on the dance floor again.

However, Jackie took note of the dancers and watched with interest as Jason danced closely with Kyra, though not exactly too close.

When the music ended, Kyra and Jason parted, each one allowing their hands to linger a little longer than necessary. Jackie noticed that, too.

"Can I get you something to drink?" Jason asked Kyra. He didn't want to leave her, but he knew that he would have to get back to Lisa and his crew soon.

"No. Thank you, though," Kyra answered. Her hands could still remember his touch, and she cursed herself for the way that her feelings for him were deepening. She knew that she was no competition for Lisa. She knew that she was setting herself up for intense disappointment later on down the line. "You'd better get back before Lisa misses you," Kyra urged reluctantly. She didn't look at him as she spoke. She didn't want him to see the disappointment in her eyes.

"Yeah, I guess. I'll call you tomorrow, okay?"

"All right," Kyra said, giving him a small smile. Jason left and headed across the floor, back to his friends.

"Hey, what's up, girl?" Renee came falling into her seat next to Kyra.

"Nothing. Find me somebody to dance with, sister girl!"

"All right, now!" Renee jumped up to begin the hunt and Kyra stood to follow her.

Kyra and Jason avoided one another for the rest of the night. Still, each never once left the other's thoughts.

Late that night, when Kyra took off her lovely dress and had taken a quick shower, she climbed into bed. She sighed. She felt tired and happy. Renee had been right; she'd had a really good time. The entire group that she went with had gone out to eat before the dance, then hung out all night. Jason had asked her to dance, and it was so apparent to Kyra now, that he liked her.

Kyra smiled in the darkness and snuggled down under the covers. Her cell phone rang then. Kyra picked it up on the first ring. She didn't want to wake her parents.

"Hello?" she said softly.

"Kyra." He spoke softly, too.

"Jason."

"Look, I know it's late. . . ."

"That's okay."

"I wanted to tell you . . . I just wanted to say that I was real glad you came to the dance."

"Me too."

They both held the receivers pressed to their ears for a few silent moments. The sweet tension between them filled the silence.

"You really were beautiful," Jason said.

"Thank you, Jason."

"I'll see you."

"All right. Bye, Jason."

"Good night, Kyra."

14

It was two weeks after homecoming when Jason pulled up outside Kyra's home. That day his father had started up with him again. But this time he hadn't been content to simply verbally beat up on Jason; this time he'd taken the liberty of pushing Jason as well. Jason could still hear his father's words ringing in his ears. He could still feel the hot humiliation and emotional hurt of the shove that his father had given him. Rage filled his throat like bile when he recalled the scene. His father had been drinking and proceeded to tear into Jason over nothing. Jason tried to distance himself emotionally, to pretend his father's words were washing over him like water off the proverbial duck's back. But as his father tore into him with how he was "nothing" and how he was "a punk," Jason felt the words "Yeah? Well I'm just like you then," escape his mouth before he even had a chance to fully realize it.

"What the hell did you say?" his father countered.

"I said, then I'm just like you." Jason kept his voice level and calm with an effort. He strained to keep any evidence of the fear that he felt out of his voice.

"Oh, so you're saying your own father's nothing, is that it, you ungrateful jackass?"

"I'm saying, why do you have to go off on me like this? Nothing I do is good enough for you!"

"Good enough? Don't whine at me like some wimpy-ass baby! You don't know what goin' off is, boy! You hear me? My daddy used to kick my tail religiously, boy. I'm soft on you. I want you to be something, see? I want you to be something." His father seemed to choke on the last words. Mr. Vincent sat down at the dining room table and looked ahead of him, unseeing. Jason stood where he was, watching and despising him. "One time," Mr. Vincent said softly and nearly to himself, "my father came home after work. I could smell that he'd been drinking before he made it home. He just walked in the door, spotted me, marched over, and slammed his fist into my face, like I'd smacked his mama. It was as though he didn't even know I was his son." He said it in a voice filled with sad wonder. But Jason couldn't hear all of that because of his own anger, fear, and sadness at that moment. His father sat for a few quiet minutes more, then pushed himself up, and headed out the front door without another word.

When his father had gone, the first thing that Jason thought to do was call Kyra. He'd been right, too. Everything she'd said had been just what he needed to hear. Kyra's soothing voice made him calm again. Her words had turned the raging tiger in his chest into a tamer creature, poised watchfully, waiting for the next confrontation. Her words had made him want to see her, too—to be near her. So he'd gotten his coat on, grabbed his keys, and left, just like that. He didn't think about why or what he'd say. He only thought about how much better he would feel if he could just be near her. *Kyra, Kyra, Kyra, Kyra,* he'd said over and over inside his head as he drove.

He got out of his car and walked over to the gate. He pressed the button of the intercom and waited.

"Yes," Dr. Evans said.

"Good evening, Dr. Evans, it's Jason Vincent. May I see Kyra?"

"Come on in," Dr. Evans responded. Jason heard the buzzer and opened the gate. Once inside he closed the gate behind him.

Dr. Evans had the door open when Jason stepped onto the porch. "How are you, Jason?" He asked pleasantly.

"I'm all right, sir. How are you?"

"Very well." They shook hands. "Kyra knows you're here. She'll be down in a minute." Kyra came down just then in gray sweats, looking so good, Jason wanted to scoop her up right then and there.

"Hi, Jason."

"What's up, Kyra?"

"Well, I'll talk to you later," Dr. Evans said, leaving the two alone in the foyer.

Jason barely noticed when her father headed away.

"I was just about to take Killer for a walk. Do you want to come?" Kyra asked.

"Yeah, sure," Jason said.

Kyra got her gym shoes from the foyer closet and sat down at one of the benches beside the door to put them on. After she put on her coat, she took a leash off a hook in the closet and whistled for Killer. The toy terrier came scrambling around a corner.

"Hi there, girl," Kyra said as she knelt and attached the leash to the tiny dog's collar. Kyra gave the dog a couple of pats and got up. "Come on," Kyra said to Jason with a smile.

They stepped out into the early evening and began their walk. It was, as always, quiet.

"Are you okay?" Kyra asked, concerned.

"I'm getting there," Jason said honestly, looking over at her.

"I saw *Victory Rising* last night. My father brought it home," she said, referring to a popular movie out on video. Jason looked at her appreciatively. Somehow she knew that he didn't feel like talking about his father right now.

"What did you think?" Jason had seen it at the theater. He had recommended that Kyra see it when he noticed it on video.

"It wasn't too bad," Kyra admitted. "It's not the kind of movie I usually pick; but you were right, I did enjoy it. I like how they had a sister in there, kicking some behind for the cause."

"Yeah, the ending was a trip, though," he said.

"A trip. It was the only real disappointment, besides there being too much violence," she countered.

"Disappointment, too much violence? You've got to be kidding," he responded. And they were off, debating the movie with good-natured energy.

"Look, I said I liked the movie," Kyra said after fifteen minutes of discussion. "I didn't say that I loved it. I could come up with ten different ways to make it better!"

"And I could come up with ten reasons why you're wasting your time doing that!"

"Or you could just shut up!" she countered, laughing. They had stopped walking and stood on the sidewalk before a house a couple of blocks from Kyra's. Killer was sniffing around the shrubbery, and Kyra held her leash in her hand. They stood facing one another, much of Jason's pain surrounding his father dissipating into the air with their words and laughter.

The autumn evening had turned cool, and the sun had begun to set. The sky was bathed in sultry hues of purple, orange, smoky gray, and pink. The crisp leaves of russet, red, gold, and green whispered, *Kiss her, kiss her.*

"Or I could just kiss you," he said softly. They stood close to one another, their warm breath held in small puffs on the cool air. He stared at her, his eyes warm and expressive.

Kyra stared back into his eyes, never wanting to see anything else. "You mean, like this?" she asked. She raised herself up on tiptoe and planted a slight, quick kiss on his cheek. She smiled.

"Or like this," he answered, giving her a slow kiss on her cheek. He smiled.

"Or like this," she said, her eyes serious. She leaned in and placed a soft kiss with her closed lips on his closed lips.

He looked at her after that. His expression was full of suppressed longing, and she felt the look, though she did not know the words for it, wash all over her and heat her from the inside. "Or like this," he said softly. He leaned in, lowering his head over hers, and kissed her in a way that she had never been kissed before. It began softly, oh so incredibly softly, with her lips closed and his closed, too. Once, then twice, then again that way. Then he touched her lips delicately with his tongue and she was surprised by its warmth and gentle moisture. She parted her lips instinctively and they brought their mouths together for a slow, deliberate French kiss, during which she thought only of him and the delicious sensations he was delivering, not just to her mouth, but to her entire body.

He wrapped his arms lightly around her, and she placed her hands upon his chest, and the kiss went on and on. She could smell the light scent of soap that he'd used and the leather of his coat. She reveled in the velvety softness of his lips and the rhythmic, circular, then back-and-forth motion of their tongues.

She drew away first.

"Kyra . . ." he began.

"Ssshhh," she said, placing an index finger softly on his lips. "Come on, Killer," she called, and the dog came immediately. She knelt to attach the leash, all the while feeling her heart thud between her ears.

Jason, she thought. I love kissing Jason.

Once the dog was leashed, she turned back toward her home and they began walking in that direction. They walked back quietly together, both involved with thoughts of one another, their kiss, and what it might mean. They were on Kyra's porch before Jason knew it.

"Kyra . . ." Jason began again.

"I don't want to talk about it right now," she said gently, looking into his eyes. "Not yet."

"Are you mad?" he asked, concerned.

"No. No, Jason. I'm so far from mad I'm scaring myself," she said seriously. Inside she was in a delicious turmoil. Jason felt the same way. "Come on in."

Once inside, the warmth of the Evans home met them. They could smell dinner cooking.

Kyra's mother walked by, heading to the kitchen. "Was it nice out?" she asked.

"Yes," Kyra answered.

"Why don't you stay for dinner, Jason?" Ms. Evans offered. Jason looked over at Kyra; Kyra looked back at him. Her expression was encouraging.

"Okay, thank you, Ms. Evans," Jason responded.

"You're welcome," Ms. Evans said and continued on her way.

"Are you sure you're okay with this?" Jason whispered to Kyra after Ms. Evans left the room.

"Yes, I really am. It's okay. I mean, I want you to stay."

"All right." They took off their coats and hung them up, then headed into the kitchen.

"Jason, Jason," Dr. Evans said as they entered the kitchen. "I need help over here. My wife tells me that I've been kind of heavy-handed with the chili tonight. What do you think?" he said, waving Jason over to the large stove. The table in the kitchen nook was set for three, and Ms. Evans was placing a fourth setting on the table for Jason. There were flowers on the table, and jazz playing, and a tossed salad sitting on the kitchen island. The room was filled with the good vibes emanating from Kyra's parents, and Jason felt his mood rising further.

Jason went over to the stove and Dr. Evans ladled a small amount of chili into a bowl for him. "Here, taste that," Dr. Evans said as he handed Jason the bowl and a spoon.

"This is tight, Dr. Evans," Jason said after two spoonfuls. "For real, it's good." Jason grinned at Dr. Evans.

"Do you see, Ashanti, it is tight! You're not going to get a rating much higher than that," Dr. Evans said with satisfaction. Kyra and Jason tried to hide their smiles at Dr. Evans's overly proper pronunciation of the slang term.

"Well, I think you've put too much seasoning salt in there," Ms. Evans said, still smiling. "But it's your chili."

"Thank you, my darling. And I look forward to watching you gobble it right up, despite your complaints," he said smugly. Ms. Evans walked over and gave Dr. Evans a playful little punch on his forearm. Jason looked on at their obvious love for one another and smiled. Kyra watched him and wished, with all she now knew of his home life, that things were better for him.

"Kyra, baby, get the corn bread out of the oven for me, will you? Jason, give her a hand getting that buttered, and we'll be ready to eat," Dr. Evans announced. Dr. and Ms. Evans went on talking to each other. Kyra and Jason washed their hands and worked side by side, stealing glances at one another, smiling from time to time, and savoring the new feelings welling up between them.

"So Kyra tells us you're a good student, Jason," Dr. Evans said.

"I work at it, sir," Jason answered.

"Good, good. What's your overall GPA?" Dr. Evans continued.

"Three-point-three."

"That's good, Jason," Ms. Evans said. "I'm sure your father is proud."

Jason glanced quickly at Kyra, then lied to her mother, "Yes. Thank you."

"Kyra also tells us you're a star on the basketball team," Ms. Evans said.

Jason looked over at Kyra again, his affections for her growing. She had discussed him with her parents, and she was proud of him. "Kyra might be exaggerating some, Ms. Evans."

"No I'm not. Jason's just being modest. He made All

City and All State in the ninth and tenth grades. And he was picked for the state All Star team both years. Last year he was the top scorer on the team, fifth highest scorer in the state, third highest in the city." Kyra beamed across the table at him.

"And a good student," Dr. Evans said, impressed.

"Well, we're proud of you, Jason," Ms. Evans said. Dr. Evans nodded.

"Thank you," Jason said.

"So what are your plans for the future?" Ms. Evans asked.

"College for sure. I want to play ball in college." Jason thought for a moment. " I don't really know what I want to be, career-wise, though."

"Well, you've got time. You'll figure it out," Dr. Evans said.

Jason relaxed into the conversation. Dr. and Ms. Evans sounded interested and caring. Jason didn't feel as if he were being grilled. He liked talking to them. Jason asked about their careers and they both gave lively accounts of what they did.

The dinner was one of the best that Jason had had in his life. Mrs. Gillman was a great cook, so it wasn't just the Evanses' food. It was the relaxed and pleasant company, the family banter, the laughter, the way they listened to Kyra when she spoke, and to him when he spoke. It was the music and the flowers and the way they all were around one another. After helping Kyra clean up the kitchen and load the dishwasher, he prepared to go.

"Can I call you tonight?" he asked as they stood in the foyer alone.

"Yes," she said. He reached up and stroked her cheek. Then he was gone.

After Jason left, Kyra went upstairs and moved around her bedroom, touching everything and fidgeting. She couldn't believe what had happened, and yet she'd been expecting it ever since the homecoming dance. She could hardly believe that *the* Jason Vincent—voted best body and most handsome in their class last year, and no doubt this year too, wanted by half the girls in their school, popular almost to a fault—this same Jason Vincent had just kissed her. She'd kissed him! He'd had dinner in her home. It was almost too much to take in at once. She felt so excited that she thought she might burst. She picked up the telephone and dialed.

"You won't believe what happened tonight!" Kyra said excitedly, even before responding to Renee's hello.

"What?" Renee asked, instantly almost as excited as Kyra.

"Jason came by this evening and we kissed. I kissed him first! Then my mama invited him to dinner and he stayed!"

"Get the hell outta Dodge!" Renee exclaimed.

"Yes, girl, I know," Kyra said. Her voice dripped with pleasure.

"Well, what was he like? How did you end up kissing?" Renee asked excitedly. Kyra told her about their walk and the little kisses leading up to the long one.

"Well, what was he like?" Renee asked again.

"Excellent," Kyra breathed. "Oh, Renee, he was excellent."

"And to sit across the table eating dinner with him in front of your parents after that! I don't know how you did it," Renee offered.

"I know, I know! I kept looking at his lips and remembering the kiss and wondering if my parents noticed me staring at him."

"How did he act?"

"He was cool, you know. I mean, I caught him looking at me from time to time, but he was much smoother than me," Kyra answered.

"Oh, Kyra, I don't believe it. You and Mr. Gorgeous!"

"And Lisa," Kyra answered wryly.

"Oh, that's right. You're messing with some other woman's man," Renee said excitedly.

"I know. Don't remind me. I feel horrible."

"So what are you going to do?"

"I don't know, exactly. I just know that I'm *not* going to kiss him again while he's with Lisa. That isn't even me," Kyra said.

"It must be you a little bit," Renee said jokingly.

"I know," Kyra said miserably. "I didn't expect that."

The telephone beeped in Kyra's ear. "Hold on, Renee, that's my other line."

"Okay," Renee returned.

"Hello," Kyra said once she'd clicked over.

"Hello, may I speak to Kyra?" Jason said.

"This is she."

"You and your mother sound so much alike, I always have to check," Jason said.

"Yeah, I know. Can you hold on a minute?" Kyra asked. Butterflies were playing a mean game of tennis in her stomach.

"Sure," Jason said. Kyra clicked back over to Renee.

"Hey, girl, it's Jason. I'll talk to you tomorrow."

"All right, Kyra. Don't get into trouble, now," Renee joked.

"I'll try not to," Kyra said seriously. She clicked back over to Jason.

"Hello, Jason?"

"I'm here," he answered. "We need to talk."

"I know," Kyra said. "I can't believe that I kissed you when you have a girlfriend."

"I've never cheated on Lisa. I've never cheated on any girlfriend, to tell the truth," he responded.

"I don't know what happened," Kyra said lamely.

"I do. I've been feeling things for you for a while now. I think about you almost all the time. I've been kissing you in my mind for too long," Jason said intently and quietly into the receiver.

Kyra could feel her insides thrill at his words. She hadn't expected him to be so direct. "It's been the same for me," she admitted. "But it can't happen again. I've never messed around with somebody else's boyfriend, and I don't plan to become the type of person who does."

"I know, I wouldn't want you to. But I can't help how I feel, either, Kyra."

"Neither can I." They sat in silence for a few moments. The same sweet turmoil that the kiss had initiated was back inside Kyra, multiplied by the electricity his admission had jolted her with. "We definitely have to stop hanging around one another," Kyra said.

"No. I can control what I do," Jason countered. He didn't want to stop being around Kyra. "We can still see each other; just keep it on a friendly tip."

"Who would we be kidding? Not you, and most definitely not me. And let's face it, that's all that matters. If we fooled Lisa, it would still be cheating because *we*'d know what was between us every time we met. We'd know why we wanted to spend so much time with one another." Kyra spoke with simple, honest conviction. Jason respected her for it. That just made him want her all the more.

"I'll have to break up with Lisa tomorrow," Jason said.

"That would be your decision. I don't want to influence you," Kyra said.

"You influence me in almost everything!" Jason said emphatically. "I can't stay with Lisa *because* you influence me. And I like it. I keep thinking about you when I'm with her, when I'm with my boys, when I get into it with my father, when I'm in class," he said with feeling. "You influence me, Kyra, and I want it that way," he whispered. She felt his words in her groin, and closed her eyes as the intense feelings for Jason swept over her.

"I didn't know," she whispered back. He didn't say anything. "Jason," Kyra hesitated, then started again. "Jason, there are things I want to say to you, I almost need to say them to you, but I can't while you're Lisa's boyfriend. You're right. We can't hide how we feel anymore, and I don't think we should even deal with one another while you have a girlfriend. I've got to go," Kyra said in a rush. She didn't want to make any confessions to someone else's boyfriend, and she knew that if she stayed on the line, she'd do just that.

"All right. Good night, Kyra."

"Good night, Jason."

15

"You're what?" Lisa asked, stunned. They stood in the back hall of the fourth floor, two floors up from the cafeteria. They'd both gotten passes for the restroom when Jason told Lisa that he needed to talk to her alone. He had planned to wait and come by her house after basketball practice. But as they all sat together during lunch, everybody laughing and talking together except him, and he couldn't take it any longer. He felt like a hypocrite. How could he watch her laugh, knowing that later that night he was planning to break up with her?

"You're what?" Lisa repeated. She stood before him, her gray eyes full of anger and disbelief.

"I'm sorry. We can't stay together." Jason said, feeling very uncomfortable. He never liked breaking up with a girl. He preferred to lead them to a place where they broke up with him.

"Where the hell is this coming from?" Lisa wanted to know.

"Lisa, we have been kinda drifting apart for a while now," Jason began.

"No, not me," Lisa interrupted with fire. "I haven't been drifting anywhere! What's this about, Jason? And don't give me some crap about us drifting apart!"

"I haven't felt the same about you for a while now," Jason said as gently as he could. He wished that this were all over. "And I want to see someone else."

"Oh, that's it, huh? Maybe you don't feel the same about me *because* of this someone else," she countered.

"No, that's not true. My feelings for you had changed before I became interested in her," he answered truthfully. "But, I don't know, I guess my feelings for you have been affected some by my feelings for her." It made him feel bad to say these things. But he wanted to be honest. Lisa would see him with Kyra in the halls pretty soon, and he didn't want to hurt her even more by having everything explained by what she saw.

"Who's the bitch?"

"She's not a bitch, Lisa."

"No, you wouldn't think so," Lisa practically snarled. "Who is she, Jason?"

"Kyra Evans."

"You're kidding me! Jason? You are not breaking up with me over some damn nappy-headed Kyra Evans."

"Damn, Lisa, why do you always have to go there? And no, I'm not breaking up with you for Kyra . . . entirely. I told you my feelings had changed for you already. So it's for both reasons, I guess. But the truth is, we would have ended up breaking up anyway because of how my feelings were changing," he finished.

"She can have you then! Good riddance! If you want *that* over *me*, I don't want you!" Lisa was fully enraged now.

"Lisa, you know that you're special to me. I don't want us to stop being friends just because we're not together. I'm not trying to hurt you," Jason said, reaching out to touch Lisa's arm.

"Keep your hands off me, Jason, and don't try any of those weak-ass lines on me! We're not friends, we're not anything to one another anymore!" She stared at him with eyes full of rage, her beautiful face contorted into an expression of pain and anger. Still, it was beautiful. "Tell me something, Jay; have you been having sex with her?" Lisa's eyes narrowed to gray slits.

"No," Jason said.

"Have you been doing anything with her behind my back?"

"We've kissed," he watched as Lisa's rage expanded. "But that happened one time, and I knew then that I had to be honest with you about my feelings and break it off."

"I can't believe you're doing this to me, Jay," Lisa said. Pools of tears made her eyes bright, and the anger fled from her face, making room for only the pain. "I love you, how can you do this to me?"

He took her into his arms. "Lisa, I wouldn't hurt you on purpose. That's why I'm being honest with you. You mean a lot to me. I'm sorry for disrespecting you by kissing her. I'm sorry for that, Lisa."

"Jay, don't leave me," Lisa cooed softly, wrapping her arms around his neck, turning her tear-stained face up to his. "Don't I make you happy? Don't you like the things I do to you?" She pulled his head down toward hers.

"Stop it, Lisa," Jason said gently, pulling out of their embrace.

"Oh, you can be faithful to her, but not me!" Lisa hissed. Her anger flared up instantly. "You can kiss my ass, Jason Vincent!" Lisa said and stalked out of the hallway.

Jason stood there for a minute thinking of what had just gone down between Lisa and him. He thought of the ways he could have handled it differently. He thought of the hurt and anger on Lisa's face, and he felt bad. But almost against his will he could feel the joy rising up inside of him because he could be with Kyra now. He felt guilty about how good he felt, but what could he do? He realized that he still had to get his books from the cafeteria, so he waited a couple of minutes before going down behind Lisa.

"What's up, man?" Greg asked when Jason came to the table. Lisa and Jackie were nowhere to be seen. The three other kids that they'd been eating with were still there. Everyone was looking up at Jason expectantly.

"Where's Lisa?" Jason asked without answering Greg's question.

"She and Jackie just hopped up outta here," Greg said. "What happened, Jay?"

"I'll tell you about it later. I gotta go," Jason said, and left. Greg, Tommie, and a girl named Sonya at the table just shrugged and looked at one another.

Jason went over to the cafeteria monitor and asked for another pass, this one to the library. Though the monitors only gave out one pass per period to a student, Mr. Lemur gave another pass to Jason without hesitation. Mr. Lemur was a regular at the Cross basketball games and admired Jason's abilities on the court.

Once he had the pass, Jason made a beeline for Kyra's fourth-hour class, not the library. He walked by the door where he saw her taking notes and looking up at the work the teacher had placed on the board. She wasn't paying the door any attention. Luckily, the girl sitting next to her was. Jason signaled her that he wanted Kyra's attention. The girl nudged Kyra and pointed to the door. Kyra looked up at the door and saw Jason. She didn't smile and neither did he. He held up his pass, indicating that he wanted her to come out into the hall. He stepped out of view when he saw her rising from her seat. Kyra went up to the teacher's desk where she wrote Kyra a pass.

"Hey, Kyra," Jason said when she walked down the hall to where he stood.

"Hey, Jason," she returned. "What are you doing here?"

"Can I come see you tonight after practice?"

"No, Jason, we went over this last night," Kyra said.

"I just broke up with Lisa," he said.

She moved to him and touched his arm. "Are you okay?"

"Yes. I just want to see you."

"Come by around eight," Kyra said. "I'd better go back to class."

"I'll see you then," Jason said.

During the rest of the day Jason was extremely distracted. He barely heard anything that was going on in his last three classes and basketball practice wasn't much better. His coached yelled at him twice, something that rarely happened.

When he got home it was nearly six o'clock. He showered, put on fresh clothes, and did homework until his father came home just after seven. They had a quiet dinner together, the television served as a talkative third, and then Jason asked his father if it would be all right if he went out for a little while.

"Have you done all of your homework?"

"Yes."

"Where are you going?"

"Over to this girl named Kyra's. I should be back by ten."

"Okay," his father said.

When Kyra opened the door for him fifteen minutes later he couldn't believe how good she looked. She'd taken down her braids and her hair was a wild mass of waves. It hung down to her chest and stood out from her head like a soft wooly cloud. It still smelled like vanilla. It framed her pretty brown face and made her eyes seemed larger, more luminous.

"Come on in," she said softly. That's all. No hello, no small talk. She couldn't get any out right now if she tried. Feeling much the same way, Jason came inside without a word.

"Mama, it's Jason. We're going to the family room," Kyra called up the stairs.

"Hi, Jason. Okay, Kyra," Ms. Evans responded from above. Jason called up hello.

"Let me have your coat," Kyra said. Jason shrugged out of his coat and handed it to her. She hung it up in the foyer closet.

"Come on," she said, leading him to the family room. Once in the room, Kyra shut the door and they settled down facing each other on one of the comfortable couches.

"What happened?" Kyra asked.

"I broke up with Lisa during lunchtime today. It's over."

"Did you tell her about me?"

"I had to. I didn't want her to trip out, and whatnot, when she saw you and me in the hall together." They sat staring at one another, absorbed in his words and what they meant for their future, for their right now.

"She's going to see us in the hall together?" Kyra asked, smiling.

"I can often be seen in the hall with my lady," he said, smiling back and moving closer.

"Your lady? I don't know anything about this. You haven't asked me anything," Kyra countered.

"Can we hook up, Kyra?" Jason asked.

"With pleasure, Jason. With pleasure." Although she hadn't believed it possible, this kiss was actually better than the first. They shifted until they were closer. He held her face gently within the palms of his hands and kissed her the way that he had imagined, fully and passionately. She circled her arms around his neck and he brought his around her back, moving his kiss from her mouth to her cheek, then her neck. Kyra's breathing became fast and heavy and she was thinking that she ought to push him back, but she couldn't think of why. Jason brought his trail of kisses back around to her mouth.

"Didn't you have something to tell me?" he asked when he pulled away several minutes later.

"What?" Kyra murmured, planting tiny kisses on his lips.

"Last night on the phone you said that you had things to tell me, but you couldn't while I was someone else's man. I'm yours now. What do you want to say?"

Kyra pulled back a little, though she remained very close, and looked into his eyes.

"I have never felt about anyone the way that I feel for you. You make something inside of me shimmer and shake and . . . I think about you all of the time, too. When I'm doing homework, when I'm talking with my friends, when I'm taking a bath . . ."

"Mmmm, I like that," he said interrupting her.

"Especially that 'in-the-bath' part," he said, pulling her into his arms again.

"Stop teasing me," she said playfully. "But don't stop kissing me just yet."

Jason leaned in to begin kissing Kyra once again. The vanilla scent of her hair was all around him. "Your hair smells so good, girl. I love your hair."

"You do?" Kyra murmured with some surprise. "I know most people don't."

"I'm not most people. I've wanted to do this for a long time," he said with satisfaction as he delved his hands into her hair. She instinctively tilted her head back as his hands played in her hair. "It's soft," he said as he stared at her exposed neck and slightly parted lips. He leaned over and kissed her neck, then brought her head up so that they could kiss on the mouth again. Kyra took the lead this time, teasing his tongue with hers. She led the kiss at a slow pace, allowing them to savor the nearness and sweetness of one another.

"Where did you learn to kiss like that?" Jason asked when they stopped.

"Why?" she asked with a grin.

"Because it's damn good," he said, grinning back.

"I just made it up," she said.

"Can you do it again?"

"Yes." And she did.

16

"Just tell me what you're thinking, man," Greg pleaded with his best friend. Jason and Greg were playing video games in Jason's den.

"You can tell what I'm thinking. I'm thinking that I want to be with Kyra." Jason responded without looking over at Greg. Greg was in the lead and Jason was up. He was intent on taking the lead.

"But why, Jay, why? No disrespect to your new woman, and all, but you got to see what I'm talking about. Lisa is fine. Too fine. She could be in music videos, man," Greg said earnestly. "She was all over you, like white on some damn rice, she was giving it up . . ."

"Watch it now," Jason warned.

"Anyway," Greg continued, "she's popular as hell, and you weren't having any real problems that I knew of. Now Kyra is cute, in her own way, but she ain't no Lisa, no disrespect. She doesn't party, doesn't hang with anybody we know, she doesn't even dress right! And of course, there's the hair thing. I mean, come on man, talk to *me*!"

Jason put his video controls down and got up from the couch. He began pacing back and forth. "First of all, everything you said about Lisa is true. But to me, Kyra is beautiful. She's smart as hell, funny, she knows a lot of stuff about a whole lot of different stuff. She's easy to talk to, she's good, you know, she's just good people inside. She's different and she's not afraid to be different. She's not worried about what you think about her hair or her clothes or her, period. I like that."

"Still, Jay," Greg said, unconvinced.

Jason stopped pacing and looked at his friend as he spoke. "I talk to Kyra about things I never, ever dreamed of telling Lisa. I've told Kyra things that I haven't told anybody else. It's like . . . it's like there's something inside of me that's been calling out, and when I got to know Kyra, I found the something that could answer it. That girl does something strong to me, Greg. Something strong."

Greg looked at his friend hard. He saw how serious Jason was; he heard him talking in ways he'd never heard him talk before, especially about a girl. And he understood Jason. "All right, bro. I hear you, I'm with you."

Jason smiled at his friend in return.

17

As much as Kyra and Jason were into one another, they couldn't block out the real world. And the real world at Cross High School was trippin' over the news that fine-as-hell, super-jock, popular-as-Nikes-in-the-NBA, can-have-anybody-he-wants Jason had dumped fine-as-hell, wickedly popular, can-have-anybody-she-wants Lisa for double-brained-nappy-headed-sweet-but-nobody Kyra. *Unbelievable* was the word, first through third hour. *For real?* was the word fourth and fifth hour, as the news began to sink in. *Damn!* was the word by the end of the day.

Lisa made a point of being at her locker every time Jason showed up that first day. She aimed her eyes at him bitterly, with all the intensity of a ray gun. Jason felt every glare, because he felt guilty about hurting her while he felt so good. Her girl Jackie was right there each time, duplicating every move of Lisa's. By the end of the day Jason had copped an empty locker in the same hallway as Kyra's. He kept his old one, but he knew he'd hardly use it. He'd rather get the extra minutes with Kyra.

Friends and classmates were stopping him all day asking him if it was true. When he told them yes, most of them asked why. He just told them to get out of his face. Why? Other than his boy Greg, they wouldn't be able to understand it anyway.

For Kyra's part, she felt that half the school was looking at her all of a sudden. Where before she had walked through the halls comfortable and relatively unnoticed except by her few friends, suddenly every other pair of eyes seemed to be checking her out, measuring her, wondering about her. She hated it. All the girls were giving her looks like, *What's she got I don't have? Nothing.* And all the boys seemed to be thinking, *What's she got I missed? Nothing much.* It was a long day.

The only relief for either of them was when they got a chance to be together. Kyra moved in Mrs. Devon's class so that she could sit next to Jason. Sixth hour they both had study hall, but in two separate halls. They made arrangements to meet in the library and spend the hour there. After fifteen minutes of hardly doing any work at a table together they moved to the stacks for a few short, tender kisses.

"Girl, I missed doing that!" Jason said, grinning, his face close to hers, his voice a whisper.

"Mmmm, I can't tell. Show me again," Kyra whispered back in a teasing voice. Jason kissed her again, more deeply, this time. "Oh, yeah, I think I can tell now," she said softly, her eyes still closed. Jason smiled down at her. Everything inside him was singing.

A student came around the stack of books and stumbled on them in their embrace. "Oh, sorry," he said, then moved on.

"Look, you're going to get me kicked out of the library!" Kyra said.

"I don't have you tied to me," Jason taunted back.

"Yes, you do," Kyra said, looking into his handsome eyes. "Right here," she said tapping first her chest, then his.

"I like that," Jason said, leaning to give her another kiss. They went back to their seats at the table and Jason pulled out a couple of sheets of loose-leaf paper. The librarians would go off on you and boot you out of the library if you violated their quiet-in-the-library rule. He pulled a pen out of his pocket and started writing.

How's your day been going? Jason wrote.

Funky. Everybody's staring. How about you?

About the same. Lisa is trippin'. But I don't blame her.

Me neither. You feel bad, don't you?

Yes. She never saw it coming.

I feel bad about her too.

I've been thinking about you all day.

Me too. You know everybody is wondering what you're doing with me.

Then everybody's stupid. I'm wondering what you're doing with me.

Then you're crazy.

Do you want to go to a movie tonight, get something to eat?

Yes. I have to ask my parents, but it should be okay.

I'll pick you up around 8.

All right.

Thank you.

For what?

For making me feel so good.

The end of the day came and Kyra was at her locker, gathering her things together for her science project. She'd spent a few extra minutes talking to her Spanish teacher after the bell rang. Now the halls were thinning out. So when a group started heading down the narrow back hallway where her locker was, she noticed. Kyra looked up to see Lisa, Jackie, and three other well-dressed girls strutting down the hall. They all carried Coach purses and had bad attitudes. Kyra's stomach tightened up and she rose from her kneeling position, leaving her locker open. Damn, I *would* be alone when this went down, Kyra thought. She was feeling a heavy sort of nervousness. They slowed when they were within ten feet of her.

"You know," Lisa said, pretending to talk to the girls around her, while looking Kyra dead in the eye the entire time. "You got to be a skank-ass skeezer to sniff all around some other woman's man. I mean, you've got to have no shame at all!" Her voice carried a hundred sharp daggers.

"You know that's right," Jackie concurred nastily. "When you can't get a man the right way, I guess a nasty piece a trash will do just about anything to get one the wrong way."

"Mmm-hmmm. Something smells like dog mess up around here," Lisa said, drawing near to Kyra. She stood just a few feet away. The narrow hallway became even more constricted as the girls circled around Kyra. Jackie and the other girls barked softly. Kyra felt the fear grow inside her and tried to think of how best to handle this. She kept her eyes fastened on Lisa. She was the only one that mattered, anyway. The others would follow Lisa's lead.

"You must've given up that nasty quick, fast, and in a hurry, huh, Little Miss Nappy Head?" Lisa asked.

"Look, I'm sorry that you got hurt, I really am, but—" Kyra began. Her voice was sincere, but not pleading in the least.

"You're sorry! What the hell do I care about you being sorry? I don't know you and you don't know me, so I don't care about your sorries, Little Miss Nappy Head!" Lisa snapped angrily. "And believe me, you don't know a damn thing about hurt yet. But I'm gonna see to it that you get that lesson. It's a good thing your skinny behind is so smart, you should catch on to the hurtin' I'm gonna give you real fast!"

"Get up out of my face," Kyra said levelly. As Lisa boxed her in, Kyra had moved to feeling less afraid and more angry. Her voice had turned hard and her large brown eyes met Lisa's angry gray ones with a look of steely assurance. "Now. You can be mad all you want, but when you mess around and think that you can threaten me, you better be ready for everything to fall down around you, sister girl. 'Cause I don't play that crap. Now, get out of my face, Lisa!"

Lisa looked into Kyra's eyes and read her conviction. Lisa stepped back.

"Whatever," Lisa responded, her bravado turned down a couple of notches.

"Yeah, whatever," Kyra said, not backing down an inch.

"We'll catch you later, Miss Nappy Head!" Lisa threw out as they headed away. Kyra was sick of that nappy-head mess.

"Hey, Lisa," Kyra called after her. Lisa and her pack of mimic hounds turned around. "Jason's hands were all over this 'nappy head' last night as he gave me some *sweet* kisses!" Kyra's voice was strong and sassy. Lisa's face grew instantly flushed and quick anger flared in her eyes. She gave Kyra the middle finger. In response Kyra slammed her locker shut and watched them go.

"What was that?" Renee asked, hurrying up behind Kyra.

"Hey, girl, you scared me," Kyra said. Her already rushing heart picked it up a couple of notches when her best girl slipped up behind her.

"Sorry. What was that?" Renee repeated, nodding toward the retreating group.

"Lisa and her crew. Called themselves stopping by to school me."

"What went down?" Kyra told her everything. "You know I got your back if anything happens," Renee said.

"I know, girl. But you know I'm not getting into anybody's fight. Shoot, I was just talking so that they'd get out of my space. I don't know how to fight!" Kyra said, laughing, much of her nervous excitement still in her voice.

"I know that's right! I sure would've liked to see you trip out on somebody, though," Renee said with a smile. "I can hardly believe it. Have you ever even been in fight?"

"No, never!"

"Are you going to tell Jason?"

"I don't know. You think I should?"

"Yeah. He needs to know what you're dealing with, maybe put Lisa in check."

"I might, then," Kyra said thoughtfully.

"Well, I just came up to get my extra T-shirt for track practice," Renee said, working her locker combination. "You all right?" She asked once she had the T-shirt and shut the locker.

"Of course. I'm on my way to Mr. Hillard's. I'll call you tonight. Jason and I are going out."

"First date?" Renee already knew the answer.

"Yep. First date," Kyra said, smiling and feeling good. "If it's not too late I'll call and tell you how it went."

"All right, talk to you later," Renee called as she hurried down the hall.

"Talk to you later," Kyra called back.

Kyra stood in the empty hallway for a few extra moments after her friend left. What did Lisa have planned? Kyra wondered.

18

"What are you all going to see?" Renee asked across the phone line. Kyra held the cordless phone cupped between her chin and shoulder while she applied clear polish to her fingernails.

"I want to see the new Jada Pinkett Smith movie. I guess we'll see that," Kyra said.

"That's supposed to be good."

"Do you think I'm skinny?" Kyra asked, a note of concern in her voice. The image of Lisa's shapely figure and her words about Kyra's weight had Kyra a little concerned about the comparison.

"What? No, not skinny. Slim. Why?"

"Lisa called me skinny."

"Don't pay that silly cow any attention. She's jealous."

"Well, she does have the body all the boys want. Jason sure wanted it for a year," Kyra pointed out, the worry still evident in her voice.

"Girl, you have a cute figure. You know that. Shoot, you're built almost exactly like Akila, and you know everybody thinks she's the bomb. Besides, Jason left Lisa to be with you, so he must like what you got," Renee concluded logically.

"Hey! You're right. He did choose me," Kyra said, mollified. Part of her still saw how good Jason and Lisa had looked in the halls together. She knew that he and Lisa had been having sex. Maybe that would still be on Jason's mind.

"What are you wearing?" Renee asked, pulling Kyra's attention back to the conversation.

"Some black Levi's and my fuchsia scoop-neck sweater," Kyra said.

"Good. You look good in that. What kind of shoes?"

"My black leather ankle boots. And I took my hair down."

"Yeah? I haven't seen your hair down in a while. I bet it looks nice," Renee said.

"It looks all right. It's really big. I hope that it doesn't rain or anything. Then it'll really be all over the place. Maybe I ought to just put it back up," Kyra said, worried about this now.

"No, no, don't do that," Renee urged. "Just put some of

those big barrettes and a ponytail holder in your purse. Then you're ready for whatever happens."

"Okay, that's a good idea."

"Are you wearing any makeup?"

"No, why? Do you think I should? I don't even know how to put any on. I'm wearing lipstick."

"Lipstick is all you need. I was just asking. You don't even need lipstick, to tell the truth."

"What time is it?" Kyra asked, turning to see her clock.

"Seven-thirty," Renee said. Kyra's clock read 7:28 P.M.

"Hey, Ky, I was just thinking," Renee said.

"Yeah, what?" Kyra asked, distracted. She stood at the mirror fussing with her hair.

"I guess you won't be in the V Club for much longer," Renee said. The V Club was what they playfully called their virgin status.

"Why do you say that?" Kyra asked. All of a sudden she was through with her hair.

"Well, you go with Jason Vincent now," Renee said, as though this sufficed as an answer. In some ways it did. Kyra prodded anyway.

"And?"

"And, let's be real. You know he was probably getting some from Lisa. They were together a year. . . ."

"Almost a year," Kyra corrected.

"Yeah, almost a year, and they weren't shy around one another in the hallway, if you know what I mean."

"Not really, I didn't pay them much attention," Kyra said truthfully.

"No, you wouldn't. But believe me, they weren't shy."

"What's your point, Renee?" Kyra asked with just the slightest bit of an edge in her voice. *What am I getting upset about?* Kyra wondered.

"You know my point, Ky. A boy, a young man, does not go from getting some on a regular basis to celibacy easily."

"How do you know?"

"I've got two older brothers; I listen to them *sometimes*, when it's convenient," Renee said.

"That doesn't mean that they never do it," Kyra countered.

"You're right. But tell me this: how often are you two kissing?"

"I don't know, every time we see each other in private," Kyra said.

"And you've been going together, what, twenty-four hours or something? Who's to say you'll be able to resist his fine butt for long? If you're starting out kissing all the time now, what are you building up to three months from now, or six months?"

Kyra plopped down on her bed, after Renee's words, her hair, nails, outfit—totally forgotten. "God, you know, you may be right. I hadn't even thought about that."

"But look," Renee offered her friend sincerely, "just take things one step at a time, Ky. You don't have to worry about that now. Just think about it some, don't worry about it."

"What time is it?" Kyra asked again.

"I've got seven-forty."

"Girl, why are you messing with my head *now*!"

"I'm not messing with your head, and you know it. I'm your best girl; I'm supposed to look out for you."

"True that. Look, I'd better get going, Renee, he'll be here in twenty minutes."

"Okay, have a good time, Ky."

"Thanks, girl. I'll call you tonight or tomorrow."

"Okay. Bye."

Kyra was all dressed and ready to go. She checked to make sure that she had twenty dollars in her wallet, "mad money." It was the money her mother made Akila and her carry when they went out, in case they got mad and had to find their own way home, independent of their date. She slipped her wallet into her purse and went over to her parents' bedroom down the hall. Her mother was sitting up in bed working on her laptop computer.

"Mama."

"Hi, baby," Ms. Evans said, looking up from her work.

"What are you doing?"

"Just going over some figures from the Chosen Vessels Foundation."

"Do you have a minute?"

"Yes, sweetie. Everything okay?"

"Oh, yes," Kyra said with a sigh as she came and stretched out across the bed on her father's side. He was downstairs in the family room with a couple of his friends. "It's just that, you know, this is my first date with Jason, you know."

"Yes, I know," Ms. Evans said patiently, a small smile playing on her lips.

"And I haven't done much dating, you know," Kyra said, looking at her mother.

"I know," Ms. Evans responded.

"He asked me to go with him, you know, be his girlfriend, last night, and I said yes."

"Did he now?" Ms. Evans said.

"Yes. He had a girlfriend, but he broke up with her because of the way that we feel about one another."

"I see. And how do you feel about one another, if you don't mind my asking?" Ms. Evans removed her reading glasses from her nose and listened attentively.

"I don't mind that you ask," Kyra said easily. "We like each other a lot. I've never liked any guy the way that I like Jason, Mama. That's why . . ." she trailed off.

"That's why what?" Ms. Evans prodded gently.

"That's why I don't want to make a fool of myself."

"How would you do that, Kyra?"

"Well, Jason's ex was, *is*, really popular at Cross, and she's talked to a lot of guys, and they had been together for almost a year. I guess what I'm trying to say is that she was a lot smoother than me, and I don't want to seem like a big baby to him."

"I don't think Jason will think you're anything like a big baby, Kyra. Maybe you've only been going together for a day, but you've been seeing each other for a couple of months now with your study project and everything. You're a very mature, sensitive, and intelligent young woman. I'm sure those are the things that Jason recognizes and likes about you. Don't sell yourself short." Kyra looked at her mother as she spoke, absorbing what she said. "And you don't have to prove anything to anyone, in any way," Ms. Evans concluded.

Kyra grinned knowingly. "Oh, Mama, I'm not going to have sex in order to prove that I'm not a baby!"

"That's not what I meant," Ms. Evans said with mock indignation.

"Sure," Kyra said in exaggerated disbelief. She leaned over and gave her mother a kiss on the cheek. "I love you, Mama," she said as she rose.

"I love you too, baby. Be careful."

"Okay. Are you coming down before I leave?"

"Yes."

"Well, its almost eight," Kyra said.

"Yes, I'll be down," Ms. Evans said, returning to her laptop.

Jason was right on time and Kyra let him in.

"Hi," she said when she opened the door.

"Hi. You look good," he said, smiling.

"So do you." And he did, too.

"Think I'll pass?" he teased right back.

"With flying colors," she said as she closed the door.

Kyra's mother came down the stairs just then, and Kyra went and got her own coat out of the closet. Jason held it while she put it on.

"Jason," Ms. Evans said. "How are you doing this evening?"

"I'm good, Ms. Evans," Jason said pleasantly. "How are you?"

"Oh, I'm doing just fine." Dr. Evans came out of the den.

"Hey, Jason, I heard the bell," he said, extending his hand for him to shake.

"Nice to see you, Dr. Evans. I'm good."

"Kyra tells us you're going to the Southfield Star Theater and to get something to eat."

"Yes, sir," Jason answered respectfully.

"Are you eating out that way?" The movie theater they'd chosen was twenty-five minutes away.

"No, not unless Kyra wants to. I thought we might come back this way and go to The Biz."

"That's fine," Kyra said.

"All right, then. Kyra has a twelve-thirty curfew," Dr. Evans said.

"Yes, sir, I know."

"Well, we'll see you then, or sooner," Dr. Evans said with a smile and a firm look at Jason. Kyra glanced over at Jason quickly. She could read her father's message easily: act right with my daughter. Could Jason? From the looks of it, he could.

"Yes, Dr. Evans."

"Have a good time," Ms. Evans said.

"Thanks, Mama," Kyra said, going over to kiss her cheek. "Bye, Daddy," she said, giving him one, too.

"Bye, Kyra," her father said. Jason said good-bye, and they were out the door. Jason took Kyra's hand as they hit the cool night air.

"How's your science project coming along?" he asked.

"Pretty good. I collated some data today and started the next stage of the experiment. It's looking really good right now."

"That's cool," Jason commented.

"How was practice?"

"Not bad. Coach is trying to kill us. He says with pretty much the same team of starters as last year, we'd better not lose the city title again. We're working harder than we did last season, though, if that's possible."

"Are you sore?"

"No, not today. Some days, usually after weight training, but not today. Why, you wanna wrestle?" he asked, grabbing her lightly around the waist. They stood beside the passenger door of Jason's car.

"Yes, but maybe we'd better wait until we get inside the car first," Kyra said, with a glance toward her house.

"You're right," Jason said. He unlocked and opened the door and then shut it carefully behind her. Kyra leaned over and unlocked his door and he got in. "Are we safe?" Jason kidded in a stage whisper.

"Yes, safe enough," Kyra murmured, just before Jason covered her lips with a kiss. "You are an excellent kisser, Jason Vincent," Kyra said happily.

"I'm only trying to keep pace with you. I love the way you kiss me," he said, shifting from kidding to seriousness. Kyra couldn't resist smiling.

"That must be because I love kissing you so much," she confessed. "So are we going to a movie, or what?" she said, gently shifting their conversation to a lighter mood.

"I checked on that Jada Pinkett Smith movie that you wanted to see. It starts at nine," Jason said. "We could get there early and play video games and get our eats."

"That sounds good," Kyra said. Jason started up his car and they were on their way. They grooved to the sounds Jason had in his ride, some R & B, a little rap, even a little jazz. They bobbed their heads to music and talked about lightweight stuff as they made the drive out to the Southfield Star theater. It was a huge space, modeled on the outside to look like an oversized, stylized 1960s theater. Inside were vast black-and-white posters of blockbuster movies and scenes of Detroit in the fifties and sixties. Video games, picture booths, and vendors lined the walls, while popcorn stations occupied the center.

They arrived more than thirty minutes before the movie and found the spacious waiting area crowded with moviegoers. They recognized a few faces from Cross and nodded to them. They stood in line talking to one another as they waited for their turn to buy tickets. Jason got the tickets, and Kyra said thank you. He looked at her, shook his head and smiled.

"What?" Kyra asked.

"Nothing," he said, still smiling at her. He doubted that it even occurred to Lisa to thank him for buying her something—she had never said thank you. He placed his arm around Kyra's shoulders and drew her in close to him. "You want to play something?" he asked, nodding toward the video games as they walked away from the ticket booth.

"Hmm," Kyra said. "Let's play the race cars."

"All right," he said.

They played a couple of games, she won one, he won the other.

"You want some popcorn or something?" Jason asked Kyra. It was about fifteen minutes before the start of the movie.

"Yeah, do you?" Kyra asked.

"Can't do the movies without popcorn or nachos," Jason informed her. Kyra smiled up at him.

"What are you having?" Jason asked as they stood in line.

"A medium popcorn and a medium Sprite mixed with a little orange. What about you?"

"A large nachos and a Sprite, maybe some Twizzlers."

When they got to the front of the line Kyra placed their order. "Right?" she said, glancing back at Jason who stood close behind her.

"That's right," he was reaching into his wallet for the money.

"No, not this time. This is my treat," Kyra said. She already had a twenty out. Her mad money was safely tucked away, untroubled.

"No, you don't have to do that," Jason said, disturbed. "I'm taking you out."

"I want to do it, okay?"

Jason looked into her pleasant, yet determined eyes and decided to give in. "Okay," he concurred. Jason picked up their cardboard food tray when the order was filled. "Thank you," he said, smiling at Kyra.

"No problem," she said.

They were making their way, side by side, to their theater when Jason saw a familiar group up ahead. It was Lisa and some of her girls standing near a wall that Kyra and he had to pass. Kyra hadn't seen them yet. In fact, Lisa's crew noticed Jason and Kyra before Kyra noticed them. Here we go, Jason thought.

"Hi, Jason," Heather Grier said when Jason and Kyra neared them. Kyra looked at the girls, looked at Jason, and said nothing. Jason and Kyra halted before the group.

"What's up, Heather?" Jason said. "Hi, Lisa," he said. Lisa rolled her eyes, looked at her girls, then stared at Jason silently and insolently.

"What are you going to see?" Heather asked Jason. Everyone was ignoring Kyra, and Kyra felt outside of it all, as though a wall had purposefully been built in order to shut only her out. Heather was thinking that if Jason asked her to be his, she'd be gone with him in a second. She looked his tall, fine frame over and felt absolutely no loyalty to Lisa whatsoever.

"The Jada Pinkett Smith flick," Jason said. "Check you later," he said, moving past them and looking over at Kyra.

"Jason," Lisa called once Jason and Kyra were several feet away. Jason and Kyra stopped and looked back. Lisa walked over to them. She walked around until she stood in front of Jason, and quite near. She lowered her head and unhooked a slender herringbone gold chain from around her neck. She cupped it in her hand and extended it toward Jason. Her beautiful face was sad, and somehow, to

Kyra's mind, even more attractive. Her gray eyes were liquid with unshed tears. "Here," she said simply.

Jason balanced the food tray on one hand and put his free hand out to receive the chain. She placed it there, allowing her small, golden-brown hand to linger momentarily in his large one. "Thanks," Jason said quietly. Then, much to Kyra's mortification, Lisa quickly placed her arms around Jason's neck and pulled his head down, placing a quick kiss on his cheek. Jason frowned down at Lisa, and Lisa glanced smugly at Kyra and then moved away.

Lisa's girls had watched the entire thing. When she got over to them they gave her fingertip plays and triumphant smiles. "Girlfriend," they congratulated her, "you know you got it goin' on!" Kyra felt like she could just crumple up and die. The night had been going perfectly. She had been so happy, and now this mess! Some other girl had just kissed her boyfriend, in her face, on *their* first date, no less! It was just too much.

Jason wiped his cheek, trying to make sure that Kyra saw it. She saw it, but it almost didn't matter. "I'm sorry about that, Kyra. It's just like Lisa to pull some crap like that. Don't let that spoil our date."

"I'll try," Kyra said, obviously hurt. Jason felt like crap. Lisa was manipulating things, ruining the night. Kyra looked so upset, when just minutes ago she had been happy. He wanted her happy again.

"Wait," Jason said. He gently pulled Kyra around with his free hand. "I don't want you to *try*, I want you to *be* happy." He took her gently by the back of her head and gave her a long kiss on the mouth. He did it in full view of Lisa and her girls, and he did that on purpose. He didn't want Kyra or Lisa to have any doubts about the kiss most on his mind. People moved all around them, most paying them little or no attention.

Kyra looked at him when the kiss was over. "What was that about?" Kyra asked.

"You know what that was about," Jason said. "I don't want you trippin' and getting confused about who I'm into," Jason said, looking into her eyes intently.

"Well, it worked," Kyra said smiling. "I'm having a good time again."

"Good," Jason said, returning the smile. "That's all I want."

Lisa and her crew looked on in disbelief. Lisa felt completely humiliated. And by Kyra Evans, for God sake, she thought. Jackie felt just horrible for her girl. The other three wore scowls just like Lisa and Jackie, but had other feelings. One thought, That's just what Lisa gets for cracking smart on me all those times. Another thought, Damn, that Jason really is too fine. And Heather thought, Kyra, you go, girl!

19

Over the next couple of months things were excellent between Kyra and Jason. They talked on the phone every night. They went out nearly every weekend. He came over to her house at least once a week, and they made a point of seeing one another at least a few times every day at school. The basketball season had just begun and it was going well, too. The Cross team was 3 and 0. Kyra had made it to every game. They'd received their first report cards, 4.0 for Kyra, 3.5 for Jason. Kyra's brother had come home to visit and Jason had met him. Akila had come home for a couple of visits and she'd met Jason, too. "You did all right," Akila complimented Kyra after seeing Jason. Jason had had dinner with Kyra and her parents two more times, and Kyra had finally met Jason's father. Jason's father seemed to be going off on him a little more often, but Jason shared no details with Kyra. His father's verbal abuse was easier to take now that he had Kyra. Soon they had been going together nearly three months.

Through it all Kyra and Jason had grown closer and closer, and more intimate. Jason could feel himself falling in love for the first time, though he'd said nothing to Kyra. Kyra felt the same way, though she hadn't said anything either. Tonight for the first time, Kyra was coming over to his house without his father or her parents knowing.

Mr. Vincent was out of town for the weekend on business. He'd taken his lady with him for company. He'd never taken Jason on his business trips.

Jason invited Kyra over for dinner. He'd ordered Chinese and bought flowers. He had some CDs lined up in the player, all romantic tunes. There were speakers in the kitchen, living room, and den that were attached to the entertainment center in the living room. He programmed the latest slow hits to guide them through three hours of the evening. She'd told her parents they were having dinner, then going out partying.

Jason checked his watch: seven-thirty. She was due here now. He felt nervous and excited at the same time. He wanted them to take things to a new level, physically speaking, tonight. He didn't expect sex—Kyra wasn't having any of that. But he was hoping for pretty much everything but. He wanted her badly, but not enough to pressure her.

He didn't doubt that Kyra was really into him. He knew he excited her, so he might be able to get her to the point where she'd have sex with him. But he also suspected that she'd hate herself, and him, later. On the other hand, he understood, too, that Kyra was extremely strong-willed. She could see what he was doing, pressing and pressing her to have sex, balk at the idea and him, and leave him and never look back. And it wouldn't be that it wouldn't hurt her to do it, but she'd see it as Jason disrespecting her by disregarding her wishes, and she wasn't going to have any part of that, either. So as far as Jason could tell, either way, he lost.

So, if some heavy fooling around was all that he could get, he'd gladly take it. With Kyra he'd found someone he could talk to about anything. They talked about everything except the full extent of his father's abuse. He'd found someone who understood his insecurities and wanted him anyway. He'd found someone who talked to him about things that mattered, who cared about him, who trusted and believed in him. He felt stronger around Kyra, he felt more at peace. He felt secure. He didn't want to lose all of that. He couldn't remember the last time that he'd felt all of those things at once. He'd felt some of those things, some of the time. But not all of them most of the time.

His mind flashed back to the conversation they'd had two months ago about sex. They'd been messing around in his car for over half an hour when Jason made his suggestion.

"Let's go to my house," he said as he kissed her neck and caressed her breasts through her sweater. She had not let him feel under her sweater yet. "My father's spending the night over at Rachel's." They were both breathing hot and heavy.

"I don't think so, Jason," Kyra had breathed.

"Why not?" Jason said, still kissing and stroking her.

"Because," she'd moaned. He stopped kissing and stroking and pulled back so that he could make out her face in the darkened car. They were parked on Belle Isle, facing the river at nine o'clock at night on a Saturday.

"Because what?" he asked softly.

"Because too much might happen over at your house, all by ourselves."

"That won't be bad, Kyra. I'll take care of you," he said persuasively.

"No, Jason," she said, not too firmly. Her lips were still tender and warm from his kisses. Her hands still lay on his chest.

"What are you scared of, baby?" he asked tenderly.

"I'm not scared . . . exactly. But that's not the only thing. I'm just not ready. It's too much. There's too much that goes with it," she said. Her voice was strained and Jason could feel her growing increasingly uncomfortable. There was hesitancy in her every word. He pressed anyway.

"Kyra, I have condoms. I'll use them a hundred percent of the time. I always have, since I started having sex. I don't play around with HIV and babies and STDs," he coaxed.

"I don't know. I'm just not ready."

"Talk to me," Jason pleaded.

"I . . . I . . ." Kyra began nervously.

"What? Go ahead," Jason urged gently.

"It's not just that I'm a virgin," she said, looking at his face in the dim light provided by a nearby street light and the full moon above. "I've never been naked with a boy. I've never let a boy touch me . . . naked."

Jason looked at her and swallowed, waited a moment, and then kissed her on the lips. "Are you scared?" he whispered.

"Yes," she whispered back between kisses.

"You don't want to do it?"

"No," she murmured.

"Ever, with me?" he asked still kissing her.

"I can't say 'ever,'" she answered. His heart leaped.

"All right, baby. Whatever you want." He stopped kissing her. "You know I want you, don't you?" She nodded, looking into his eyes. They looked like shiny black pools in the darkened car interior. "I want to feel myself inside you, feel what you're like on the inside. I want to make you feel good and bring us even closer."

Every word was a whisper, a verbal caress stroking Kyra on the inside and outside. He meant every word, and she could feel each word planted inside her ears, her heart, the pores of her skin. "But if you say *no*, or *wait*, I'll do that. You don't ever have to worry, okay?" She nodded again, mesmerized by his words, his voice. "Whatever you want, Kyra," he murmured, kissing her softly on the lips. "Whatever you want," he said, kissing her again, less softly. "Whatever you want, baby," he repeated. Each time he kissed her more passionately and thoroughly.

He'd taken her home afterward and thought about her all night. He thought about what he'd just committed himself to, and had to admit to himself that it would probably drive him insane. He'd been having sex since he was fifteen. Girls gave it up easily to him, even back then. Now, two years later, girls, and even some women, were still very willing. Some girl was always slipping him her digits. Some knew he was with Kyra, others didn't go to Cross and maybe they didn't know, so he'd tell them. It didn't seem to matter to them anyway. He threw all the numbers away.

It hadn't been easy. He didn't mind resisting the other girls. He noticed them, but he didn't want anybody but Kyra. No, what hadn't been easy was resisting Kyra. Or, to put it more accurately: resisting pressuring Kyra. She was smart, beautiful, and all caught up in his heart, and all of that made him want to feel himself inside her even more.

So here he was, nearly three months into the relationship, happy as hell. He checked everything one more time, turned the music down and headed over to look out the window and see if she was pulling up. The doorbell rang before he got to the window.

"Hey, Kyra," he said when he opened the door.

"Hey, Jason," she said. She looked a little nervous to him.

"Come on in. Let me take your coat," he said, playing the host. He helped her out of her coat and took a long look at her. She wore a sheer blouse over a thin cashmere camisole paired with boot-cut pants. "You look beautiful, Kyra," he said as he admired her.

She blushed. "Thank you, Jason," she said nervously. She rubbed her hands on her thighs and got a good look at Jason. She swallowed. He looked extra fine tonight. His haircut was new and she could smell aftershave on him. He had allowed a mustache to grow and he kept it neatly trimmed. She reached up and touched it lightly. "This looks good," she said, her fingers still grazing it. "You look good," she said.

Something inside him shifted as he stood there with her touching him, his eyes on her face, her eyes on his lips. He kissed her fingers and felt the muscles in his groin constrict involuntarily. She closed her eyes, allowing him to kiss her fingers. She moved her hand to his cheek and he lowered his head, kissing her mouth. She returned the kiss, bringing her other hand around to the back of his head.

"Just dinner, a video, and spending some time together, okay, Jason?" she said after the kiss. She'd had to take a deep breath before speaking.

"That's right, Kyra," he assured her. Whatever you want, he thought. "Come on in, everything's ready." He took her hand and led her into the dining room. The table was set with the Vincents' best dinnerware: bone china with a gold border, real silverware, linen napkins, long-stemmed wineglasses, water glasses, and a small bouquet of deep pink, white, and red roses, with baby's breath and dark green foliage.

Her eyes lit up when she saw the room. "It's beautiful, Jason!" she exclaimed. "Thank you."

"You haven't even eaten. Don't thank me yet."

She turned to him. "No, I mean it. Thank you for caring about me enough to do all of this."

"I'd do anything for you," he said, staring into her eyes. "Sit here," he said, leading her to her seat. She sat down and he extracted a pink rose from the bouquet and presented it to her. She took a deep breath; it was opened wide, each delicate petal perfect.

"Thank you," she said again, looking up at him.

"You're welcome," he said. "I'll be right back." He headed off to the kitchen and Kyra sat at the table feeling her insides flutter. She was so nervous, her hands were shaking slightly. She hoped he hadn't noticed.

She'd lied to her parents, something she rarely did. She was sneaking around to a boy's house with his parent not only not around, but out of town! She had good reason to be extremely nervous. The only person who knew was Renee. Kyra had told Renee their plan a couple of days ago.

"Oh my God, Ky! What are you going to do?" Renee asked excitedly.

"I told you, dinner, a video, mess around a little," Kyra said, feigning calmness. They were over at Renee's house, upstairs in her bedroom, under the pretense of getting some studying done. Her older brothers had loud rap music going next door.

"You know, this could be it! This could be the night you do it," Renee said.

"No it's not going to be it. I'm not ready yet, Renee," Kyra stressed.

"Then don't do it. Don't do it until you're absolutely ready."

"I know."

"Still, girl, alone at his house, after the way you all have been gettin' on these past months, the way you two feel about each other . . ."

"I know . . ." Kyra said, her voice in anguish.

"You should be prepared," Renee said.

"What do you mean?" Kyra asked.

"Condoms. You should get some condoms," Renee said confidently.

"No!" Kyra said, laughing and shaking her head.

"Yes!" Renee retorted, laughing and nodding her head.

"He should have them," Kyra asserted.

"I'm sure he would, except that he doesn't expect to be getting any. You made that perfectly clear, remember?" Renee pointed out reasonably.

"I know, but—"

"No buts, Ky. Not having a condom would be stupid in this situation. You could be playing with your life," Renee said seriously.

"You're right."

"I mean, yeah, you're telling yourself that you're not going to have sex, and you're telling Jason you're not going to have sex. But you could get over there, all alone, late at night, extra romantic, and your body and heart may be telling you, 'Oh yes, you are going to have sex!' Then, there you are without a condom and in a fix."

"You're right," Kyra said thoughtfully.

"Don't lie to yourself, Kyra. Despite your best intentions, you could end up doing it. Don't lie yourself into a baby, or worse."

Kyra leaned over and hugged her best friend. "God, Renee, you're so right. Will you go with me?"

"You know it. Let's go now," Renee urged. Kyra said all right, and so, nervous and embarrassed, they drove to a gas station outside Renee's neighborhood and purchased three condoms. Renee made Kyra ask. "I'm not the one who might be having sex," she'd said.

So even though Kyra was still committed to keeping her virginity, at least through the night, she had three condoms tucked into the zipper pocket of her small purse.

"Here we are," Jason said, bringing in two serving plates of Chinese food. "I've got to get a couple more, and then we can eat."

"Do you want some help?"

"No, you just relax, and I'll get it." Jason came back with two more steaming plates of food.

"Everything looks delicious, Jason. Where'd you get this?" Kyra said as she admired the meal before them.

"The Mandarin Box," he said proudly. They served themselves and ate silently for a few minutes.

"It's delicious," Kyra said after another mouthful.

"Well, I didn't cook it, but thank you," Jason said. "I'm glad you like it."

They continued their quiet dinner. Kyra was too

nervous to talk about anything, and Jason was thwarted by her mood. The minutes stretched into agonizing rubber bands of tension. Every clink of silverware on a plate seemed to echo above the quiet music. They became self-conscious about their chewing and posture. They both knew that they were thinking too much, but neither seemed to be able to stop it and relax.

This is perfect, Jason thought sarcastically. It could only get worse.

This is horrible, Kyra thought. At least I won't be in any danger of losing my virginity at this rate.

20

"Are you thinking what I'm thinking?" Jason asked after five more minutes of uncharacteristic, miserable silence.

"That my first and only romantic dinner is going to be my worst?"

"Exactly," Jason said with a small smile. "We can't let that happen. You know what we need?"

"What?" Kyra asked, genuinely at a loss.

"A way to relax," Jason answered, his smile growing. "First of all, we may have one too many plates over here." He moved his plate aside and placed Kyra's plate between them. "Sharing always builds friendships—at least that's what my first-grade teacher taught me." He maneuvered some shrimp fried rice onto his fork and moved it toward Kyra's mouth. She leaned in, mouth slightly opened to receive it. She chewed slowly.

"Now, you," she said, placing some of the rice onto her fork. She brought it to his full, sensual lips. After several mouthfuls of the various Chinese dishes, they had noticeably relaxed.

"That's better," Jason approved.

"Yes, much," Kyra returned. They ate for a little while longer.

The CD switched over and a young man's rich voice began to croon about his love for a beautiful woman.

"May I have this dance, Kyra Evans?" Jason asked formally. He rose from the table, hand extended to her.

"Why yes, Mr. Vincent. I'd love to dance with you." Kyra smiled as she played her part, placing her slender brown hand in his. "Mr. Vincent, I hope you don't mind my making a small request," Kyra began.

"Anything for you," he said sincerely.

"May I have a peppermint?" she said, breaking into in a grin.

Jason laughed softly. "All right. I'll get one for myself, too. Just a moment; don't move," he said, and hurried to the kitchen. He returned sucking on a peppermint and with one in his hand for Kyra. "Here you are," he said, handing her the candy.

"Thank you," she said. She unwrapped it and put it in her mouth. The sweet taste and scent of peppermint began to replace that of their Chinese dishes.

Jason extended his hand again silently. Kyra took it and rose.

"Do you remember the last time we danced together?" Kyra asked.

Jason held her pressed close to him, her head rested on his shoulder. "Of course. It was the only time we've danced together," he answered. "Homecoming."

"That's right."

"I was so surprised to see you there. You kept saying that you weren't coming. I had been thinking about you so much that when I saw you I thought I was dreaming," Jason said.

"Yeah, right," Kyra said.

"No, really. I had to do a double take. You looked so good," he said softly.

She began kissing him softly and slowly. Jason slowed their dancing way down and they swayed in one another's arms. Their kissing grew increasingly passionate. They pulled away from the kiss and looked into one another's eyes. Kyra saw so much emotion in Jason's eyes that it made her catch her breath. No one had ever looked at her that way. There was desire, and joy, and peace, and sweet anxiousness, and . . . Kyra shook her head gently. She couldn't be seeing what else she thought she saw, could she? Would she recognize it? She didn't know, she'd never felt it before herself.

"Well, I'd say we're relaxed now," Kyra said in an attempt to inject some humor into the scene.

"I don't know if I can call myself exactly relaxed." Jason

had danced them right over to the couch in the family room. He smoothly moved Kyra down onto the couch. They never stopped kissing as Jason eased Kyra onto her back. Her hands were on his neck, then she placed one on the back of his head, her tongue moving in and out, around and around. Jason propped himself up onto his forearms, being careful not to place his full weight on her, and gently pressed her legs apart. He lowered his body between her legs and began to slowly, rhythmically rub himself against her. They'd never done this before.

Kyra felt her heartbeat quicken. She moved from feeling comfortable, secure, and aroused to feeling a delicious jolt of fear. Is this what it would be like to make love with Jason? She began moving instinctively to his rhythm. "Jason," she moaned softly. It all felt so dangerously new and forbidden. She moved her hand along the muscles in his shoulder, down the hard muscles that stood out in his arms, then began stroking the sides of his torso and along his back. He felt so perfect. She wanted to feel his skin warm against the palm of her hand.

Their kisses never stopped as their rubbing became grinding. Kyra tugged at Jason's shirt until it slipped from his pants and she began stroking his skin. It was warm and smooth, like some sort of firm, silken fruit. He moaned softly as her hands played down the center of his spine, and the hairs stood up, poised and alert. He shifted onto his hands so that he was propped up at arm's length above her.

He looked down and saw that her eyes had taken on a

look of sultry, languid heat. "Do you like this?" he asked, his voice husky.

"Yes," she whispered. She closed her eyes and arched her back, then eased herself down again. "Do you?" she asked.

He nodded, unable to speak as he looked at her. She was so natural and instinctive. He loved that about her. She did the thing she felt when they were together instead of trying to do what she thought he wanted. He knew that she'd never done anything like this before. He knew that before him she'd done no serious necking, just a few French kisses with a boy the year before, and she'd let that boy touch her breasts through her top. Over the last few months they'd kissed intensely and he'd caressed her breasts outside and inside her blouse. But that was about it. He knew just how much trust she was putting in him right now. Knowing that and seeing the way that he was pleasing her made him feel powerful and protective all at the same time. He wanted to feel himself inside her and shield her from any hurt.

"You make me feel so good," Jason said as he stared into her eyes.

"I love the way you make me feel," Kyra responded and closed her eyes.

Jason eased off her, and Kyra opened her eyes. Jason began undoing her buttons. "Do you mind?" he asked. She sat up. Kyra shook her head no. Once he'd unbuttoned it, he moved the whisper-light, sheer blouse over her bare shoulders and off her arms. "My turn," he said, and began undoing his own buttons. Kyra watched as though mesmerized. What did this mean, she wondered, almost frantically. Would we do it? Would we make love tonight? Will this be the night I lose my virginity? she wondered. Underneath he wore only his rich brown skin stretched across exquisite muscles. She had never seen him like this. If a guy took off this much clothing, did it mean that he thought he was going to have sex? His chest had a small patch of silky black hair placed in an almost perfect diamond in the center. His stomach bore the evidence of all of those workouts in the form of washboard abdominals. His broad shoulders and tapered waist offered a lovely silhouette.

"Jason," she whispered, her voice filled with wonder. "I've never touched a naked man before."

Jason swallowed. "I'm not naked yet." The *yet* echoed in both their minds. "Are you scared?" he asked.

"A little," she said, nodding.

"Don't be," he said as he stroked her cheek with the back of his hand. "I've never undressed for someone I loved before."

"You love me?" she asked, stunned. So she *had* seen that in his eyes earlier!

"Yes," he answered simply.

"Oh, Jason, baby. I think I love you, too." She was sitting on the edge of the couch with her legs parted, and he was on his knees on the floor between her legs, his hands resting lightly on her thighs. "I've never felt this way," she continued. "I *do* love you." He closed his eyes and allowed his emotions to move through him. Kyra Evans loves me, he thought. She knows all that she knows, and she loves me. The sweetness of it made him want to jump up and shout it, but he didn't. He kissed her hard and deep, wanting to be a part of her. When they stopped kissing, she spoke. "I was scared to say it, Jason," she confessed.

She leaned over and kissed his left cheek, then his right. She kissed one eyelid, then the other. She did exactly what she felt, and trusted herself, trusted Jason. She did not think this time, as she had sometimes before, this is Jason Vincent, every girl wants him, he has kissed so many others before me, he has had this better before. He had never loved before. She knew that he had never been kissed when he was in love. Everything was always so new for her, but *this* would be a first for him. She kissed his neck. It was warm and smelled clean. She sucked his neck gently, then more insistently, then stopped. She didn't want to mark him; she didn't want it to be anybody's business but theirs—what they did in private.

"What are you doing to me, Kyra, girl?" he asked. The words seemed to be coming from deep within his throat. He brought his hands up her thighs and around her hips and gripped them firmly. He slid his hands under the feathery softness of her cashmere top and up her back, pressing her chest firmly into his own. As his hands rose he pulled back, separating their torsos. She wasn't wearing a bra. "Can I take this off?" he asked. She didn't have to ask him what he meant. She swallowed and nodded silently. In the background Janet Jackson urged her lover to make her moan real loud. The single lamp lit in the room was turned

183

down to its dimmest setting, bathing them in its subtle coral glow. The rest of the room rested in semidarkness, watching and waiting.

As Jason began to lift her sweater, Kyra closed her eyes and extended her arms above her head. She kept her eyes closed, even when she felt the sweater gone and herself exposed. She had never, ever been in any way naked with a boy. She felt self-conscious.

"You're beautiful, Kyra," Jason said in a voice soft with honesty and love. Her large brown eyes fluttered open to find his eyes on her small breasts, and a quiet smile on his lips. He looked up into her eyes. "You are, you're beautiful," he exclaimed softly. He lowered his head and she caught her breath with a sense of anticipation thick with want and fear. She closed her eyes again just as his full lips met her right breast. His lips were unbelievably tender, and he began to circle her breast with a ring of kisses. Then he ringed the other with an identical glowing circle of kisses.

She allowed herself to slip from the couch until she was on the floor on her knees, just as he was. She placed her hands on his bare chest and felt his heart beat beneath her hands, faster but even. "I love you, Jason Vincent," Kyra said.

"And I love you." He hesitated for a moment. "You know I've never been in love before," he confessed. "I've never trusted anyone enough to fall in love." He took a deep breath and swallowed; he swallowed the fear along with the air. "I trust you, Kyra, deeply." Everything inside Kyra seemed to expand; each and every particle of her being became full of colors, vibrant and moist and touchable.

He kissed her again and they stretched out on the couch. Their kisses and stroking and grinding began once again to escalate. He moved his hands over her breasts, her thighs, and between her legs in a way that brought moans to her lips despite her best efforts to bite them back. Kyra felt her yearning for him mount and become a wild thing that she did not want to catch and cage. She wanted to feel it burst forward and take charge. She wanted to allow it to direct her.

Kyra spoke into his ear. "Jason."

"Yes." He was focused entirely on pleasing her and trying not to make himself too crazy.

"Go get my purse for me, it's on my chair." She heard her own heavy breathing, mingled with his.

"What?" He sounded a little confused.

"Go get my purse. I have some condoms." Jason paused in his motions and his heart seem to take the same pause. He could hardly believe it himself, but he actually grew even more excited.

"Kyra," he said, a warning in his voice.

"I know," she said, "I want you to get them." Her voice sounded edgy with excitement and fear to Jason's ears. Did his sound like that?

"Are you sure?" he asked, wanting so much to hear her yes.

"Yes, I am," she said. Her voice, always so confident, shook slightly.

Jason moved himself off her, and knew, in spite of what he wanted, what he had to do and say. "No."

"What?" Kyra asked, more than a little surprised.

"No, baby. You know I want to. I want you so badly," he said, pressing his forehead to hers, glancing down at her breasts. "So badly," he said, moving his head back so that he could look into her eyes. "But not like this," he explained.

"It's all right, Jason. I want this," she urged.

"And I want it, too. But I want you to come to me at the start of the evening, when you're your regular cool, smart, levelheaded self and say, 'Tonight, Jason, I want you to make love to me.' I want you to do it before I've had my hands all over you."

"Why?" she asked, genuinely perplexed. "What matters is that I want you, not when."

"It does matter. I don't want you doubting. I don't want you scared about whether you really should do it or not."

"But I'm not—" she began.

"Sshh," he said gently. "Yes, you are. And that's all right. Hell, I'm a little scared myself. I want it to be special with you; I want it to be perfect. But like I said, I don't want you doubting. Because if you're doubting a little bit before we make love, you could be doubting a whole lot the next morning. And your bad feelings could start to drive us apart."

"Jason—"

"Let me finish, Kyra. You're the best thing that's ever happened to me. A lot of fellas my age might say that and it wouldn't mean much. They've got mamas that'll do anything for them, they have daddies or brothers or sisters or somebody. I don't. My mama's dead and my daddy hardly gives a damn about me. For me it's the truth, you're the best thing that's ever happened to me." She kissed him, then, and he buried his hands in her fragrant hair and relished all the love she was sending him. "You're my best friend now," he whispered. "You know almost every important thing about me. Because of you everything is better. The blue in the sky, the music I like, the food I eat, the shots I take. Everything. I look forward to each day because I know you're in mine. I don't want to lose that, Kyra. I'm saying stuff out loud to you that I hardly ever even thought in my head before you! So as badly as I want to be inside of you the way that you're inside my heart and soul, I don't want it to tear us apart. It's not worth it. And believe me, it's worth a lot," he said, grinning. "But it sure as hell ain't worth losing my Kyra over."

When he'd finished, she sat staring at him with eyes that glimmered with unshed tears. "Jason . . . Jason . . ." He kissed her lips. "Are you the best boy in the whole wide world?" she asked.

"No," he answered seriously. "But I aim to be the best one for you."

21

"Now, do you have enough gasoline, Jason?" Ms. Evans asked.

"Yes, a full tank, Ms. Evans," Jason reassured her. They stood beside Jason's car on the morning after the first real snow. A thick blanket of fresh white powder bedecked the rooftops, tree limbs, and vehicle tops along the street. Three new inches had been added overnight to the two that had arrived yesterday afternoon. The sidewalks were not shoveled yet, and the streets bore slushy gray ribbons made by tire tracks.

"I know you'll drive carefully," Ms. Evans said. She didn't look all that confident. "Just take your time. You know that some people don't know how to behave in the first snow, even in Michigan, and they're zooming all over the place." Kyra's mother was trying hard not to look as worried as she felt.

"Yes, Ms. Evans. We're in no hurry, so I will be sure to take my time and be extra careful," Jason said respectfully.

"I'm sure I don't have to tell you the story of a boy I grew up with who was so busy trying to impress the girl he was dating that he didn't notice the semi edging its way into the road." Ms. Evans paused for dramatic effect as she held Jason's eyes and Kyra tried hard not to sigh out loud. "He smashed right into the truck. Of course, he lived, but the girl died, and he spent the rest of his life tortured by the thought. When I think of the nightmares he suffered for the rest of his life. He couldn't even talk about what happened to him—too, too painful."

"How do you know about his nightmares if he couldn't talk about it?" Kyra couldn't resist asking.

Ms. Evans cut Kyra a cold look. "He could *rarely* talk about it, I should have said," Ms. Evans corrected herself. "Rarely, Jason." Her voice was extremely prim, as though the correction of her own sixteen-year-old child were a difficult burden to bear.

"We'll be fine, Mama," Kyra added. "We'd better go while it's early and the roads are still fairly empty."

"That's right," Ms. Evans said. "Good idea. Get going, you two. Call me, Kyra, when you get there."

"Yes, Mama," Kyra said. She leaned over and gave her

mother a kiss on the cheek. Jason opened her door for her, and Kyra climbed into the passenger seat.

"Good-bye, Ms. Evans. Please tell Dr. Evans that I'm sorry I missed him." Dr. Evans was in Chicago at a medical convention.

"I will, Jason. Be careful," Ms. Evans couldn't resist adding.

"I will," Jason said again.

Jason climbed into his car, started the engine, shifted into gear, and pulled away from the curb. Ms. Evans stood watching them for a couple of moments, then turned and headed back to the house.

As they began the quiet drive, Jason's thoughts drifted to the night before when he and his father had gone to see the new exhibit of Romare Bearden's work at the Detroit Institute of Art. His father hoped to "broaden Jason's horizons," as he liked to put it, at least several times a year. They visited the DIA and the Museum of African American History, heard visiting jazz greats at Orchestra Hall, and saw several plays every year. The art exhibit had been unexpectedly pleasant. Usually the art thing bored him slightly, but Bearden's work drew him in. His father, as usual, had done some research on the man and his art, and every once in a while Mr. Vincent would break their quiet staring to impart some piece of information. It was usually helpful information, so Jason didn't mind. He just wished that he and his father could be relaxed together more often.

"So you had the car checked out for this trip tomorrow, right?" Mr. Vincent asked.

"Yes, sir, everything's fine."

"What time are you expecting to get back?" Mr. Vincent regarded the portrait of a troubled man before him.

"Oh, about nine-thirty tonight."

Mr. Vincent turned and lifted his eyebrow at his son. "That's quite a long time to have somebody's daughter out of town."

Jason got his father's meaning. "It's all right, her parents know. They said that it was all right."

"You've been seeing a lot of this young lady. Is it pretty serious?"

"Yes." Jason swallowed once, but kept his eyes on the painting just as his father did.

"Well, be careful," he instructed mildly. "Don't get too serious too quickly."

Whatever that meant, Jason thought. "Yes, sir," he said aloud. Then they'd gone on, as though the conversation hadn't occurred at all. That was his father, cool and caring. But too often cool.

Jason drew his attention to Kyra as she interrupted the comfortable quiet and began speaking.

"You'd think we were going to be gone a month, traveling across the Alaskan wilderness," Kyra said in an exasperated voice.

"I think it's sweet," Jason said with a smile. "Your parents are cool, you know that?"

"Yeah, I know," Kyra agreed.

"I mean, they watch out for you, but they don't try to give you a million and two restrictions. That's cool."

"True. They trust me, I'm a good kid," Kyra bragged.

"Yeah, you're all right," Jason said, squeezing her thigh. They were headed up to a tiny town called Greystone, about an hour's drive from Detroit. It had lovely, old, quaint houses on tree-lined streets. There were inns, restaurants, fudge shops, gift and craft shops, and a few tame ski slopes. The Cross High School annual ski trip was being held here for the twelfth year in a row. Kyra had not gone during her previous two years of high school. Jason had gone last year for the first time.

In the backseat they had extra jackets, long johns, sweaters, snow pants, socks, hats, gloves, and mittens, and everything else packed. They would rent skis once they got there. Jason had picked up a thermos of white hot chocolate and some cheese Danishes. The car was nice and toasty and pulsed mildly with R&B rhythms. They were leaving at seven o'clock, and the Saturday roads were quiet. The sky wore a coat of bright blue. It was cloudless, with the beginnings of a pale new sun. The air outside was cold and mild. They eased out of the neighborhood and onto the freeway, then out of the city limits, with few words. Kyra rested her head back on the headrest, while Jason handled his sporty car easily.

"You know what I wonder about?" Jason began.

"What?" Kyra asked lazily. She felt wonderful. An entire day alone with Jason, off someplace different, all in a beautiful winter wonderland.

"I wonder about if I'll become everything I want to be."

"Of course you will," Kyra assured him.

"Why 'of course'?" Jason wanted to know. "No, really," he said when she looked his way. "My father spends almost no time with me. So he's not guiding me. I'm not sure of what I want to do, career-wise. I don't think I'm good enough to get into the NBA. I don't even know what I do well enough to make a living at, Kyra."

"What do you like to do?" she asked, giving Jason her undivided attention.

"Nothing that pays."

"What, though?" Kyra pressed.

"Write, I guess. I like to write," Jason admitted.

"You can make good money writing," Kyra said.

"Yeah, doing what?" he asked, unconvinced.

"Writing novels, articles, screenplays, writing for television, writing for advertising agencies, a bunch of stuff."

Jason nodded appreciatively. He considered what she said. "Maybe. I could write a novel or a screenplay about us," Jason allowed. "I envy you, though," he admitted.

"You do? Why?"

"You're so smart, for one. You can do anything. You know what you want to do. That's excellent. It's almost as if you can already see your future in medical research."

"Not exactly," Kyra said, trying to play things down.

"Almost exactly. You're so confident, too."

"You're confident, Jason."

"Yes, but I'm not different. You cut your own path and you're confident. You're not worried about what other people think about your hair, your clothes, your brains. I'm not quite like that."

"Okay, but you're smart and you're the best junior in the state on the basketball court, one of the best in the state in any grade. College scouts are checking you out already. You're kind and thoughtful and loving. You're a very good writer. You're going to have a great future," Kyra reassured him.

Jason looked over at her and smiled. The miles slipped behind them as they talked, the village of Greystone drawing closer, mile after mile, minute after minute. His face lost all traces of a smile as he spoke again. "But what I envy most is your family life. Your parents are there for you, you know they love you. They're good to you. Not to mention, you have a mother."

They drove on in silence. Kyra didn't know what to say to all that.

"I know that my whole life would be different and better if my mother had lived." Kyra's heart ached for Jason and the pain she knew that he was experiencing. She released her seat belt and leaned across the seat and began kissing Jason's cheek with multiple soft kisses.

Perched up on her knees she whispered in his ear, "I love you, Jason. I love you." Jason felt his love for Kyra pressing against his rib cage, pulsing in his fingertips. I wish I could always have her buzzing in my ear like this, he thought.

"I know that you can do anything, be anything you want. You're strong and that's what it takes, more than anything!" she whispered fiercely.

"I love you," Jason said, looking over at her. Kyra looked at him and realized that he needed her. He didn't just want her, he needed her. It made her feel wonderful. She had never felt needed by anybody in her dynamic, capable family before. Especially as the youngest. But Jason needed her.

The rest of the ride up they talked about lighter topics and listened and sang along to the music. They devoured the Danishes and hot chocolate and arrived safe and sound in Greystone village.

"It's lovely," Kyra breathed as they entered the small town. Everything was quiet, no busy traffic, no sidewalks jammed with tourists . . . yet. They had arrived about half an hour before Cross students were supposed to get there and meet up. It was only eight-thirty.

"Yeah, it really is," Jason said as he drove slowly through the streets.

"Let's go for a walk, Jason," Kyra said excitedly. It would be so romantic, she thought.

"All right. But call your mother first."

"Oh, yeah." Kyra pulled out her slim cell phone and made the call. It was a quick one.

Jason began looking for someplace to park. He pulled over at the foot of a sparsely wooded trail. They got out of the warm car and were greeted by the cold morning air. They pulled on hats, and put mittens over their gloves, and headed out at a leisurely pace. The woods were quiet all around them and the snow, a couple of inches thicker here than in the city, crunched lightly beneath their thick boot soles. In their long johns and corduroys they were not cold at all.

The sky still bore remnants of the pink-and-purple

sunrise on its pale blue facade. The trees stretched high over-head and held an outline of fresh white snow upon their branches. When they looked up it appeared that they walked beneath an intricately woven lace-covered cathedral.

"Isn't it beautiful, Jason?" Kyra said as she looked up.

"Yes," he said. "So are you," he added, remembering all of the things she'd said to him on the ride up here. She was the most beautiful thing in his life, the most beautiful per-son he'd ever known. He took her arm, wrapped in its bulky ski jacket, and gently pulled her over to him. He wrapped his arms around her shoulders as she slipped hers around his waist. Then he tried to tell her, in a kiss, just how much she meant to him. They could hear the quiet all around them. Jason hoped this incredible girl could hear his heart calling out to her in all this quiet.

When they stopped kissing they stayed with their bodies pressed together, buffered by the layers of warm clothing. Jason and Kyra looked at one another for a long minute without speaking. Then Kyra said, "I want you to know, Jason, that if you ever need to know that someone believes in you, just think about me. I believe in you, Jay. We were friends before we went together, and that's going to be there no matter what. I know what kind of person you are. You'll make it, Jason. I know you will." She spoke with utter con-viction.

She told him what no one told him. Certainly not his father. Not even his friends or his crew, who already thought he knew it. No one had bothered to speak those words to him since he was a really little boy in Mrs.

Mooreland's second-grade class. The words seeped into him like a longed-for elixir, healing and soothing him.

"Thank you, Kyra," he said. "Thank you."

"You don't have to thank me for telling you the truth. You deserve much better than what your father gives you. You're special. I was stupid not to see that at first."

"You saw what I wanted you, and everybody else for that matter, to see. Smooth, cool, and collected. And I do feel that way most of the time. But not always, not always," he said, shaking his head slowly. "But I never feel as good, as right, as when I'm with you. Do you know that?"

She nodded. "I feel the same way. I can hardly believe that I feel like this about you so soon, so fast. But I do," she said with a grin. "I do!" she shouted into the quiet woods.

Jason laughed as he looked at her, his first love, and Kyra laughed for joy in return.

It wasn't long before groups of kids from Cross arrived in the small town. Kyra and Jason joined Greg and his date, Aretha, on the small slopes and winding wooded trails. Renee had an indoor track meet in Toledo, Ohio, and couldn't make it. None of them were very experienced skiers and much tumbling and laughter ensued. The day had turned into a bright and sunny one and the snow was a brilliant landscape of white. In no time at all, Greg, Aretha, Jason, and Kyra were familiar with the feel of the powdery white stuff on their behinds.

"God, I've got to get some hot chocolate in me before I freeze to death!" Aretha said around eleven o'clock.

"I'm with you," Greg said, planting a wet one on her cheek. "You two coming?"

"Sure," Jason said with a look over to Kyra. She nodded.

The lodge was spacious and spare. Four fires blazed at four different points of the great room. Seating was arranged near each fireplace and in the room's center. A café occupied the rear of the room. The group took off much of their gear outside and got a table in the cafe.

"Mmmm, it feels so good in here," Aretha said as she rubbed her hands together.

"It smells good, too," Kyra said.

"You got that right! Man, I'm hungry. I'm getting lunch," Greg said. "You want some lunch now?" he asked Aretha.

"Sure." Aretha began scanning the menu. Everyone else followed suit.

Once they'd placed their orders, hot chocolate and tossed salads arrived right away. The group wasted no time digging in.

"So what do you think of Taylor, Jay?" Greg asked his friend.

"They have a good team. But they depend a lot on Vern Hill and Keith Ramsey. If we can shut them down, we shut the whole team down," Jason answered.

"Yeah, that sounds right. So we can knock them out?" Greg asked.

"No doubt," Jason said confidently. "Everybody on our

team is playing hard, feeling dedicated. We keep our heads straight, stay focused, keep that hustle on, we'll be able to handle it all the way to the city championship."

"We just have to take one game at a time," Greg said.

"One game at a time," Jason concurred.

"That championship is just four games away, Jay. That's nothing."

"You're right. That's why it's all about focus now. The training is done. We're physically ready. It's a matter of staying on top of our mental game. And we've got the edge there. We won last year. We know what it feels like to go all the way and win the championship."

"That's right," Greg said, giving his boy a play. "So what have you thought of our games, Kyra?"

"I love them. I'm sorry I didn't make it to some games over the last two years."

"I see you over there in the stands," Greg said. "You get pretty rowdy, girl!" he said with approval.

"I know. I get kinda excited watching you all play."

"I like that," Jason said as he looked over at Kyra. She touched his arm without thinking. Just a small caress, but totally natural. Greg took it all in and felt good for his boy.

"So I hear you're a semifinalist for the Hamilton Science Scholarship," Aretha said.

"Yes, I am," Kyra said, a little surprised. She hadn't realized that many students paid that sort of thing any attention. Many probably didn't, Kyra figured.

"I'm an aide in your counselor's office. I heard Ms.

Thymes bragging about you on the phone to a counselor at another school."

"That's cool," Kyra said.

"Yeah, that's straight, Kyra. Jason was telling me about your competition. He said it was some pretty serious business." Greg drank some of his hot chocolate after he spoke.

"It is," Jason jumped in proudly. "She's been working on the project for what, ten months?" he asked Kyra.

"Nine," she said, smiling.

"Nine months, man. Hard work, too. I barely understand her project. It's got something to do with medical research. It's over my head. How many people entered this year?"

"Almost fifteen hundred," Aretha said. "I heard Mrs. Thymes say that on the phone."

"What's it down to now?" Greg wanted to know.

"About one-fifty," Kyra said. "They make massive cuts at the quarter-final level."

"How many do they take to the finals?" Aretha asked.

"Fifty. The semifinalists win saving bonds, then the last fifty compete for various scholarship amounts," Kyra said.

"What's the top prize?" Greg asked.

"A fifty-thousand dollar scholarship to the college or university of your choice—fifty thousand dollars!" Jason said with feeling.

"Damn!" Greg said.

"Damn is right!" Aretha said. "I heard Mrs. Thymes say that no junior had ever won the top prize, though."

"Yeah? What did she say after that?" Kyra asked.

"She said that didn't matter. She said that you would definitely be one of the finalists and win one of the top prizes, even if you didn't win the big one."

"Is that right?" Kyra said with interest.

"Then she said that if the judges didn't feel that it was 'politically incorrect' to give the top prize to a junior, you'd probably win the whole thing," Aretha said.

"Hell, yeah!" Jason said emphatically. "My baby is crazy smart."

Kyra laughed and nudged Jason with her shoulder. He pulled her to him and kissed her cheek.

"So when do you find out?" Greg asked.

"They announce the finalists in about six weeks. Then all the finalists come up for a two-day session of interviews about our projects by all these different people in the science field."

"That sounds hype," Aretha said.

"Yeah," Greg said with a look of respect toward Kyra. "You nervous?"

"Not yet," Kyra said.

"Six weeks, huh? That's right after state regionals, Jay," Greg said.

"Yeah, I know. I'm going up there with her, if my father lets me."

"You-all staying in the same room?" Greg asked, interested.

"Naw, man. Don't be crazy. There will be teachers and kids everywhere. Plus, her parents will come. I want to stay in the same hotel, though."

Their lunches arrived, and everybody got right to the task at hand. After lunch they hit the snowy trails for a couple of hours, kicked it with some people they knew from Cross for a while, and met at four o'clock, tired and happy.

"Well, we got to get on, man," Greg said.

"Why are you leaving so soon?" Kyra asked. Her mother wasn't expecting her home until around nine o'clock.

"Aretha has to go to work," Greg said.

"Oh. It was nice meeting you," Kyra said.

"You too," Aretha said with a smile.

"See you later," Jason spoke to his friend and Aretha.

"What about you?" Kyra asked after Greg and Aretha pulled away. "Are you ready to go home?"

"No," Jason said, shaking his head. "I've got a better idea."

After turning in their rented ski equipment, they both headed to the locker rooms to clean up and change into fresh clothes. Without telling Kyra where they were headed, Jason led Kyra to his car, stowed their bags in the trunk, got in, and starting driving.

"Jason, you have to tell me!"

"Trust me," he urged.

Kyra decided to give the trust thing a try and sat silently and excitedly beside him. Jason hummed the tune playing on the radio. A few minutes later they pulled up outside a small restaurant with large windows. Kyra could see a fire blazing inside.

"Do you mind an early dinner?" Jason asked with a smile.

"Jason," Kyra said.

Once inside they were met by the fragrance of excellent Italian cooking, the warmth of two blazing fires in huge fireplaces, the sight of people clad in casual and ski clothes, and a maitre d'.

"Good afternoon," the latter said.

"Good afternoon. We have a reservation," Jason said. Kyra looked over at him in surprise.

"Your name, please." The maitre d' was pleasant and professional.

"Vincent."

"Right this way, sir," the maitre d' said after checking his book. Jason grinned at Kyra. They were seated near one of the fireplaces. The table was covered in a thick, cream-colored tablecloth. It held wineglasses, heavy silverware and napkins, candles, and a low, fragrant floral arrangement. The restaurant was dimly lit and elegantly decorated. Classical music floated around them in muted tones.

"Jason, this place is gorgeous."

"Yeah, it is."

"Sir, the sparkling cider you requested," a waiter interrupted quietly. The waiter poured and left.

"Jason, how did you arrange all of this?" Kyra was immensely impressed.

"I asked around, you know, trying to find out about some nice restaurants up here. I made some phone calls and here we are."

"You did all this for me?"

"You know it."

"Thank you." She got up and moved to the seat beside him. "Thank you, Jason," she repeated. She leaned over and gave him a long kiss.

"You're welcome. I wanted to be somewhere special when I gave you this." He went into his jacket pocket and pulled out a slim, gift-wrapped box.

"Jason, you didn't have to," Kyra said, surprised. She unwrapped and opened the box carefully as Jason looked on. Inside she found a gold charm bracelet that shone in the warm firelight. "It's gorgeous," Kyra said quietly. She lifted the bracelet from the bed of pristine white cotton. Four golden charms dangled from it and caught the light: a solid heart, a sweet 16, and the initials K and J. "Thank you, Jay. But why?"

"Because I love you."

"I love you, too."

Jason clasped the bracelet around his girlfriend's wrist. It was the most expensive gift he'd ever given. He'd been looking for just the right thing for two weeks.

When the waiter returned they ordered dinner. That late afternoon they talked, laughed, ate, and talked some more. All the while Kyra was warmly and sweetly aware of the symbol of Jason's love that encircled her wrist.

22

"This is it! You understand? This is it!" Coach Henderson shouted these words above the crazy noise level of the Cross and Handover crowds. This was the last regular season game and the score stood at 58 Handover, 56 Cross. The clock stood patiently, waiting the restart of the game at forty-eight seconds. Cross needed to win to be assured the right to battle for the city championship. A loss and they'd have to wait to find out who was the victor of the Gregor–Bingham game, five days from now. If Bingham won, Cross would be out of the city championship game, but if Gregor won, Cross would face Roper two weeks from now. Roper had a 12 and 0 season,

Cross had 11 and 1, and Bingham had 11 and 2.

"Jason, you take it. Run number seven, don't let up, no matter what you do. Everybody, stay focused, be energized, and pull from way deep inside yourselves. Let's hear it!" Coach Henderson commanded.

The team joined hands as they stood in a circle and shouted "Mighty Cross! Mighty Cross! Mighty Cross!" Catching the team's cheer, the Cross fans joined in on the second call so that the final "Mighty Cross!" was a rousing, rowdy cheer. The coach grabbed Jason's arm just before he followed his team onto the floor.

"I'm counting on you, Vincent," Coach Henderson said. Jason looked into the eyes of this coach, whom he both respected and loved, and gave him a look of confidence. "Go get 'em, son!"

Jason rushed out onto the court, ready to receive when his teammate gave him the inbound pass. Every nerve in Jason's body felt alive, yet he felt remarkably still at the same time. He knew exactly what he had to do, and even better, he knew that he could do it. He glanced up and to his left, and there she was: Kyra was on her feet, her expression fierce and excited.

"You got it, Jason!" Her voice rang out in an unaccustomed lull in the crowd's loud buzz. Yeah, baby, Jason thought. He was so focused that he could not afford to acknowledge her, or break into the smile her words and enthusiasm inspired.

The pass came in and Jason had the ball in his hands, dribbling expertly. He saw the court and all its occupants in a glance. He saw the moves of each player, on his team and his opponents, now and several moves ahead. He moved the ball swiftly toward the hoop, seeing the Cross players shift gracefully, smoothly into position for play #7. Suddenly, Chris Klein got caught up behind two of Handover's big players and couldn't get to his position. Jason needed Chris in position—that's where he was supposed to shoot the ball for a three-point play. While Chris struggled to find an opening, Jason scanned the floor for another viable option, all the while fending off the man assigned to check him. All of this took only seconds. Quickly Jason signaled Greg to make a move, give him an option. Greg moved his large frame with the sort of grace, confidence, and speed that made opponents say "Aw, sh—!" and signaled for the ball. Jason shot to his boy, Greg, who caught the ball, stepped back, and took the shot. He got it, but it was only a two, and the score stared down at them, tied at 58. Jason called the time-out that his coach wanted, and both teams cleared the floor. The clock stood at thirteen seconds.

"Foul as soon as their man gets in. It's a one-and-one free-throw situation. If their man misses, snag those rebounds and lob it out to Jason. Jason, you be gone to just about half court. Get it down to the paint area. Take the shot yourself or get it to Greg or Chris, whoever looks best for the shot. Everybody else, pick those screens up, clear a lane out. Everybody got it?" The team nodded all around. The cheer of "Mighty Cross!" rang out all over the gymnasium. The gym was alive with the energy of the spectators and players. The cheers from the crowd and cheerleaders echoed all around. Kids were practically bouncing all over the place, rockin' the house with electric screams and calls.

Kyra looked down at Jason from where she sat. He looked entirely poised and sure. She was a bundle of nerves. She knew how much this game meant to the team, but more important to her, she knew how much it meant to Jason. He had played the game beautifully. Kyra, new to paying attention to basketball for more than five minutes a month, was still amazed at the way her boyfriend played. On the court her handsome, low-key man was all controlled, aggressive power and finesse. He gave this direction, he called that play, he scanned the floor constantly, bumped bodies, and took shots. He gave plays, shouted pleasure and frustration. The crowd loved him, kids and adults alike. Cross didn't necessarily have the best all-around team in the city or the state, but they had Jason and Greg, both of whom everyone figured would make All American this year. Then they had Chris Klein and Joshua Temple, two solid seniors. What gave them the edge, and everyone agreed on this, were three important things: the Cross coach and team had a tremendous work ethic, Jason knew how to run his team on the court, and Jason hated, hated, hated to lose. He wasn't thinking about class, or a test, or his father, or her. He was thinking about winning. And she was right there with him, in spirit and mind. "God, please let them win," she prayed aloud softly.

The teams returned to the court, and Handover took it

out of bounds. As soon as they inbounded it, the Cross team swarmed into action. When it looked as if one of the Handover players might shoot for two, with seven seconds left on the clock, Greg committed his fourth foul. The Handover player missed the first shot, and Jason, who'd already been in position, took off running down the court. One of his teammates threw the ball out his way, and Jason caught it effortlessly, swooped it behind his back to the other hand without even thinking, kept his stride, and saw the hoop dead ahead and no Handover player in sight to stop him. Jason powered ahead, planning to close in and take the easy shot, no showboating, just take care of business. He checked behind himself—Greg and the top Handover player were behind him—he had time, though. Jason was in flight, headed toward the easy, careful layup, when his arm and the ball were slapped from the rear. Damn, Jason thought. He lost his balance, stumbled, and looked around for the ball. Where was his foul? he wondered. The Cross crowd was in an uproar as they wondered the same thing. The Cross end of the court was now full of players chasing the ball in the other direction. Jason joined the hunt. As he approached Handover's paint, he watched, his stomach tight with a sense of doom and disappointment, as the ball went in for two. Jason turned to look at the clock. Four seconds. The Handover crowd was going insane. Their stands rocked, literally and figuratively, with cheers. To beat Cross was a sweet victory.

Chris took the ball out. He threw it in to Jason. Jason passed it to Greg, who stood at midcourt. Greg took two steps on the dribble and let the ball loose on the buzzer and it flew vainly in the direction of the hoop. The crowd seemed suspended, on some insane hope or fear that it might actually make it. But it didn't go in, and the gym roared. Jason stood on the court looking at the clock, then the hoop.

Jason turned toward the Cross stands, trying to find his girl. He found her and locked eyes with her. Kyra tried to send him all the love and comfort she could from a silent look. Oh baby! she thought. I'm here, it'll be all right. Jason turned and headed off the court with his team.

Forty minutes later the school bus pulled up before a darkened Cross High School. Players filed out quietly into the cold February night. The sky was a frigid, dark dome, encasing them in its shadowed splendor. Fellas said their good-byes and went to cold cars or warm rides. Jason spotted Kyra's Jetta when they pulled up and made a beeline for it. She was standing outside the car before he got there. Without a word she surrounded him in her embrace and held on tight.

"Hey, baby," she said. His answer was a kiss.

"Where do you want to go?" she asked.

"My place. My father's over at his woman's house."

"We're gone, then."

They held hands in silence as Kyra drove them to Jason's house. Tupac Shakur rapped rhythmically, angrily as they moved through the city streets. Kyra parked up the street and they walked to Jason's house, just in case. Once inside, Jason dropped his bag and took Kyra's hand. He led her to his room wordlessly, his fingers intertwined with hers. He closed the door behind them once they were inside his room.

Then he did what he'd wanted to do from the instant the last Handover ball went into the hoop; he took Kyra's face gently between his hands and kissed her. He searched her mouth softly and longingly for something to soothe his frustration and disappointment. He found it. She tasted so sweet to him, her lips and tongue moved so willingly with his, and he wrapped one arm around her and drew her in close. When their lips parted she spoke his name.

"Jason."

"Can we lie down?"

"Yes." They took off their jackets and shoes and climbed into his bed fully clothed. Jason felt a sense of disappointment that was thick and layered over him like a coating of sticky caramel. Kyra wrapped her arms around him and he embraced her as they began kissing again. The familiar stroking and rubbing became insistent and intense. Kyra moved her hands to Jason's face and looked at him in the muted light of his bedside lamp.

"It wasn't your fault, Jason. You played so well."

Jason didn't say anything, he just looked into her eyes as she spoke.

"I was proud of you, Jay." He kissed her lightly on the lips, then one cheek, then the other. He rose up to his knees and began to undo the buttons of her shirt. She didn't stop him. Instead she began undoing his shirt buttons, starting at the bottom edge.

"I love you, Kyra," Jason said as he looked down at her. Her braids were spread across his pillow. His pillow would smell like vanilla tonight.

"I love you." He came out of his shirt and she came out of hers. He unfastened her bra, then slipped it off. He ran his hands along her skin, feeling its softness and warmth. He'd never been filled with such conflicting emotions at once. There was the ripping pain of losing the game and the intense, almost breathless love he felt for this girl.

"I wish we had won."

"I know."

"I wanted to win so badly."

"I know, Jay, I know." He shook his head, his hands still stroking her, her hands now on his torso.

Jason heard it first and the sound stilled his hands.

"Was that a key?" Kyra whispered.

Jason nodded. "Ssshh." Jason got up soundlessly and Kyra followed, picking up her bra and shirt. He grabbed her purse and jacket and pointed to his closet. Kyra scooped up all of her things and hid inside his closet.

"Where are you, dumb-ass?" Mr. Vincent called. "Woman said she won't take off a thing until I get that damn Luther Vandross CD over there."

Damn, Jason thought. Not tonight. His stomach tightened and his throat constricted as he realized the helplessness of his situation. Everything inside him went still and he tried to prepare himself for the humiliation. Damn! His father was going to slice and dice him in front of his lady.

"Jay, do you hear me, boy?"

"Yes, sir."

"Then dammit, answer when I call your sorry ass!"

Jason thought to go out and meet his father, maybe keep Kyra from hearing everything; but it was too late for that now. His father opened his bedroom door.

"What are you doing up here?"

"Getting ready for bed."

"Why the hell are you going to bed so early? It's only nine o'clock."

"I had a game, I'm tired."

"Oh, that's right." Mr. Vincent sounded as though he had genuinely just remembered that Jason had had the most important game so far this season today. "Which one was it?"

"Last one of the regular season."

"Well?"

"We lost."

Mr. Vincent snorted. "Figures. You sure are a weak-ass captain, Jason. I'm not surprised you lost." Kyra wanted to punch Mr. Vincent in the mouth. She was so angry, she was shaking. "You sure are sorry." Jason stood there feeling his insides shrivel up. Go away, Jason thought. Go away. He sent the silent message to his father and Kyra. "What a waste," Mr. Vincent said with disgust as he left the room.

Kyra and Jason heard him go downstairs. There was a pause while he mumbled about the CD, then they heard the door close behind him and the sound of his Volvo starting up and pulling away. The condo was silent.

Jason closed his eyes and wished he could leave, too. Kyra came out of the closet, still topless and holding all of her things. She dropped everything and went to Jason. Without words she came before him and placed her hands on his chest. Jason kept his eyes averted from her face. He looked at a spot just beyond her shoulder.

"It's all right, Jason." Her voice was soft, an angel's caress upon his heart. "It's all right, Jason. I love you." She touched his chin and shifted his face so that he was fully facing her. His eyes followed and he looked into her eyes. His eyes were so sad that Kyra wanted to cry.

"You should just go," Jason said.

"No, I shouldn't." She kissed his neck, his chest. "I should be right here." He brought his hands up and touched her hair, tangled his hands up in the warm softness of her beautiful braids. She kissed his lips, then his mouth. Jason's hands moved to her pants and unfastened them. He slid them from her hips and they dropped to her ankles. Kyra's heart began to drum violently against her chest, and she nearly felt her pulse move through her body. She stepped out of her pants. Jason got rid of his pants and socks. Then he sat her down on the bed and took her socks off for her.

"It's all right, Kyra," he whispered. "I just want to hold you and touch you."

Kyra nodded. They turned off the light and lay together on the bed, nearly naked, fully touching. They kissed, and touched, murmured and talked. They aroused one another and cooled one another down until they grew sleepy. Kyra turned until her back was up against Jason's chest and he wrapped his arm around her. "I love you, Jason," she murmured in the darkness.

"I love you, too."

23

After a good day together filled with roller skating, driving around Belle Isle, and dinner at Kyra's with her parents, Jason and Kyra once again found themselves at Jason's condo. Once they'd starting messing around with only their underwear on, they kept doing so whenever they got the opportunity. It felt good to Kyra and Jason, but the amount of time they spent on top of one another was becoming dangerously long to Kyra. She was finding it harder and harder to stop their necking. Not because Jason pressured her, but because it felt wonderful to be so close to Jason and she didn't want to stop. They touched just about any- and everywhere. She had started wondering more and more about what it would be like to go farther, to actually make love with Jason. Then, too, she could tell that Jason was getting more and more into it. She didn't think he'd be able to go on like this much longer.

The truth was, it was all starting to scare her. This time, when they were going hot and heavy, she pushed him off her, telling him to stop. She hadn't intended to be so rough or speak so abruptly, but she had.

"What's up with you, Ky?" Jason sounded frustrated.

"What's up is that we're doing too much! I need us to slow down."

"We're just doing what feels good. What's the big deal? We're not doing anything that can get you pregnant or get you some disease!"

"I know, but I still want to slow down!"

"Fine, fine, we'll slow down. Why are you starting this tonight? Huh? We've had a good day, everything is going so well, and we were having a good time. Then you have to go and start this again."

"Not again."

"Yes, again. You brought it up the last time we were here and that time when we were at Belle Isle messing around."

"Whatever."

"Yeah, whatever." He got up and started putting on his clothes. "Ky, you're the one who's always throwing limits up in our faces."

"Because I know you want more!"

"Yeah, I want more. But do I bother you about it? No. I want you, okay? I keep telling you we should just relax and enjoy what you're willing to do. It can be really good if you let it."

"I know, it is good. But it'll only make you want more."

"Yeah, it makes me want some more, but I'm not a damn animal, Ky! I can stop myself. You're the one who's always talking about sex, but you don't want to do anything about it."

"Jason—"

"Forget it."

"Don't do that."

"Well, you stop doing this."

"Why are you yelling at me?" she demanded.

Jason looked across the room at Kyra where she sat on his bed in only a pair of purple panties. His look of utter frustration turned to one of contrition as he took in the look of pain and worry on her face. "Look, I'm sorry, Kyra. Really," he said, going over to her. "But you have to stop doing this to us, okay?" Kyra nodded. "Do I want to make love to you so badly I could cry sometimes? Yes! Of course. You're beautiful and I love you. But you're not ready yet, so all right. I'm okay with it, really. Believe me, you're worth it, all right?"

"Okay. I'm sorry I tripped out."

"That's all right. You want to watch a video?"

"Yeah."

"All right. Then you'd better get on some clothes before I'm all over you again," Jason said with a smile.

24

"I'll tell you this," Angela said to Kyra as she snapped a piece of strawberry-scented bubble gum. "I wasn't the only one surprised when I heard that you were going with Jason Vincent. Hell, after all this time, I'm still trying to get used to it."

They were sitting together with Renee, Portia, and Crystal at their usual fifth-hour lunch table. The table was littered with books, empty chip bags, trays of half-eaten French fries, pop cans, and the remains of Renee's and Kyra's bag lunches. In the center sat Kyra's huge bouquet of mixed blossoms propped up on a stack of books. The voices of more than three hundred teenagers collided under the high vaulted ceiling, making the noise level even higher than it would have been in a low-ceilinged room. A pale, pale yellow sun, the color of sliced lemon, struggled valiantly to flood the cavernous lunchroom with its mid-February afternoon light.

Angela, Portia, and Crystal knew about half the stuff between Jason and her, while Renee knew a little better than three-quarters. No one knew it all but Jason and Kyra.

"Now you know that I know that you're a sweetheart, Kyra, I mean that," Angela asserted. "You are!" she added for emphasis. "But still, you and Jason don't really seem like a match. He's so . . . you know . . . God, how do I say this?" How about not saying anything more? Kyra thought with a groan inside. "He's so, everything you want, you know? Shoot, this isn't coming out right. I mean, look, he's, like, extra fine, he's built like a GQ model at sixteen, for God's sake!" This she said at a near shout. The girls gave one another high fives all around the table. Kyra just shook her head and smiled. "He *dresses* like a GQ model. He is cool in all block letters, underline it and put it in bold!"

"You're stupid," Kyra said, laughing with the other girls.

"He's kinda smart from what you say, which sure as hell ain't fair. I don't think I want a boy that fine to be smart, too," Angela said with energy. The girls just kept right on laughing. "And his skills on the court! Colleges are already looking at him, aren't they?" she asked needlessly. Kyra just nodded and grinned. Everyone at Cross knew about the college scouts who attended the basketball games so they could check out the seniors and look over Jason on the down-low. "Didn't I hear they were thinking about dedicating an entire page of the *Detroit News* sports section to Jason this season, he's in there so much?" Angela joked. "The boy can write his own ticket in almost every area!"

"You're right," Kyra concurred.

"Now, I love you, Kyra, but you know that you're about as brainy as they come! What's your IQ, girl? One-sixty? One-seventy?"

"Shut up, Angela, you talk too much," Kyra said, laughing with the others. Angela wasn't too far off, though.

"No, seriously, you're so smart it's kind of scary. Not to mention all that loot your family has." Angela lowered her head and spoke in a dramatic whisper, "It's okay, I'm keeping that low-key," she said, smiling. "And you're, like, entirely your own person on top of it. What are there, like, ten sixteen-year-old girls with that kind of confidence? I just never pictured the two of you together."

"Well, we are," Kyra said, smiling. Four months and they were still a couple and going strong, Kyra thought with pleasure. Then Angela unwittingly hit upon the only sore spot in the relationship for Kyra.

"Not to mention everybody at this table knows the kind of lock and key that you're keeping the virginity box under. What's your saying, girl—'Abstinence is the best defense'? I know your boy Jason isn't used to putting up with those kind of defenses. He probably says '*condoms* are the best defense'!"

Everyone at the table burst out laughing. All except Kyra, who sat there with a wan smile. Kyra shivered a little, Angela was so dead-on.

It had turned out that Jason had been exactly right that night a little over a month ago. Kyra wasn't ready for sex yet. She was scared. She was scared of crossing that line and never being able to go back. She was scared of getting pregnant and ruining her life. She was scared to even think about having an abortion, her thoughts on it were so conflicted. She was scared of getting some sort of STD that left her unable to have children when she was grown, or with all sorts of symptoms she'd have to explain to any potential lover for the rest of her life! She was scared of getting HIV and dying a slow, horrible, painful death from AIDS. She was scared of what sex might mean between Jason and her. How often would they do it once they started, where would they do it, when would they do it? Her mind whirled every time she thought about it. Jason's mind seemed as steady and still as the Rock of Gibraltar on the subject. Kyra tried to laugh with the other girls to cover her anxiety.

"I know he was getting some from Lisa, and probably every other girl he's been with since he's been wanting to have sex," Angela said, crunching on a potato chip. She sipped her soda thoughtfully to wash down the chips. "I know it hasn't been easy for him, giving that up."

"Of course," Kyra said on a falsely happy note. "You would know," she added sarcastically. She picked up her backpack from the back of her chair as she got up to leave. It was ten minutes before the bell. She scooped up her flowers after she had everything else properly adjusted. "I've got to go, I'll talk to you all later."

"All right, I'll call you after practice," Renee said. She

could sense her best friend's discomfort. She knew that this was a touchy subject for Kyra.

"Okay," Kyra said, extremely ready to leave.

"Catch you later, Ky."

"Later, girl."

Kyra left the lunchroom and used her pass to the library. She walked with thoughts of Jason and everything Angela had said traveling through her mind. Everything seemed perfect in their relationship, except the issue of sex. Jason wanted some; he was very, very, very ready, and Kyra was just as much not ready. Things were still good between them, quite good, but it could be even better if they were in agreement on this critical issue.

Today was February 14, Valentine's Day, and Kyra had a card and a box of dark, rich Godiva chocolates wrapped in thick, lustrous golden paper tucked in her bag for him. She had not wanted to give it to him in third hour in some sort of rush. Instead she'd met him outside class and presented him with a small, individually wrapped chocolate encased in thick silver paper. It was tied in red string from which dangled two velvet hearts. I LOVE YOU was etched in black into each heart.

She had been only a little surprised, but extremely pleased, when a Sweet-O-Gram showed up third hour for her. It was a Cross tradition that singing Sweet-O-Grams could be hired on Valentine's Day. Three young men dressed in black tuxedo pants and crisp white shirts with red ties and cummerbunds sang of love and sweet caresses in beautiful harmony. She'd blushed and grinned at Jason as he beamed back at her in pride and pleasure. The trio had ended by handing her the large bouquet of mixed flowers she carried now. It must have cost a lot of money.

Other than those tiny valentines kids handed out in elementary school, Kyra hadn't received a valentine from a boy. She had been proud and overwhelmed by Jason's public expressions to her. In fact, up until Angela's reminder of her biggest problem, Kyra had felt as though she were floating on air. Well the fact was, she wasn't floating on air, she was walking right here on earth where her boyfriend wanted sex, very much, thank you very kindly, and she wasn't giving any up. He wasn't pressuring her for sex; in fact, he wasn't even asking for it. But she still felt that she was letting him down.

She walked slowly through the hallway, thinking, until she ended up outside Jason's fifth-hour class. He soon noticed her outside his door and got a pass to meet her. He took her hand and they moved into a nearby closet doorway, out of sight.

"Hey, sweet thing," he said, kissing her neck. "What are you doing here?"

"I was just thinking about you," Kyra said with concern in her voice.

"What's the matter?" he asked as he looked into her eyes.

"Nothing, I guess. I just wanted to see you,"

"Nothin' the matter with that," Jason said as he kissed her lips.

"You'd better go on back," she said, returning his kisses. "I'll call you tonight, all right?"

"All right. You know I've got to be down at the club early. You want to come then? Or do you want me to cut out and pick you up later?" Jason and some of his boys were giving a Valentine's party.

"No, neither. I'll come with Renee later on and meet you there."

"Don't come too late, I want to see you as soon as I can."

"Okay. I'll come around nine o'clock."

"Okay."

"I might have a surprise for you," Kyra said with a sly smile.

"What kind of surprise?"

"You'll see soon enough. Here, I got this for you," she said, digging into her book bag for the box of chocolate and card. He took them both.

"Thank you, Kyra," he said, touched. It had been a while since he'd received a Valentine card or present from anyone he cared about. Lisa had expected Jason to get her something, but didn't think it fitting for the girl to give the guy a gift. "Do you want me to read it now?" he asked, indicating the card.

"Yes," she said a bit shyly.

He opened the card and read it aloud softly.

> Kiss the new day with our love,
> And hold your dreams in mine.
> I will wrap my love around you
> Until the end of time.

He looked at Kyra, who stood very near in the tiny doorway. "I can feel it too, your love all around me."

Kyra felt much better. "Happy Valentine's Day, Jason."

"Happy Valentine's Day, Kyra. I love you."

"I love you, too," she said. "I'll see you tonight."

25

"I don't believe it," Akila said, shaking her head.

"Well, believe it," Kyra assured her. They were sitting in Shear Pleasures, an expensive salon in the downtown area.

"You're getting your hair pressed," Akila said in wonderment. "All that hair."

"All that hair is right," Vivian the stylist retorted. "I've been after you to let me put a perm in your hair for three years now. I don't know why you're still wearing your hair natural. A good perm would make your hair so easy to take care of, girl!"

"Well, I still don't want a perm," Kyra said hurriedly.

"Just a press." Kyra watched in the massive wall mirror as Vivian carefully blow-dried her hair. One half of Kyra's head was thick, woolly, and wet. The other half lay across her chest and halfway down her back in hot, blow-dried straightness. Kyra's stomach was doing all kinds of flips and flops. God, I hope it turns out right, she thought.

Akila had come into town for the weekend and joined Kyra at the salon. Kyra had told her how nervous she was and what kind of look she was going for that night. They'd been there since four-thirty, and it was already six o'clock. Vivian was taking her time, getting it done right, she assured Kyra. Kyra had taken down her braids the night before and wound her hair into two thick, graceful twists on each side of her head that ended in an intricate figure-eight–style bun. Kyra had skipped out on working on her science project today and had arrived home just before three o'clock. She'd taken her shower early because she knew she didn't want to mess with the steam after she'd gotten her hair done—it would ruin the style. She'd laid her clothes for the night out on her bed and left with Akila for the appointment. Vivian shampooed her hair gently, then put in a leave-on conditioner. "I'd better let that sit for half an hour with all that thick stuff," Vivian said. So Kyra had ambled on over to one of the nail technicians who didn't have an appointment, and had a simple manicure done. Now they were almost halfway through the process.

But what Kyra had planned to be a pleasurable experience had turned out to be pure torture for her. She had moved through all of her preparations for tonight with a sense of gloom.

"Don't worry, pretty thing," Vivian advised. "It's going to be beautiful when I get done. Shoot, you'll probably want a perm after seeing it like this."

"How long has it been since you've gotten it straightened?" Akila asked.

"Six years, I think," Kyra said. She thought a few moments. "Yep, six years."

"All this for Jason, huh?" Akila asked.

"Yeah, I guess so," Kyra said. She sat facing her sister now, who sat in the neighboring styling chair. Vivian had turned Kyra away from the mirror.

"He must be really special." Akila looked at her little sister seriously.

"Yeah," Kyra said, lowering her eyes to the hairstyle book in her lap.

Akila considered her sister silently for a moment. Kyra had called and told her that she had a boyfriend, but they had not talked long about him. Now, looking at Kyra face-to-face, Akila could see that her baby sister was—in love? Could Kyra, so young, so serious, so in the books, be in love now? And could he feel the same?

"You know, if you ever need to talk, about anything at all, you can talk to me?" Akila told her sister.

"Yes, of course," Kyra said easily. "Everything's cool right now." She couldn't explain why, but she wasn't ready to discuss her relationship problems with Akila.

"Okay," Akila said as she rose and playfully slapped

Kyra's thigh. "I'm starving. I haven't eaten all day. I'm going down the block to that Chinese food place to get something to eat. Do you want me to sneak you something back?" Shear Pleasures had a no-food-or-drink policy.

"No, thanks. I'll see you later." Akila took off, and Kyra allowed her mind to drift back to what had led her to the miserable mood she was in now.

Jason and a group of his friends had been planning to throw a Valentine's Day bash for a couple of months. It was an excellent way to make some quick cash. It would be open to the coolest city and suburban high schools. Small, glossy, white-black-and-red handbills circulated among eight different high schools advertising the promoters, date, time, place, cost, and attire. Everybody at Cross was talking about it.

Kyra, of course, was planning to attend. She had even intended to surprise Jason with this new look, at least for a day. But all of that had changed. She was walking down the main hallway at the end of her day, preparing to head on out. She had to make a quick stop in the restroom and then she'd be on her way. Just as she approached the girls' restroom door, she noticed Lisa and her crew down the hall. They didn't seem to see her.

Wasting no time, Kyra headed right into a stall in the empty restroom, and quickly did her business. Just before she could flush the toilet, though, she heard voices as some girls entered. She recognized Jackie's voice right away.

"So did you talk to him last night?" Jackie asked.

"Yeah. He sounded pretty good. He reminded me

that he and his boys were getting a party together for Valentine's Day tonight. Like he needed to remind me. He asked if I was gonna be there," Kyra heard Lisa respond. Kyra stood perfectly still as her stomach and throat constricted. They must be talking about Jason, Kyra thought.

"What did you tell him?" That was Heather.

"I asked him, did he want me to come."

"What did he say?" Jackie prompted.

"What do you think? He said yes. I said, What about your girlfriend? Is she coming? And he said yes, but that he wasn't too worried about that."

"I wonder why he told you that?" Heather asked.

"I don't wonder at all," Lisa said in a cocky voice. Kyra leaned over so that she could peek out of the tiny space between the door and its frame. Lisa was applying lip gloss as she spoke. Her next words were contorted by the posture of her lips. "He wants to see me for a little bit before she comes."

"Are you coming early?" Jackie asked.

"Mmmm-hmmm," Lisa said. "I love the way that boy dances. God, Jason can move. And I'm not just talking about on the dance floor!" Lisa and her girls started giving one another plays. "You know, he came over a few weeks ago."

"What? You never told me that," Heather said.

"I knew," Jackie said confidently.

"What happened?"

"Well, I was having some problems with my parents and I needed to talk to somebody. We broke up, but Jason is still my boy. You know, he's like one of my best friends. So anyway, I was telling him about what happened with my parents and I started to get upset, you know. Then he came over to me on the couch and started holding me and trying to console me, and then we started kissing and, well, you know. We'd been together for a year, longer than that if you count when we were just talking to one another. We're close. You're not just gonna get rid of all those feelings and attractions in a couple of months. It's not possible."

"You're right," Jackie agreed.

"So we made love right there."

"Where were your parents?" Heather wanted to know.

"My father was at work and my mother was over at my auntie's," Lisa informed them.

"So go ahead, what happened?" Gillian urged. She was the fourth wheel of their sorry little bus, Kyra thought. She'd been quiet up till now.

"Well, it was like old times. Neither of us had forgotten what it was like to be together like that," Lisa said in a confidential voice. Kyra leaned over again and saw that Lisa was now turned in her direction, resting her hips against the wash basin. Her three friends were grouped nearby, but they didn't block Kyra's view of Lisa. "Jay's real strong, you know, but he can be so tender when, you know. . . . He was gentle with me, made me want to cry." The other three, and Kyra listened raptly. Lisa appeared to be in a dreamy reverie. "You know what he told me?" Lisa asked her audience.

"What?" Gillian asked with her mouth hanging half open.

"He told me that he missed me. Said he missed my style, you know, my hair, my clothes. He said he missed how soft and silky my hair was," Lisa touched her reddish hair for added effect, then smoothed her perfect outfit over her lovely figure.

"What did you say?" Heather inquired.

"I told him that I missed him too, but that he'd made his choice. He gave me this pitiful look." Lisa's girls stared at her with eager looks. "You know what else he said?"

"What?" Heather asked.

"He said he'd really been missing gettin' my lovin', if you know what I mean." Kyra grimaced, she knew. "I told him he could have some of this anytime he wanted. He said he was glad to know that. Then he started to show to me how much he missed it."

"Damn!" Gillian said.

"The Brain must be doing something all wrong, 'cause Jason was eager as hell," Lisa said laughing.

"Girl, you could probably have him anytime you wanted," Jackie volunteered.

"Probably," Lisa said nonchalantly as she turned back to the mirror for another quick check. "Probably." They strolled out of the restroom.

Kyra stood shell-shocked in her little stall. She felt as though she were about to throw up. Jason slept with Lisa a few weeks ago? she wondered incredulously. They'd been going together for almost three-and-a-half months by then. How could he do this to me? Kyra wondered. She couldn't believe it—but what else could she do, except believe it? It wasn't as if Lisa had told Kyra all of this news. Lisa hadn't even known Kyra was in the bathroom. No, she was confiding in her friends, privately. Or so Lisa thought.

Kyra thought about the conversations that she and Jason had had about sex. She thought about how understanding he had been, how patient. She thought about what Renee had said about the fact that boys didn't go from having sex regularly to having none very well, if they adjusted at all. Then she thought again about how patient Jason seemed. Of course he's patient if he knows he can get with Lisa any time he pleases, Kyra thought furiously.

So he thought he could just make a fool out of me? she wondered. Well, he's dead wrong. We'll see who gets played!

That's when she'd begun to hatch a plan to get back at Jason for his betrayal. She wouldn't give him the chance to explain or lie. If he tried to do either she'd just hate him entirely. Or worse, believe him. Kyra was so sick of hearing about girls who got played this way and stayed with the guy. Weak, she'd always thought. That wasn't her. She'd get herself all fixed up the way that he *missed*, and she'd come to his stupid party, and then she would dump him. In front of everybody, if she felt like it. Then he would know how it felt to trust somebody, trust something, and have it yanked from up under your feet, leaving you flat on your behind with the wind knocked out of you.

That's how she felt right now, as though someone had knocked the wind out of her. Her mind became flooded with memories of Jason's touch on her body, his mouth on her mouth, his words whispered in her ears while they lay pressed together. Then, unwillingly, she became tormented by those same images, but this time it was Lisa happy and satisfied on the receiving end of Jason's romancing. Kyra shook her head over and over. She slapped the bathroom door and mumbled, "Shit" as tears began to fall from her eyes. "How could you do this to me, Jason?" she whispered aloud. "How could you hurt me like this?"

Kyra flushed the toilet, grabbed some toilet paper, and left the stall. She washed her hands, threw some water on her face, and got out of school as fast as she could. What to do? she wondered. What to do?

She was in her car by now, heading home. Her eyes began to fill with hot tears and her throat constricted in pain. Jason, Jason! Was he thinking about Lisa sometimes when he was with me? The thought made her so angry and hurt that she screamed, "No-o-o-o-o!" inside her quiet car. She grabbed the wad of toilet paper she'd taken from the restroom and wiped the tears as they fell from her eyes.

All the good and beautiful parts of their relationship never even crossed her mind.

26

"You look good, Ky," Akila said. She lay across Kyra's bed, watching her sister primp in front of the mirror. "What time is Jason coming to pick you up?"

"I told you, he's not. He had to go to the party early and help set up."

"Oh, that's right. Well, what time is Renee coming?"

"She's not." Kyra had talked herself to a point of moderate stability. She repeated the things Lisa had said over and over until her heart had hardened, although only a little, toward Jason. "She's got a date. I told her to go ahead and have a good time."

"You going to be okay driving there alone—at night, I mean?"

"Yeah. It's only ten minutes away, luckily. Otherwise, you know Mama and Daddy would never let me go alone."

"You sound funny." Akila had noticed how odd her sister's mood was, considering she was heading out for a Valentine's Day party to meet her boyfriend who she was crazy about.

"I'm a comedian, I guess." Kyra's tone was entirely without humor.

"No, silly. Not funny ha-ha, funny odd."

"I feel kind of odd," Kyra said, staring at herself in the mirror. She turned from the mirror and looked at her sister. "Jason and I are having a couple of problems."

"Oh."

"Yeah, oh."

"Do you want to talk about it?"

Kyra walked over and gave her big sister a hug. "Thanks, but no. I can work this one out."

"All right. I hope you feel better soon."

"Thanks." Kyra glanced at the watch on her wrist: ten o'clock. I guess he's had enough time to dance with Lisa, Kyra thought bitterly. "I'd better go." Kyra picked up her purse and looked at herself in the mirror once more. The snug-fitting red sweater exposed her navel and the short black miniskirt fit perfectly. Her hair fell all around her in a cascade of dark, shiny brown curls. She'd put on red lipstick. She'd had to pick it up today just for the occasion, because she normally only used lip gloss. Some occasion, she thought.

Kyra arrived at the hall and found a parking spot. She took her coat off and left it in the car. A group of kids were heading to the door and she walked near them for safety. Once inside, she was assaulted by the weighty beat of the bass rhythm. The corridor was lit well and kids lined the walls, talking and waiting for friends, enemies, whatever. At the end of the hall she could see double doors flung open on the party. It was darkened in there, with flashing lights providing fleeting illumination.

It's just too loud in here, she thought. That was one reason she didn't go to parties like this anymore. Some people from Cross nodded at her. Most looked at her hair and outfit in mild surprise. Kyra just nodded back at whoever nodded to her and kept on walking. Once at the door to the party she was met by two doormen. They were in their thirties, burly and immovable.

"What's up, cutie?" one of them said.

"Nothing. I'm Kyra." The doorman sat next to the tiny, tall table that held a cash box, stamp pad, stamper, and a tiny spiral notebook. He flipped the spiral open and read a brief list of names.

"Go 'head."

Kyra walked into the semidarkness of Jason's Valentine's Day party and felt her heart quicken. Despite what had happened today, she wanted to see him. She still loved him. She was nervous about his reaction to her appearance. She wanted him to like it, but not too much. Because maybe that would mean that Lisa was right, he truly preferred her look to Kyra's. But most of all, she was scared about pulling the breakup off. God, don't let me cave in, she prayed. But half of her mind was praying that she would cave in, and hard.

She moved along the rows of spectators who stood near the wall. The floor was jam-packed. The party was hype and the DJ was making all the right noise. A couple of wallflower fellas asked her to dance. Kyra just shook her head no and kept on walking. She hadn't been to a party like this in over a year. Only one person had asked her to dance then, and it had been well into the night. Another reason she didn't go to parties like this.

After working her way in a good distance, she stood still and looked around. She spotted Renee dancing nearby. She waved, trying to catch her eye.

Renee came over dragging her date once she noticed Kyra. "*Girl*, look at you!" Renee exclaimed. She picked up Kyra's hair on both sides and let it fall. She checked out Kyra's outfit. "Look at my girl, Ky! When you said to expect a couple of changes, I wasn't expecting anything like this!"

"Hey, Renee. Hey, Brandon. Do you like it?" Kyra asked Renee. They both leaned in and shouted to each other. The music made it hard to hear even with these adjustments.

"Oh, yeah. You look good, Ky. But I like the old you better," Renee said with a smile.

"Thanks, Renee." Kyra returned the smile. "Have you seen Jason?" Kyra felt so nervous, her hands were sweating.

"Yeah. Here and there."

"What's he been up to?"

"I don't know. Checking on things around the party and stuff."

"Has he been dancing?"

"Mmmm. Yeah, a couple of times."

"Who with?" Kyra's heart was beating up the inside her chest. How many sixteen-year-olds die of heart attacks? she wondered.

Renee looked at her friend then. "What's up, Kyra?"

"I'll talk to you about it later. Who with?"

"Gillian and Lisa."

Kyra just nodded knowingly. She set her jaw and hardened her heart a little bit more. Ol' Lisa knew how to work, Kyra thought.

"Where's your coat?" Renee asked.

"I left it in my car."

Renee nodded. "Smart," she shouted.

"Look, Renee, I'm not staying long. So don't look for me. I'll talk to you tomorrow, okay?"

"What's going on, Kyra?" Renee asked, concerned. Why would Kyra go through all of the trouble of fixing herself up this way and then plan to leave early? "You and Jason going off together?"

"No," Kyra answered simply. "I'll talk to you about it tomorrow. Don't worry about me. I'm straight."

Renee was still worried, but she decided not to press Kyra.

"Go on and dance. You look good out there," Kyra told her friend.

Renee and Brandon headed back out to the dance floor and Kyra resumed her stationary search for Jason. She saw him across the dance hall. "Here goes," she whispered to herself.

Jason stood across the hall with Greg and a small group

of well-dressed young men. He wore black jeans and a black polo shirt with a red collar. He was dressed simply but well, and Kyra found herself admiring his handsomeness all over again. He stood in profile and didn't see her approaching. The bass in the fast-beating R&B rhythm propelled her forward; she felt carried on its hard, persuasive notes. As she neared, Greg turned, saw, and admired her. His expression of attraction changed to a look of surprise as he recognized her. Kyra watched as he nudged Jason and shouted something in his ear. Jason turned and looked her way, spotting her quickly. He looked entirely surprised.

Kyra's heart and stomach flip-flopped as he looked her up and down. He smiled slowly at her, and before she could stop herself, she smiled back. He walked to meet her.

"Hey, baby!" he shouted when he reached her.

"Jason." That's all she could say. With everything that she was feeling, she could only speak his name.

"What have you done?" he questioned with a smile.

"Do you like it?"

He nodded yes, the look of surprise still on his face. He leaned so that his lips brushed her ear softly. "You're beautiful." Kyra felt like crying. So this is what he'd wanted all along, just as Lisa had said. "But you already were."

She felt some relief. "Thanks."

"Come on," he said, leading her over to his friends. He introduced her to the ones she did not know. "This is Ian Striver, Mike Morris, and Christian Hull," Jason told her. She spoke to Greg and the couple of boys she did know.

"Kyra, you look fine!" Greg shouted, still admiring her.

"Heel, boy," Jason cautioned his friend in a joking tone.

"Your girl has been hiding under all those clothes, man," Greg said.

"I could see her just fine," Jason said, looking at Kyra. "Let's dance."

Kyra, instead of growing more resolute in her decision to break up with Jason, was weakening, quickly. And he isn't even trying to convince me of anything, she moaned inside. I know that I can't let him try to talk to me about Lisa and him; I'll believe anything! She allowed him to take her hand in his. She noticed some girls checking her out as she walked with Jason. She imagined that some of them had been getting an eyeful of Jason, plotting how to get a dance or two out of him and slipping their numbers in his hand. Jason took them over to the DJ's table and shouted something to him. The DJ nodded. Kyra couldn't make out what they said.

As Jason led her to the dance floor, the last song ended and a popular slow song began. The male vocalist began to call out to his woman that he loved her, and he wanted her, always. "This one's for you," Jason said into her ear. Kyra felt his lips, tender against her ear. Jason pulled her close to him, one hand fitted into her lower back, securing her against him. She could feel the strength of his hips pressed against her. She drank in the warm, clean scent of him.

Jason led them into a slow, grinding groove, the sweet, romantic rhythm of the song binding them together. Kyra allowed herself to relax into Jason's embrace. And she wanted to enjoy it thoroughly, because it would be their last time like this, even if she was the only one who knew it. But

242

try as she might she couldn't push Lisa's words, and the image of Lisa with Jason, out of her mind for a full five minutes at a time. The image came rushing back to her mind's eye, and before she could stop herself, she was crying softly.

"I could hold you like this all night," Jason said into her ear. He pulled away slightly in order to kiss her lips. He tasted salty tears. "What's the matter, Ky?"

Kyra just shook her head.

"Tell me, baby," he said.

Kyra shook her head again. "Let's get out of here and talk," she said. They made their way out of the crowded dance hall, Jason holding her hand as he led her out of the room. He didn't say anything again until they were one floor up in a quiet, empty hallway.

"What's the matter, Ky?"

"I want to break up, Jason." Kyra looked into his worried dark eyes, her brown eyes sparkling with tears.

"What? What are you talking about, Kyra?"

"I'm breaking up with you." She didn't want to do this while crying, but she wasn't able to stop the tears on command.

"Why? This doesn't make any sense. Why?"

"You already know why. I'm the one who's just finding out."

"Just found out what? Why are you trippin'? Talk some sense!"

"Whatever, Jason. It's over. That's all the sense I feel like talking right now. Except to say, as much as I care about you, I'm not willing to let you play me."

"What the hell is going on? Am I in the twilight zone?"

"Oh, it's funny, huh? You can crack jokes, right?"

"Do you see me laughing?"

"I'm gone," Kyra said as she turned and began walking away.

Jason grabbed her arm. "Wait a minute. Tell me what this is about."

"I know you'd better let me go! Now!" Jason dropped her arm. "I'm not telling you anything. You know everything. Or at least you thought you did. We start talking and you'll just start running game on me again. No thanks!" She turned away again and hurried down the stairs. Jason was hot on her trail. The door to outside was at the foot of the stairs. Kyra swung it open and Jason held it for her without even thinking.

"Kyra, this is crazy! Hold up a second." She never broke her stride.

She got her keys out and got the car door open. Jason held on to the door. "If you think I've done you wrong, why are *you* the one running?"

Kyra looked at him, then. He was just as handsome now, angry and confused, as he was at any other time. She looked at his lips, his jaw line, and felt sick when she thought about Lisa taking pleasure from them while he was supposed to be hers. "Because I can't wait to get away from you," she said. She got in the car and slammed the door.

She was gone before Jason had a chance to recover. He stared as her taillights fled into the night.

27

"Kyra, the phone. It's Jason," Akila called.

"I'm not taking any calls tonight, Akila."

"She's not taking any calls tonight, Jason," Akila spoke into the receiver.

"Thanks, Akila," Jason said. He sounded just as perplexed as she was.

"No problem," she said into the receiver. Akila walked over to Kyra's room and stood in the door. Kyra, home only five minutes, was changing out of her party outfit. "What's up, Ky?"

Kyra turned around and looked at her older sister. Tonight they looked even more alike, since Kyra's hair and outfit were more similar to what Akila would choose. Kyra's beautiful, serious dark eyes met the matching concerned pair of her sisters. "I don't even feel like talking about it yet, Akila. It hurts too much." Kyra looked down at the small fabric puddle that her skirt formed around her feet as though wondering how it got it there. She stepped out of it as she spoke. "I don't know, I . . . I guess I just want to be alone for a while. I don't want any of Jason's calls, okay?"

"Okay," Akila said helplessly. Akila walked over to her sister and placed her hands on Kyra's shoulders. "You can tell me anything, you know that, don't you?"

Kyra nodded yes in response. "I won't judge you, or tell Mama and Daddy, anything like that. I'll listen. And tell you what I know, if you want to hear it."

"I know. Thanks, Akila." Akila pulled her younger sister into her embrace. Kyra wrapped her arms around her sister in return and allowed herself, for a moment, to be comforted.

Once Akila had gone, Kyra finished getting out of her party clothes and into her pajamas. Jason rang her line again, as he'd done from the moment she got in the house, and she turned the ringer off. He called her cell phone and she shut it off. She turned her radio on and listened as Janet Jackson crooned about loneliness. It was an old hit that rang absolutely true for Kyra. Kyra climbed into bed and took a deep breath in the dark room.

Kyra hadn't spoken to anyone about what had happened in the bathroom. She hadn't opened her mouth to tell a single soul that Jason had slept with Lisa while he and Kyra had been going together. It was still too raw, too painful and humiliating. But she felt as though she were about to burst with the news. She wanted to tell someone. But not Akila, not yet. Kyra couldn't imagine any boy doing that to her sister. Akila was too desirable. It seemed that whatever Akila gave her boyfriends, and Kyra wasn't sure how far her sister went, it was enough to keep boys calling again and again and again.

But Kyra needed to tell someone. She'd tell her girl Renee tomorrow.

Slowly, against her will, one warm tear rolled down her cheek as though testing the air. Kyra sighed as the painful, hot lump that had been growing inside her belly began to dissolve into warm tears. She allowed them to come, unchecked, silent, and fast.

Oh, I still love you, Jason! Even though you've hurt me, and even though you've given yourself to someone else, I still love you. I still want you, too. But if I allow you to hurt me this time, you'll just hurt me worse the next time. I know it, Kyra thought.

You know what it's all about too, don't you, she continued in her thoughts.

Or are you still frontin'? The thing that really hurt, though not necessarily the most, was that the one person who could understand her best, comfort her best, was the one who'd caused the pain.

Greg saw Jason standing in the nearly deserted hallway as

he headed back to the party. He'd just made a quick run to the john.

"What's up, man? You been gone almost twenty minutes. I thought you two were out in the car, or something. Where's your girl?"

"I don't know."

"What? Don't tell me a brother has lost his woman," Greg joked. "Where'd she step to, Jay?"

"I said I don't know!" Some of the frustration Jason felt flared out in his words.

"What's going on, Jason?"

"I don't *even* know, Greg. Kyra's gone."

"What do you mean, gone?"

"I mean gone. Gone from the party. Gone from the hall. I think gone from me."

"What? Naw. Jay? That can't be right. Where is she? Out in the lot? Let me go talk to her for you."

"Can't. She got in her ride and jetted."

"Damn." Greg looked out the glass doors into the darkened parking lot with his friend. "You two get into it?"

"I guess. Shoot, Greg, I don't even know what happened. I've called her about three times already and she won't pick up."

Greg looked at his best friend, remembering how good Jason and Kyra had looked together. They were so right together, happy and in love. What could have happened to make Kyra trip out like that?

"You coming up?" Greg said, indicating the party.

"What's the point?"

"Yeah, I guess."

"Look, I'm just going to get my coat and go. I don't even know what the hell happened, man."

"All right. I'll call you tomorrow."

"Bet," Jason said as he gave his boy a play.

What *had* happened? Jason wondered. What the hell had happened?

28

"Girl, you look a mess. Tell me what happened," Renee said.

The morning after the party Kyra and Renee sat in cross-legged positions facing one another on Kyra's bedroom floor. Hip-hop music pulsed from Kyra's CD player and sunlight streamed in through the blinds on the windows.

Kyra told Renee about overhearing Lisa talk in the girls' bathroom. "I don't believe it!"

"Believe it. I was there. Unfortunately."

"What? You wish you never knew?"

"I don't know. In a way, I guess." She thought

for a moment. "No. I'd rather know the truth than live a lie."

"Yeah, I guess."

"I mean, that's what made me so angry. Just thinking about the fact that he had this secret, that he was keeping this from me, made me furious."

"So that's why you broke up with him?"

"Not just that. I also broke up with him because he cheated on me."

Renee nodded. "What did he say when you threw it up in his face?"

"Nothing."

"Nothing!"

"I mean, I didn't throw it up in his face, so he didn't get a chance to say anything." Kyra told Renee everything that happened at and after the Valentine's Day party.

"What are you saying, Kyra—that you didn't even talk to Jason about it?"

"What is there to talk about, Renee? He can't go without getting any and I'm not giving any up. He thought he could get a little on the side and I'm not having it! End of discussion, and I had that one all by myself!"

"But you should have heard his side of things, Kyra."

"For what? So that I could look into his gorgeous face while he lied his way out of it? Renee, I'm crazy about Jason. God, I love Jason! If he got me alone and told me he didn't do it . . . I'm liable to believe it."

"What's so bad about that?"

"Are you kidding? I'd be believing a lie, that's what

would be so bad, Renee. If he could get me to believe this, he could get me to believe any lie."

"Do you really think he's like that, Kyra?"

"That's what's truly tearing me up, Renee. I thought I knew him. It's like I can't even trust my own instincts. And no, this doesn't seem like him at all. But I can't just ignore what *actually happened*!"

Renee shook her head in confusion. "Still, maybe you should just talk to Jason. To cut him off like this, not even telling him why. That's harsh, girl."

"No, what's harsh is sleeping with one girl while you profess to being *in love* with another."

"True that," her friend concurred.

Kyra nodded. Yeah, true that.

29

"I'm not even supposed to talk to you about this, Jason," Renee said.

On Thursday, almost a week after the party, Jason had cornered Renee at her locker just after his lunch hour. Kyra had pulled a disappearing act on him. Even when she was physically present, like in AP English, she wasn't there for him. She said hi if he spoke, and he'd spoken every day this week, but she said nothing else, no matter what he said. Once, on Wednesday, she'd turned and looked him in the eye, the first time since that crazy night of the Valentine's Day party. Her eyes were moist with tears.

"Look, Jason, it would be better if you just left me

alone. I don't have anything to say to you, and I don't really want to hear anything you have to say." Her voice was weary and pained. Then she'd just walked away.

"I need somebody who knows something to talk to me, Renee."

"What do you want me to say?"

"Come on, don't play games. Why did she break up with me?"

Renee leaned against her locker, holding her book bag on her shoulder. Jason looked utterly confused to her. He didn't look as if he had a clue. That didn't make any sense to Renee, unless he was the world's best actor. It had been a weird week, and there was still Friday to get through. Kyra was running around avoiding Jason like the plague, and Jason was running around chasing Kyra like a winning lottery ticket. Renee had been spinning, answering the questions "Have you seen him?" and "Have you seen her?"

Renee was still confused herself. Kyra couldn't tell her Jason's side of things, because she hadn't bothered to talk to him. Maybe Jason could tell her a few things.

"So what's up?" Jason said, breaking into Renee's thoughts.

"She found out about you and Lisa."

"Me and Lisa? There's nothing to find out."

"There's plenty to find out, from what Ky told me."

"Like what?"

"Like she knows you two did it since you and Ky were together."

"Did what? Sex? What the hell are you talking about, Renee?"

"Kyra overheard Lisa tell her girls that you two slept together about a month ago."

"When did she hear this?"

"That Friday of the party."

"Well, it's a lie. I don't even believe this. Why didn't she come talk to me?"

"She figured she'd believe anything you said once you got her alone."

"Oh, now she thinks I'm a player. Now she wants to act like she doesn't even know me. Damn! Why did she trip out like this?"

"Are you going to go and talk to her?"

"Hell no! If she wants to believe that crap without even talking to me, when she's supposed to love me . . . later for Kyra!" It hurt him to the core to even say the words. He swallowed, took a deep breath, and paused. He almost wanted to cry, but he wouldn't, of course. He shook his head as Renee watched him. "You can tell Kyra that she doesn't have to avoid me anymore. I won't be looking for her."

Kyra's science project had been delivered out of her hands to the district judges two weeks ago. Since then, she'd been getting out of school earlier. She would usually go home, knock out her homework, and wait for Jason to get out of practice. Then they would talk on the phone for a while, or he would come by, or they'd go to The Biz, or go driving or mess around over at Jason's house. On the weekends they went to the movies or rented videos, or Jason had dinner over at her house. She had been so very, very happy. The only cloud on her horizon had been worries about how much Jason must be missing sex. Now the afternoons, evenings, and nights stretched before her as boring obstacle courses of useless minutes and hours. She could hardly think of what she used to do before Jason.

"Kyra, could you play something else?" her father asked. He had appeared suddenly in her bedroom door. A trio of male voices bemoaned the pain they felt at losing a love. Kyra had programmed her CD player to repeat this and four other pitiful ballads over and over.

"Daddy . . . please. I'll turn it down." She had changed out of her school clothes into a pair of faded, ripped jeans and an old sweatshirt. Her hair, still straightened from the press, was falling from the bun she'd put it in and lay spread across her back and chest. She sat curled up on her bed, writing in her journal. She'd rarely found the time to write in it when she and Jason were together. Flipping through the pages, she realized that she usually wrote when she was unhappy. It didn't have a lot of pages filled . . . until now.

"Why do you listen to it if it just makes you sadder?"

"I don't know, Daddy. I don't know."

Mr. Evans looked at his youngest child. He wished that he could shield her from this heartache, just make it go away. He'd felt the same when it had first happened to his son and older daughter. But he couldn't.

"Can I do anything, baby?"

"No. Thank you, Daddy."

"Play something cheerful. Maybe it'll make you feel a little better."

"Maybe." When her father left the room Kyra turned the volume down and opened her journal again. She read over her last entry.

> *I cannot believe how hard this week has been. I miss Jason so much that I can taste it. It's a sourness in my mouth that seeps into my motions and speech. I think about him a million times a day. I scurry around in the back halls so that I don't see him. I've moved my seat to the front in AP English and I hurry to get to class early so that my back is to the door and I don't see him come in. I drag most of my books around so that I don't have to stop at my locker. I've stopped going to the library because he might be there . . . or is it because I'm afraid he won't be there?*
>
> *I see or hear something funny and the first thing I think to do is call Jason. I know that I could tell him and we would laugh at it together. Telling him and hearing him laugh made it funnier to me. I hear a romantic song, a good one, and I want to be with Jason the next time I hear it. Holding him, kissing him, caressing him.*
>
> *How can I still feel this way about him after what he did? How can I still love him? I don't understand.*
>
> *Then at other times, in the same day, the same hour, sometimes in the same <u>minute</u>, I want to run him over*

with my car! He cheated on me! I torture myself with ideas of what he did with Lisa. I see him coming over to her house, talking to her, looking down at her, kissing her, at first hesitatingly, then fully, really into it. I see him taking her in his arms, telling her in a whisper in that voice I love so much, that he's missed her, that he's been wanting her. I can see them get undressed and then they're having sex. That part is all dark and foggy, because I'm not sure what it would look like, but the pain is crystal clear.

I've never hurt like this before in my life. I don't know how to make it stop. Almost every minute of my day is spent hurting like this. God, I want it to stop. I want to be over Jason.

I never want to stop loving him.

Jason walked into his empty home around six-thirty that Thursday evening. He was tired and still had homework to do. Practice had been hard, but tomorrow's would be light. The city championship was on Saturday. He had been looking forward to it all season. It had been his best season ever. He held the school record in assists now, and he was the highest scorer on the team. He had been written up in the school paper every week since preseason started, and he had appeared in the city newspapers eight times—more than any other player in the state. He was ranked as the top point guard in the state.

And Kyra had been with him every step of the way. She hadn't understood the game at first because she hadn't bothered to pay it any attention before. But she'd said that she wanted Jason to teach her everything. She'd watched the videos he had from last year's March Madness, the NCAA college finals. He'd had fun teaching her the lingo, the terms, the fouls, the technicals, the plays, all of it. She was so bright, she picked it all up fairly quickly. She would have learned even faster if she hadn't had the excellent idea that every time she answered one of his questions correctly he had to give her a kiss. They did a lot of kissing. He tutored her all during preseason and during the season. Toward the end of the season she was a bona fide couch coach.

Today was one of those days when he hated the quiet of the condo. Before, during these past months when he'd felt that way, he would take a quick shower and call Kyra. That would energize him for the rest of his night. He'd get his homework done, and if his father came in trippin', Jason wouldn't let it phase him too much. If his father was in a decent or good mood, well, having Kyra made that even better. Having her in his life had made everything better.

They talked about everything. Since Kyra knew how nasty his father could be, Jason told her any and everything that was on his mind. They talked on the phone, they passed notes in the library, they talked in the hall, they talked during drives, over at his house, over at hers. He loved it over at her house. Her parents were cool and supportive. Kyra had rules, but they didn't treat her like a baby. A couple of times Jason and Kyra had sat around with her parents watching a television show after dinner. He had dinner over there about four times a month. They had just pulled him into their lives. When Kyra left, she took all of that away from him.

Now his home seemed even lonelier. He didn't have the one person that he could talk to about the hurt that happened in this place, or the one who took him to another, better home.

Jason dropped his bag into the closet and hung up his coat. He smelled the fried chicken that Mrs. Gillman had cooked. At least dinner would be good, he thought glumly. He checked the machine. Four messages. He played them back. One from his father: he'd be home late. One from Lisa: give her a call. Yeah, right, Jason thought angrily. One from some girl at school. How did she get his number? How did any of them get his number? The last one was for his father. No Kyra, again.

Well, good, he told himself. He didn't want to talk to her now. Now that he knew why she had broken up with him, he was mad at her. When she'd broken up with him he had been crazy with worry and confusion. All that he'd wanted to do was talk to her, hold her, fix whatever it was that was bothering her. He hadn't cared about playing it cool, about putting up a front. He wanted Kyra. Period.

But when he'd found out that she had dropped him because she'd *heard* that he had cheated on her. When he realized that she had believed something so bad, had done something so serious as break up, all without even *talking* to him, he had been furious. He had felt almost as angry as he'd ever felt in his life.

He had loved . . . hell, he *still* loved Kyra more than he'd every loved anybody. He trusted her more than anyone. Certainly more than he trusted his father. The only person even close to how he trusted and cared for Kyra, was his boy Greg, and even he was a distant second. Jason had never been in love. Not even close. He had liked a couple of girls a lot, but other than that, he just liked this girl or that one. But not with Kyra. Right from the beginning everything that he felt for her had been more intense than anything he'd felt for a girl before.

He'd buy her anything, but she wouldn't let him. He'd take her anywhere, expensive restaurants, or at least as expensive as he could afford, but she didn't care about any of that. She said that being with him, wherever, doing almost whatever, was enough. He just shook his head, remembering when she'd said that. Damn, that girl made him feel so good! She made him feel complete, as though he were enough, just as he was. He'd never felt that before. If he had, it must have been when he was too young to remember.

That's why he couldn't understand why she would do this to him—to *them*. He loved her completely. He trusted her. And he just knew that she trusted him. Or at least he thought that she trusted him. But the truth was she couldn't have trusted him all that much if she could dump him based on what someone else said, without even talking to him. She had cut him deeply. More deeply than he even knew he could be hurt by anyone other than his father.

If she was like that, even with the way that he loved her, he didn't need her. If she hurt him like this once, she'd do it again.

30

It had not been a good day for Jason. He'd gotten a C- on an easy trig quiz because he'd forgotten that he even had a quiz coming up, so he'd failed to review. He'd run into Kyra three times that day—*three*, besides seeing her at English class —and each time made him more and more agitated. He wasn't worried about letting any of his feelings show, though. If he could emotionally maneuver around his father as they lived under the same roof, he could certainly handle seeing Kyra for two minutes at a time in the hallway. It hurt, but he could hide it.

The cafeteria lunch had been inedible, even for him, and the four bags of chips, three candy bars, and two juices that he'd gotten out of the vending machine as a substitute lunch had worked against him. He had felt a surge of energy for two hours after he ate, but by the time he went to practice he'd felt as though he were running and jumping through water. The coach had noticed, benched him, cussed him out when his play didn't improve much when he returned to the court, and pointed out to Jason, entirely unnecessarily, but no less dramatically, that the most important game of the season was so close he could reach out and slap it.

On top of all of that, Jason had come home to find that his father, who had been home sick with the flu these past two days, must have gotten better, because he'd eaten all the food that Mrs. Gillman had left the day before for today's dinner.

"Shit!" Jason said.

"What was that?" Mr. Vincent said as he came into the kitchen, opening a piece of mail that Jason had placed on the foyer table on his way in the house.

"I said, you could have *at least* left me something to eat for when I came home."

"Oh, sorry about that. I was feeling a lot better. You wouldn't believe how hungry I was." Mr. Vincent said casually. "Just run out and get something."

"I don't want to. I have an unbelievable amount of homework to do and I'm already getting home real late from practice. I need to eat right quick and get to work, period. Not run all over the city trying to scramble up some dinner when I thought I already had some!"

"Damn, boy, it's not the Red Sea. You don't need God to part this one for you. Open a can of soup, have a microwave dinner, or something—lighten up," Mr. Vincent said as he turned to leave the room. Jason could feel all of the anger and frustration that he felt for his father, for Kyra, and the day rise up in him and wash over him. He wanted to smash his fist against his father's face and see the shock register after the impact. At that moment he hated his father. He always acted this way, dogged Jason out when he was drunk, and sometimes even when he wasn't drunk, then went on acting as if nothing had happened once *he* was no longer intoxicated or angry. But so often, it wasn't over for Jason; the feelings remained, sometimes at a low simmer, other times at an ugly boil, and at still other times, like now, pumping like a steam engine. Always, Jason had bit back any retaliation against his father. His father, he had thought, was all that he had. Until Kyra. Then he'd thought that he'd found another family in her. Well he didn't have "another family." This really was all that he had, and he was fed up with it.

"It is the damn Red Sea for me, Dad! But you wouldn't know it because you can't be bothered with knowing much of anything about me. You're not even coming to the city championship, *the city championship*, for God's sake. I'm the captain of the current city championship team, heading to our next title game, and my father has made *arrangements* to be elsewhere. Why couldn't you take a day, no, hell, not even a day, a *night* off and come to the game. Why? Because you don't give a damn! That's why!" Jason was breathing as though he'd run up and down the court, full speed, seven times.

"Watch your mouth, boy," Mr. Vincent ordered. His voice was like tempered steel and his eyes took on that look of cold rage that so often made Jason quake inside. This time, though, Jason felt only a tremor. He met his father's look and tone of voice with nearly the exact same qualities on his own face, in his own tone.

"No," Jason said slowly and deliberately, "you watch it. I'm sick of *watching* it around here." Jason twisted the word *watching* into an ugly, venomous sound. "I have to 'watch it' when you leave me here alone for two, three, four days. I have to 'watch it' when you've had a bad day at work. I have to 'watch it' when you and your woman have it out. I have to 'watch it' when you've had too much to drink. I'm sick of *watching it*—it's your turn. You watch it." Jason felt relief come over him with his last words; he felt pressure lift from his chest and from behind his eyes, and his breathing, though still fast, slowed some. His father might hit him, but he didn't care, not at this moment. His father might kick him out, but he doubted it. Jason didn't think that it would make his father treat him better, but that didn't matter so much. He had one year left here, just one. He could make it through that, probably a little better now that he'd gotten that off his chest.

"Did you know that Kyra and I had broken up?" Jason asked.

"No, I didn't."

"Yeah, well, we did. She was my first love, you know?

It's over and I don't even understand what happened. But you're too busy to even notice all of that. *That* I've got to figure out on my own. But almost every time things are going really wrong for you, *I* know about it, right? Because you come home pissed." Jason's words and worries washed over his father, overwhelming him. Jason turned to leave the kitchen by the passage that led to the family room. His father still stood holding the mail by the entrance to the kitchen near the front door.

"Jason, wait." It was the change in his tone of voice, more than the words, that halted Jason. Jason turned and saw on his father's face what he'd heard in his voice, shame and uncertainty. Jason just stood where he was, waiting.

He stood there staring at his son as if they'd just been introduced. "I'm not coming to the city championships because I have an incredibly important meeting in Colorado tomorrow. It's a two-million-dollar account and it's in serious trouble."

"I thought kids were supposed to be priceless."

Mr. Vincent shook his head and, for a moment, let his head drop. "Shit," he whispered when he lifted his head. He stared at his son for a few silent moments. "I don't know how to fix this, Jason." Just then, when Jason heard the utter helplessness in his powerful father's voice, he felt exhausted, and alone. More alone than he'd ever felt before. It was hopeless, this thing with his father and the thing with Kyra. It was all hopeless and draining, and bottomless. He could count on no one. So when his father said

"I don't know how to fix this," Jason didn't know if his father meant his schedule or their relationship, but his answer would have still been the same.

"Neither do I," Jason said before he turned and left his father standing there.

"Have you heard from Jason?" Renee asked Kyra across the phone line.

"No, you know I'm not talking to him."

"No, what I mean is, has he called?"

A Friday night comedy played in Renee's background. Kyra sat in the family room with an unread magazine on her lap.

"No, not today."

Renee said nothing.

"What's up, Renee? Why are you so quiet?"

"I talked to Jason, Ky."

"So, it's a free country."

"Oh, well, I'm glad you think so." Renee sounded relieved.

"What did you talk about?"

"What do you think?"

"Just tell me, Renee."

"Why don't you call him yourself, Kyra? You know you should."

"We've been over this. I'm not calling Jason. Now are you going to tell me or what?"

"I told him why you broke up with him."

"I'm sure he wasn't surprised to hear why."

"Actually, I think he was."

"No. He was just acting for your benefit. He knew you'd tell me how surprised he was and I'd believe it coming from you. Then I'd call him, and he'd come over and we'd make up."

"Oh, I see you've played the entire little fantasy through in you mind, huh?"

Kyra blushed. "Whatever. All I'm saying is, it's an act."

"Like I said, I don't think so."

"Trust me on this one, Renee. He's just trying to get me back."

"Let me ask you again then, has he called? Did he try to talk to you this afternoon at school?"

"No."

"Kyra, the last thing Jason said to me was that you didn't have to worry about avoiding him anymore, he wouldn't be looking for you." Kyra felt her insides sink. She should have been glad, but she wasn't.

"So. Good."

"He said it was a lie. He hadn't cheated on you."

"And you believed him?"

"Well, yes. I mean, he seemed sincere. But that doesn't explain what you heard, and that still has me confused."

"Well I'm not confused by the truth. I know what I heard."

"Maybe what you heard was a lie, Ky."

"But why? She didn't know I was there."

"I don't know. Maybe she was lying to her friends."

"That doesn't make sense. Those are her girls. She

shouldn't need to lie to them. They already worship her," Kyra reasoned.

"Yeah, you've got a point. Still, something isn't right."

"The whole entire thing isn't right, Renee. I miss him so much."

"Call him, then."

"No."

"Call him, Kyra."

"No, I can't. I can't."

"So what do you want to talk about?"

"Let's talk about you. Tell me what happened when you called Brandon."

They talked on with Kyra only half listening.

"Come on, Jay, you're bringing me down," Greg told his best friend. They were over at Greg's house listening to CDs and playing on Greg's PlayStation.

"Maybe I'll just go home."

"No, you said you wanted to come over and kick it, do something to get Kyra off your mind."

"Well, it's not working. She's on my mind. Still. All the time."

"Damn, boy, she worked a whammy on you. I ain't never seen my brother like this."

Jason just shook his head and smiled weakly. Jason's father had given him permission to spend Friday night over at Greg's house. Practice, as the coach had promised, was light and over quickly. Jason and Greg had gone to The Biz, eaten, chilled with some of the fellas, and headed to Greg's house for an early evening. The game was at one-thirty, but they had to meet at the team bus at Cross at nine-thirty. They were all going for breakfast at the International House of Pancakes on East Jefferson, then they would head to Roper High School for the city championship game. They would do all the pregame stuff and get their heads right. Roper was tough, but they were tougher. They planned to win, but it wasn't guaranteed and it wouldn't be easy.

"Aaaargh," Jason moaned and threw himself across Greg's full-size bed.

"Now, don't start that again," Greg complained.

"Let's watch a video," Jason said.

"Okay. Something funny, right? You definitely need to have a couple of good laughs."

"Definitely. You've got *Friday* right?"

"Yeah. Come on." The boys headed to Greg's den where a large-screen TV and DVD system were housed along with an extensive video collection.

"Here we go, *Friday*," Greg said after a brief search.

"Cool, pop it in. I'm ready to be cheered up."

"What are you doing?" Renee asked.

"Making a call."

"Obviously. Who are you calling? We're in the middle of a game of spades."

"I know. One of the best Fridays I've had in a while," Kyra said sarcastically.

"Who are you calling?" Renee didn't seem all that interested as she examined her hand and sipped her Vernors.

"Jason."

"What!"

"You heard me. The city championship is tomorrow. I want to wish him luck."

"At eleven o'clock?" Renee said, glancing at her watch.

"Yes, Renee, at eleven o'clock. Now be quiet. You're making me even more nervous than I already am."

Renee watched her friend dial and listen. She watched Kyra replace the receiver without saying a word.

"What?"

"No answer."

"Maybe he's asleep."

"Maybe." Kyra felt totally deflated. She hadn't admitted it even to herself, but she was anxious about hearing Jason's voice. She wanted to hear it, even for a moment, even if he hung up after hearing hers.

"Let me guess, you don't feel like playing anymore?"

Kyra sighed deeply. "I'm sorry, Renee, no, I don't. I don't feel like doing anything right now."

"Are you still going to the game tomorrow?"

"Yeah, I guess." Kyra hesitated, thinking. "Do you think he's with Lisa right now?"

"I don't know, Kyra. I don't think so."

Kyra wished that she didn't believe differently.

"I'm glad that she decided to go over to Renee's house for the night," Ms. Evans said. She and Mr. Evans sat cuddled up on the sofa in the family room. Classic jazz played and they each held books, forgotten for the moment. "Maybe it'll cheer her up a bit."

"I hope so. Did she tell you anything?"

"No. Only that she and Jason had broken up. When I asked her why, she just shook her head. I didn't press."

"He was calling every day. I don't think he called yesterday or today."

"I didn't take any messages."

"I guess she broke up with him," Mr. Evans concluded.

"I guess. But I can't imagine what it was about. They seemed so happy."

"Who knows what dramas they play out. We only know about half of what's ever going on with our teenagers."

Ms. Evans chuckled softly. "You are so right. But seriously, I hope that they work it out or that she gets over it soon. I hate seeing her like this."

"Me too. You know what?"

"What, baby?"

"I kind of miss Jason."

"Yeah, me too. He's a good kid."

"He is. Real respectful, smart, too."

"Yeah. I don't understand it."

"I know. Me either."

"Lisa, you are so-o-o-o-o bad!" Jackie said with delight.

"I know," Lisa said with a grin. "It's not easy, but I do what I can."

"Girl, she dropped Jay just like you said she would. I have to admit, they seemed pretty tight. I wasn't so sure your plan would work. But she bought it, she really bought it," Terri said. Lisa, Jackie, Terri, and Imani occupied a booth at The Biz. The place was packed with a Friday crowd, but the girls kept their voices down.

"That's right. I usually know how to read people. She was just the little self-righteous Goody Two-shoes I thought she'd be. Not to mention, Jay *will* always get what he wants. If he couldn't talk her out of breaking up, he must not have wanted to stay with her that badly," Lisa assured the girls.

"So, have you made your move yet?" Imani wanted to know.

"No, she's giving him just a little time, first," Jackie piped up.

Lisa smiled at her best friend. "Yeah. I'm going to talk to him right after the game. Jason used to like to celebrate, if you know what I mean, after a big win." Lisa's smile turned to a smirk. The girls gave each other finger plays all around.

Heather had decided not to go to The Biz with Lisa and the crew. She wanted to be by herself. Jason and Kyra had been on her mind all week. Her plan had been to try and get with Jason herself if he and Kyra actually did break up. She had always liked Jason. She had not been too adverse to Lisa's underhanded plan to break the two up.

But something, actually a couple of unexpected things, had happened. The first was that Jason really seemed hurt by the breakup. He wasn't trying to hang with his old crew, and he was down every time Heather saw him. The second thing was that she felt bad for him. She began to feel that what they had done to Jason and Kyra was . . . dare she even think it? Wrong.

But the fact was, Heather rarely had to do something deceitful in order to get what she wanted. Her parents spoiled her and she was so pretty that the boys loved to spoil her too.

I can't believe this, Heather thought. I actually feel guilty.

Heather wasn't used to that. Not at all.

31

Kyra went to the Cross/Roper City Championship just as she had been planning to for months. She wore an evergreen-and-white sweat suit to support her school and her love. She sat with Renee and some other kids from the track team. Cross won 67 to 56, but the game was a lot more exciting than the eleven-point spread might lead one to believe.

All during the first half, Roper and Cross batted the lead around, never being more than three points apart. But when they came back from halftime the Cross team rallied around its star point guard, who played with renewed fire and determination, and Cross pulled ahead to its biggest lead of the game, five points, within the first four minutes of play in the second half. Five minutes before the end of the game the Roper team buckled under the pressure and supplied the Cross team with more than a few holes in its defense and a tired offense. Cross surged ahead for the decisive lead and the city championship.

Kyra's heart was protesting the excitement for the entire game. She wanted Jason to win even more than she wanted Cross to win. She knew, from talking with Jason during better times, that Roper had a good chance of winning the game. They weren't as deep as the Cross team, but they were scrappy and exciting, not to mention that they had an All-City, All-State scorer in their top senior. The only thing that kept her from screaming and hollering like a lunatic was her desire to not reveal her presence. She didn't mind entirely if Jason knew that she was there, but she didn't want to make a spectacle of herself. She never saw Jason look her way. Admittedly, he had very few minutes on the bench.

Kyra enjoyed watching every motion that Jason made. She admired the evident strength of his muscles and his swiftness and agility. She was proud of the way that he handled the ball and the team. He knew what he was doing out there, and everyone knew it.

When the buzzer rang for halftime, Greg had looked directly at Kyra across the court and nodded. She'd nodded back, discreetly.

On the way into the locker room, Greg strode next to his friend.

"Kyra's here," Greg told Jason.

"Yeah, I saw her just before the buzzer," Jason said glumly. "And she's not the only one," he mumbled as he nodded toward the other end of the Cross stands.

Greg scanned the area until his eyes landed on Mr. Vincent, dressed in tailored brown tweed pants and a camel-colored turtleneck. Though Greg didn't know the full extent of Jason and Mr. Vincent's relationship, he knew that it wasn't too good. Mr. Vincent in the basketball stands was a seriously rare sight. "How are you doing?"

"All right. My game feels good."

"No, I mean with them here."

"Oh, it ain't nothin' but a thang." Jason had noticed his father at the game ten minutes into play, and for ten minutes afterward it had made him feel as though he were trying out for a team. His flow was off slightly, and an unexpected nervousness swam inside his stomach. He knew that his father was here at the city championship instead of in Colorado because he had challenged him. Jason always played hard for himself and his team, and he had to fight mentally to keep that focus and not make it about proving something to his father. It took ten minutes of play to pull it off.

That's all the time there had been for talking, but Greg had noted the tension in his friend's face, and his zeal and focus once they returned to the court. Jason was on fire. All of the anger and frustration that Kyra and his father inspired in him was funneled and focused on the Roper team and his job of directing the Cross team.

After the game Cross students and supporters swarmed onto the court to congratulate the team and celebrate. Greg, still concerned for his friend, quickly searched the floor crowd for Kyra. Not seeing her there he looked to the stands. She wasn't there either. He looked over to Jason, several feet over from him, surrounded by Lisa and a bunch of other kids. Jason was looking the same way into the stands. Jason saw what Greg had seen and returned his attention to the people surrounding him.

"All right," the coach yelled above the noise, "let's get into the locker room!" Those players close by who heard the coach immediately turned and left. Those who couldn't hear the coach above the noise saw their teammates leave and quickly followed.

Once inside the locker room the coach led the team in a rousing cheer. When it finished, the team erupted in spontaneous screams and shouts. Jason joined in, feeling a strange sense of being there and yet outside himself. He was, like the rest of his teammates, glad to have proven their team to be the best in the city. That felt right. He had worked hard for most of his life to earn this honor. At the same time, though, he felt incredibly sad. As good as it was to win, it really wasn't that much without the person he loved most to share it with.

Why had she shown up at the game? he wondered. He realized that she probably hadn't come to just support the entire team —but to support him. But could it mean something more? After thinking about it a little, while he moved about giving his teammates plays and small comments of praise, he decided not. No, if it had meant something more, she would have stayed after. She came to the game because she knew how important it was to him and because she still cared for him. That didn't mean that she wanted to be with him. Anyway, he didn't want to be with her anymore, right? And what about his father? What was he trying to prove? His only sense of relief on that score came with the realization that his father would probably be gone by the time he got out of the locker room.

The coach delivered a brief congratulations speech, admonished the team to celebrate wisely without alcohol, drugs, or unprotected sex ("Actually, you've got no business having sex at all," the coach said sternly, "but if you're going to do it, use a condom!"), then left the team alone in the locker room.

"You going over to Howie's?" Greg asked Jason.

"Yeah, I'm gonna check that out." Howie, a forward on the team, was having a party to celebrate their victory. If they'd lost, it would have been just a low-key get-together at his house. His parents were out of town.

"Bet. Well, let's get cleaned up and get out of here. You know that there are going to be all kinds of honeys at his crib tonight," Greg grinned.

"All right." Jason didn't feel enthusiastic at all. He could not shake his feeling of loneliness. He told himself repeatedly that he was better off without someone who jumped to serious conclusions and trusted him so little, but he couldn't shake his feelings for her. When Greg and Jason came out of the locker room, they found Lisa, Jackie, and their entire crew, boys and girls, parents, teachers, and other supporters all bunched together in the hall, waiting for them to emerge. His father was there, standing beyond the crowd. Jason felt a twinge of hope and gladness tug inside him. But a wary voice warned him not to expect too much. The crowd immediately began cheering and clapping when they saw Jason, Greg, and the other players. Jason grinned, genuinely moved by this support. Lisa moved swiftly and easily into Jason's arms. Jason turned his head just in time to force her kiss, planned for his mouth, onto his cheek. Lisa was only momentarily thrown.

"Hey, Jay! You were excellent, baby!" Lisa praised him.

"Thanks," Jason said, still holding Lisa. He really wanted to let her go, but he felt a little bad about blowing her kiss off in front of everybody. He figured he'd have to hold her for a few moments longer in order to allow her to save some face. He didn't want to hurt her; he just didn't want to give her the wrong idea.

There was lots of noise around them as a small crowd congratulated all the players. Everyone seemed to be talking at once.

"Hold up," Jason said to the group. He approached his father, uncomfortable and nervous, hoping that his father would speak first, because he had no idea what he was supposed to say. All that buzzed through his mind were questions.

"Hey, Jay," Mr. Vincent said as his son neared.

"Hey, Dad." It did not console him to see that his father seemed as uncomfortable he did.

"Great game." Mr. Vincent offered a half smile, and Jason felt a small smile ease onto his lips.

"Thanks. I'm glad that you could make it." There was suddenly an outburst of laughter from behind Jason. He glanced around and saw the group riveted to something that Howie was saying. Lisa's gray eyes flitted toward him for two heartbeats, and he turned back to his father. "What about your meeting? Two million dollars?"

"I sent my assistant ahead of me, and I'll fly out tonight," he checked his watch. "In an hour and a half, actually. It'll work out. Somehow. Anyway, I'm glad I came and got a chance to see you play tonight."

"Me too." He wanted to hug his father, to say more, but they were both so out of practice that the one step it took to be that close proved, really, to be too far.

"Come on, let's get out of here," Howie said.

"Well, go ahead. I'll call and check on you tomorrow."

"All right." Jason half turned to go, then turned back to his father. "Good luck . . . on your work crisis, I mean."

"Thank you," Mr. Vincent said as he held his son's eyes.

"You coming, Jason?" Greg called over.

"Yeah, just a sec." Jason returned his attention to his father. "I'll see you."

"Yes. I should be back in two or three days."

"All right. Bye, Dad." Jason rejoined his friends and everyone, en masse, began making a relaxed exit from the school. Jason gave Greg and several other players a ride to Howie's. Rap music filled the interior of the car along with the overly loud voices of the excited players. His father's words and Kyra's face filled his mind. Once at Howie's, everyone tumbled out of their vehicles into Howie's place.

Howie had stocked the place with chips, sodas, and beer. Everybody dropped $5 into Howie's girlfriend's bag, a way of helping out with the cost of the party. BET was on, and barely-clad, beautiful black women danced raunchy move after raunchy move, as pseudo-angry black men strutted and shouted their lyrics.

Loud, but not too loud—Howie didn't want the neighbors complaining—R&B and rap music emanated from visible and concealed speakers. Couples began grinding together in what passed for dancing. Jason checked the scene out—a scene he had been in so many times in the past and had had little problem with—and wished he were somewhere else. He wished he were with Kyra, and he was mad at himself for thinking that again. He realized most of the kids here were looking for what he *thought* he had with Kyra: someone to belong to, to trust, to love. He was tired of feeling sorry for himself and just about to tell Greg that he was ready to jet, when he felt a small, firm hand on his shoulder. Lisa mouthed the words "Let's dance." Jason nodded and let Lisa head him to the dance floor.

Lisa turned him around gently and looked into his eyes. Seeing her again made Jason's mind slip back to how he had gone to Lisa after school a while back and confronted her.

"Lisa," Jason had said. "I need to talk to you."

Lisa had nodded to her girls and they told her they'd see her out in the parking lot. Jason had told his coach that he'd need to be fifteen minutes late for practice. He needed to have some questions answered. "What's up, Jay?"

"I know you heard that Kyra broke up with me."

"Yes." She looked up at Jason with innocent eyes.

"Yeah, well, her girl Renee said that Kyra heard you saying that you and I had slept together, and that's what set Kyra off."

"Where was this? Was she spying on me or something?"

"No. The way I understand it, you and your girls came in the bathroom when she was there and she overheard you."

"Sounds like eavesdropping to me."

"Did you say that?" Jason said, ignoring Lisa's last comment.

"Well, we did sleep together, Jason."

"No, Kyra heard you say that we'd done it in the last month or something." Jason was walking around in a constant state of frustration and pain since the breakup. If it turned out Lisa had told those lies, he planned to make certain that she knew how he felt about her.

"Well, I do seem to remember a conversation like that." Lisa paused. She seemed to be delving into her memory. "But Kyra must have misunderstood. I was reminiscing about how good it *used* to be to make love with you." Lisa gave a small, almost shy smile, and stepped in closer to Jason.

"Is that right?"

"Mmmm-hhhmmm. Don't you remember?"

"I was talking about what you said in the bathroom."

Jason took a step back. What she was saying could be the truth. Lisa played games with her parents, but he didn't think she'd play such a serious game with him.

"Oh. That's right. Still, don't you remember? Us, making love?"

"To tell you the truth, Lisa, I hardly even think about it." Jason held his ex-girlfriend's eyes.

"Yeah, right," Lisa said sarcastically. "Sell it to somebody else, Jason. I was there, remember? When nobody else was there, I was there, in your arms, in the dark, in the light. I was there. And I remember, and I know you do, too."

Jason had just turned and walked away.

Now here he was again with Lisa right in front of him.

What the hell, he figured. He was here, single, and Lisa had never hurt him like some people he could name. They began the slow, grinding, rhythmic motions of the dance. Jason could feel himself growing aroused, yet strangely detached. His body felt good, but his mind wasn't into it. He could walk away right now, and it wouldn't even matter to him.

So that's what he did.

Greg and the other fellas told Jason that they could find their own way home. "Don't worry about it," they said. "Go home, get some rest, you deserve it," they all said. "You gonna be all right?" Greg had asked. Jason had reassured him, yeah, he just needed to get out of there.

At home Jason took off his clothes, which smelled of marijuana and cigarette smoke, something he always hated about house parties. He tossed everything in the hamper and put on clean underwear and a T-shirt. He was exhausted. He plopped onto his bed and planted his hands behind his head and lay in the dark.

He went over the way that he had planned to spend this night. Kyra would run into his arms after the buzzer rang, and they would kiss, deep and sweet. He'd mess around in the locker room, celebrating for a little bit with his team, then go out into the hallway, where Kyra would be waiting for him. They would kiss again. Kyra would take him to The Biz, and they would get a booth with friends. Afterward, they'd make a brief appearance at Howie's, then they would end up right here at Jason's. He would relish every moment of having her in his arms; relish the way she loved him in her arms. Just thinking about how perfect it would have been made him shake his head in the dark.

He rolled over on his side, sleepy, worn out, painfully sad. Jason fell asleep, and then, for the first time all day, he was truly happy. He dreamed of Kyra.

And he was kissing her.

32

At the end of seventh hour on Wednesday, Kyra made her way through the longest hallway in the school to Mr. Hillard's science class. Sure, Kyra reasoned, it was technically the same length as all of the other front and rear hallways, but it felt like the longest hallway since Jason and she had broken up. That was another thing she hated since breaking up with Jason (the list was growing rapidly): there were placcs in the school she dreaded going to now. The third-floor hallway where Jason was back with his crew, the athletic area where she used to wait for Renee, the bank of vending machines, the school store—all places where she might run into Jason, Lisa, or their friends.

Before she and Jason were together she could go anywhere. Pretty much no one had noticed her. She moved easily, unselfconsciously through the halls, and through her life. Now, Kyra actually felt herself being aware of how she was walking when she saw Lisa or one of her friends! That was so unlike her. Lisa would be certain to have a smug look of knowing and satisfaction on her face whenever Kyra saw her. Running into Greg was horrible because, although they spoke, Greg always acted as though he had something to ask or tell her. She dreaded whatever it might be.

But of course, the worst was when she would come across Jason. At first, before he knew why she'd broken up with him, he would leave whomever he was with and step into stride with her. But since she refused to talk to him, after a couple of days he stopped chasing her. Then, still not knowing why she'd broken up with him, he would silently watch her pass. While she strained not to stare at him, she could feel his eyes on her as she walked. When he learned why she had broken up with him, he changed radically. She saw him avert his eyes from her, and when she watched him (she didn't want to the first couple of times, but she couldn't seem to help it) she saw that he made certain not to lay eyes on her at all.

All of the reactions had caused her pain. They had pained her because what she wanted was to be with him. She wanted the time back that they had before she'd found out he had cheated on her. She missed talking to him; she missed listening to him, laughing with him, and touching him. She missed looking at him as much as she liked, he was so beautiful. When she considered going back to him, when she felt particularly weak, she would remind herself that *he* had been willing to sacrifice all of that in order to have sex with Lisa. That could usually strengthen her resolve long enough to avoid embarrassing herself.

Still, she missed him all the time. Even though seeing him in the halls was torture, those times also thrilled her. She could, after all, see the person at whom she most loved to look. Thus, she went through the day both dreading and longing to see Jason. In fact, when he did appear, it felt almost as though she had made him materialize because she thought of him so much. The city championship game had been wonderful because she had been able to look at him, and look at him, and look at him without feeling that others were watching and measuring how much she still loved him. She had the perfect excuse to stare at him! He was the center of attention.

Now, though, as she made her way to Mr. Hillard's classroom, she had no excuse to stare at Jason, and she hoped he wasn't in the hall. It had been a long day, and she was tired. She didn't feel like dealing with the strain of avoiding eye contact with him. As she passed the most coveted lockers in the school, the very ones Jason had left with ease in order to be nearer her, she noticed with the now familiar mixture of relief and regret that he wasn't there. Neither was Lisa, a definite bonus.

But Heather was there, just putting on her coat to leave. As far as Kyra was concerned, Heather was just another one in Lisa's pack. Every time Lisa had pulled a whammy on Kyra—kissing Jason on his and Kyra's first date, confronting Kyra in the back hall, and bragging in the bathroom, about Jason's cheating—Heather had been there, supporting Lisa. Kyra could do without ever seeing Heather again, too. Kyra tilted her head just a little higher and kept walking.

"Kyra," Heather called. Kyra kept walking. "Kyra," Heather repeated in the nearly deserted hallway. There was no way that she could think Kyra didn't hear her. Kyra didn't care what Heather thought. Heather caught up with Kyra. "Look, I just want to talk to you for a minute."

Kyra stopped walking and looked over at Heather. Kyra's eyes were full of contained anger and obvious irritation. "I've got somewhere to be."

"Fine," Heather said. "This won't take long, though. Five minutes maybe."

"I don't have five minutes for you."

"It's about Jason. Do you have five minutes for him?"

"Maybe you haven't noticed, but Jason and I aren't together," Kyra said sarcastically. "So no, I don't have five minutes for him, either."

"Well, I'll take even less time." Heather paused and took a deep breath. "It was all a lie. Jason never cheated on you with Lisa."

Kyra's eyes narrowed. Now what were they trying to pull on her?

"Lisa made it all up. She just wanted to break you two up so that she could get back with Jason," Heather continued.

"I don't know what kind of game you and your girls are up to now." Kyra looked around to see if Lisa and her girls were lurking somewhere nearby. "But I'm not playing, okay?"

"I'm not playing any kind of game. At least not anymore."

"Maybe you don't know it, but I overheard Lisa talking. Nobody told me she slept with Jason; I heard *her* say it with my own ears."

"I know."

"Okay, so you know. Somebody did tell you."

"No, nobody told me. You heard it in the first-floor bathroom. You were in the third stall. Lisa planned the whole thing."

"I don't understand."

"Yes, you do."

"She set me up?"

Heather simply nodded.

"Oh, God, what have I done?" Kyra whispered. She looked into Heather's eyes and saw the truth in them, and something else, a little pity.

"I'm sorry, Kyra. I never should have been a part of it. I should have told you or Jason right away."

Kyra just looked at Heather, shaking her head from side to side, barely hearing a word Heather said. "What have I done?" Kyra whispered again.

"I know you probably hate me. I don't blame you. But I'll go talk to Jason for you, get it all straightened out. It was our fault, Lisa's, and all of us who knew what she did and didn't say anything."

"No, don't."

"I want to. This has been messing with my head."

"No, really, don't."

"No, you don't understand. Jason has been *really* hurt. Seriously. He's not the same. I thought you two were maybe some sort of lightweight relationship. But you weren't, were you?"

"No."

"Then I read this, and I knew that I had to say something. Did you see this?" Heather pulled a copy of *The Cross Herald* out of her book bag. It was folded neatly to an inside page.

"What's this?" Kyra asked as she took it. Heather pointed to an untitled poem and Kyra read it.

> Sadness swells and sometimes slices
> across old hurts.
> What do you do when the one you trusted does not
> trust you?
> Betrayal bites like a bee's indifferent sting
> and causes
> Sadness to swell and sometimes slice
> across old hurts.
> I'll say this:
> It can make you tired of trying.
>
> By Jason Vincent

Tears sprang up in Kyra's eyes, but she fought them back. "No, I hadn't seen it."

"And I hate thinking about the fact that I helped to hurt Jason. I like Jason; he's always been cool with me."

"No. *You* don't understand. *I'm* the one who hurt Jason. Lisa, you, none of you could have done anything to hurt Jason. I was the one."

Heather just looked at this girl that she'd practically ignored for over two years. She was kind of pretty. Kind of. She obviously really cared about Jason; he wasn't just a social status toy to her. Heather had been concerned for Jason during this time, but when she'd read the poem she'd thought that she'd fallen a little in love with Jason herself. But she'd noticed the pain on Kyra's face, too, as Kyra walked through the halls.

"Look, thanks for telling me," Kyra said. "At least you *did* tell me."

"I am sorry."

"Thanks for that, too. I have to go. Don't talk to Jason, please. I'll do it. Okay*!*"

"Okay." Heather was relieved, to tell the truth. She didn't want to see Jason's face when he realized what she and the other girls had done to him.

Kyra continued to Mr. Hillard's room as though in a daze. She listened through a fog as he reminded her that the finals for the Hamilton Science Competition were in less than two weeks. Hotel accommodations had been confirmed, he assured her, and there was an allowance for meals. He reminded Kyra to pack a couple of professional-looking outfits for the competition days. He told her how proud he was of her and her work. Kyra just nodded her head from time to time.

"Are you okay, Kyra?" Mr. Hillard asked.

"Mmm? Oh, yes, Mr. Hillard. I'm fine. I've got to go, though, if that's all right."

"Sure, Kyra. Are you certain that you're all right?"

Kyra made herself focus on Mr. Hillard for a moment. "I'm fine, really. I'll see you next week. And thanks for the information," she said, holding up the packet he'd given her with all of the trip and competition finals information in it.

"All right then," he said, unconvinced. "I'm really proud of you for making the finals, Kyra. You've worked hard all year for this. I'll see you on Tuesday."

"Thank you."

Kyra wandered out of the classroom and the school, barely seeing anyone or hearing herself speak to people she passed. What have I done, she kept asking herself? How can I fix this? What if I can't fix it?

When she got home her mother was there in the kitchen watching TV and reading a magazine.

"Hey, Mama."

"Hey, Kyra. What's the matter with you? You look so upset."

"Oh, Mama, I've really messed up this time!"

"What, baby?" Ms. Evans was instantly concerned. Kyra rarely looked like this, all distraught and out of sorts. What could have happened?

"You know that I broke up with Jason."

"Of course."

"Do you know why?"

"No."

"Because I overheard his ex-girlfriend say that Jason had cheated on me with her."

"Oh . . . oh."

"So I broke up with Jason without even talking to him about it. On Valentine's Day, Mama!" A feeling of desperation and fear welled up inside of Kyra. She did her best to keep it at bay.

"Ouch."

"Right. Ouch. Huge ouch. Anyway, guess what?"

"What?"

"It turns out it was all a lie. Lisa set me up. She planned for me to overhear her, she made the entire thing up to break Jason and me up!"

"How do you know this now?"

"Because one of Lisa's friends, Heather, just confessed. She said that she felt guilty for hurting Jason this way, and she just had to confess."

"Well, then, why didn't she tell Jason?"

"I don't know. But I think she was afraid to face him."

"Makes sense. So what are you going to do?"

"Crawl under a rock!"

"Well, after that, then?" Ms. Evans's voice was all reason and patience.

"Call him?"

"I think you should. Maybe you two can straighten it all out."

Kyra felt just a tiny glimmer of hope. "He won't forgive me."

"He may not. But you should at least give him a chance this time."

Just after ten o'clock that night, just two days and two nights before the state regional playoffs, Kyra got up the nerve to call Jason.

"Hello," she began nervously, "may I speak to Jason?"

"Is this Kyra?" Jason's father asked.

"Yes. Hello, Mr. Vincent. How are you?"

"I'm fine, Kyra. How have you been?"

"Okay."

"I haven't heard from you in a while."

"No, not in a little while."

"Well . . . I'll get Jason for you."

"Thanks, Mr. Vincent." Kyra waited the seconds it took for Mr. Vincent to tell Jason that the call was for him. She had wanted to tell Mr. Vincent not to tell Jason who it was. Jason might not even pick up the receiver if he knew she was on the line. But if she did that, she'd look like a perfect jerk. So she waited, anxiously.

"Hello?" Jason's voice was as deep and rich as she remembered. Her stomach tightened with nervousness and excitement. Maybe she should have waited to see him in person. If she could touch him it might be easier. "Hello?"

"Hello, Jason." The line went totally silent. For a full, painful minute. Kyra was too ashamed to speak again.

"Hello, Kyra."

"Can you talk for a few minutes?" Her voice was all hesitation and caution.

"Not really."

"I— How have you been?"

"What did you call about?"

Kyra swallowed and tried not to cry. "I know that you didn't cheat on me. I wanted to—"

"How do you know that?"

"Heather told me."

"Heather? And you believed her?"

"Yes."

"That's rich." He snorted a cruel, humorless laugh. "That's really rich, Kyra. You believe Heather, who you hardly even know, and you didn't believe *in* me enough to even talk to me about it!"

"I know, Jason, I feel horrible about that. I want to tell you how sorry I am and . . ." She paused, fumbling for words.

"You feel horrible about that, huh? You're sorry? I'll tell you what, Kyra. I'll make this easy on you. You don't have to feel bad or sorry on my account, okay? You did me a favor, really, you did. You taught me how stupid it is to let my guard down. I should be thanking you rather than looking for an apology. So, thank you, and later."

With that, he hung up the phone and cut the connection between them.

33

Renee asked Kyra if she was sure that she wanted to do this—to come out to Dearborn for Jason's state regional game. Kyra assured her several times that she most definitely wanted to come. Kyra told Renee everything that had happened with Heather and Jason, and Renee felt for her girl. Renee did not want to see Kyra humiliated by Jason in public, or in private, for that matter. But Kyra explained to Renee that she had to see Jason, communicate with him somehow, because he wasn't taking her calls and he ignored her in school.

"I can hardly sleep, Renee. I have to tell him everything that I need to say."

"But at the big game, Kyra? Can't you wait, try to catch him privately?"

"No. I can't explain it, but if I don't speak to him soon, I feel like I'll explode. Plus, I want to see him play."

So they stood in the huge stands with throngs of other people there to support Cross and Josiah High School from Dearborn. Cross was about to claim another victory, with thirty seconds on the clock, and a six-point lead. Kyra watched the clock tick away those final seconds, then stop for a team's time-out, then begin again, then stop again, until the thirty seconds on the clock stretched into five minutes in real time. She played back in her mind what had happened Thursday night, the night after she'd called him.

It was just before midnight, and she was getting her things together for school the next day. She'd already had her bath and put on her nightgown. She heard her parents go to bed an hour before, their light going out not long after that. As she moved about her room gathering things together, she thought that she heard a light tap on her window. Then she heard it again, much more definitely this time. She looked out the window and saw Jason in his Cross varsity jacket standing in the dark March night. With the light behind her, the thin nightgown was nearly transparent from Jason's vantage point. Kyra didn't know this.

"Wait, I'm coming," she called softly, but clearly. She hurried downstairs without grabbing a robe, excited and afraid at the same time. Please, God, don't let Mama or Daddy wake up. She went to the study, which was directly below her bedroom, and opened the French doors that led outside. Jason was waiting there. He came in quickly and shut the door behind him. Kyra went and turned on a light on an end table. The light shone through her gown again and the sight held Jason's eyes. She was so beautiful, he thought, and she didn't even realize it.

"Turn the light down," he said, his voice husky. The light fell to a dim golden glow. He didn't want to be distracted by how much he lusted for her. "Come over here." He still stood in the shadows by the French doors. Kyra came to him without hesitation and stood before him, near and waiting. She breathed deeply in an effort to calm her excitement and nervousness, but her breathing continued soft and fast.

Jason stared at the girl he loved and felt all of his emotions rush over him, weaken him. She was staring at him in a way that made him feel weak and powerful all at the same time. If he touched her, if he touched her . . . But he hadn't come for that. How long had it been, he wondered, since he'd kissed her lips.

"Jason." She said his name like a breath, as though his name itself were air.

He closed his eyes and opened them to see her there before him, barely dressed, wanting to be his. He wanted to make love to her right here, right now. But he couldn't, for so many reasons now.

"Don't call me anymore, Kyra."

"Jason," she breathed his name again. He could hear pain in it.

"I mean it," he strained to control his voice, his hands. "It's over. You made me feel loved—"

"I did love you," she cut in. "I still love you."

He shook his head no, trying to convince himself, to tell her. "You made me feel loved, then you snatched it away. Without talking to me, without warning me, you left me alone. That hurt, Kyra. You knew what things were like for me, and you left me without even giving me a chance. How can I count on you after that?"

"I know, but—"

"I can't, Kyra. I can't." He whispered the words to her. "I was better off before I knew what it was like to love somebody like this." Kyra heard *this* instead of *that*, which gave her hope. "You got me to needing you, then told me I couldn't have you, without even trusting me enough to talk to me. I can't get that out of my head, Ky. How could you diss me like that?"

"Jason, I'm sorry, I'm so sorry," Kyra said.

"First, to think that I would cheat on you, then to not even trust me enough to come to me with it? I thought you were better than that."

They stared at one another in the shadows of the room. Kyra could say nothing, and Jason felt he had almost nothing left to say.

"Don't call me again. Don't try to talk to me at school. Don't come to my games. We can't be friends either. I love you too much for that."

Kyra had been standing so near him in the darkness, close enough to smell the peppermint on his breath, the clean soapy smell that he always seemed to have, which she loved so much. She heard what he was saying, she understood his words, but she could feel him, too. She could feel that he wanted her, to be with her, to hold her, to kiss her. She could feel him in the semidarkness without touching him. Everything she heard from him and everything she felt from him, made her ache with wanting him. She, who had caused him the pain, ached to soothe it.

"Jason," she whispered, moving still closer, until her chest touched the front of his jacket, "I love you. I love you. I love you." Each time she said it, she moved her face to kiss him. Gently, slowly. Each time she moved, he evaded her mouth, gently, slowly. She was not put off. She understood, and she didn't mind. "I love you."

Jason felt himself moan inside, or did he moan aloud? He brought one hand up to cup the back of her head and pulled her forward to kiss her. The kiss was so intense, so fast, that Kyra did not even have a chance to bring her hands up to hold him.

"God," Jason whispered, his lips now against her forehead. "Don't call me, Kyra."

Then he left into the night with a wind whipping behind him.

And so here she was at his game with a letter in her pocket for Jason. A letter that she had to get into his hands, and that she prayed he'd read. It said everything that she thought and felt, as well as she could write it. She was here, clutching it in her pocket and praying for a victory for Jason and a chance, even a small one, for herself.

"You'll never make it down there!" Renee shouted. Cross had just won the game and the court filled with spectators, who surrounded the players. Kyra was trying to make her way to Jason. He stood surrounded by screaming, cheering spectators near her end of the court.

"I have to," Kyra said. She never stopped moving. "Excuse me, excuse me," she repeated as she pressed through the people before her. Renee stayed on her tail. Kyra glanced down at the court again. Jason was looking her way, at her. She stood still, momentarily arrested by his eyes locked onto hers.

"Go, go! Hurry up, before the coach moves the team to the locker room."

Kyra moved on again at her friend's urging, losing eye contact with Jason as she watched the people ahead of her and her footing. Finally they made it onto the floor and neared Jason. Lisa, Jackie, Greg, and bunches of other kids stood all around him, shielding him from everybody else.

Kyra pressed herself past all of them until she was close enough to touch Jason. He looked down at her, neither of them speaking.

"Here." She pulled the letter out of her pocket and handed it to him. "Congratulations, Jason. You were so good out there," she said.

"Thanks," was all that he could manage.

Kyra felt a lump forming in her throat. She turned and

started making her way out of the crowd and the gym, Renee always close by.

"Well, you did it," Renee said once they made into the hallway. It was crowded, too, but not quite as much as the gym.

"Yeah. I just hope it does some good."

"Me too," Renee said, hugging her friend. "Me too."

34

"I don't believe it," Akila said.

"It's true, though. All of it," Kyra assured her sister.

Kyra had made the fifty-minute drive up to Ann Arbor to visit Akila. After the game Kyra had dropped Renee and several other kids off at The Biz, where they said they'd catch rides home. Kyra went home and asked her parents if she could drive up to Ann Arbor and spend the night with Akila, and they'd said yes. She called Akila to make sure it would be all right, then packed a quick bag, a cell phone, some CDs, and gotten out of town. She used the drive up there to think about Jason and herself. When she'd gotten there, Akila had given her a big hug and welcomed Kyra into her dorm room. Akila had a single, so there would be no roommate to interrupt them.

Kyra told her big sister everything. She told Akila about the way that Jason and she had fallen in love. She told Akila of how sweet it had been to be loved by Jason. She told Akila everything that had happened since she had overheard Lisa talking in the girls' bathroom. When Kyra finished, Akila sat staring at her sister for a few stunned moments.

"I cannot believe all the drama you've been living, girl!"

"I know." Kyra allowed a small smile to slip by.

"So, you're in love, huh?"

"Yes."

"What do you think he's going to do?"

"I don't know. He might not even read the letter."

"He'll read it."

"I can't be so sure, Akila. I hurt him, really badly. I mean, you don't even know what Jason has been dealing with. I can't tell you that, because that's his business. But suffice it to say, he already had a lot going on in his life, and he was counting on me. I sort of helped him to deal with it all."

"I see. Well, still, I think he'll read it."

"Why?"

"Because he loves you. When you love somebody, you can't help it, you want to talk to them, to hear, or in this case, read what they have to say. Everything inside of you calls out for it."

"Sounds like you know."

"Oh, yeah. I've been there before."

Kyra nodded.

"But little sis', even if he does read it and comes back to you, that won't solve all of your problems. You need to deal with why you tripped out so quickly and so badly."

"I won't let Jason down like this again. I'll talk to him when I'm worried about something like this from now on."

"No, Kyra, I think it goes deeper than that. I think that you were worried about more than Jason cheating on you."

"No, I was worried about Jason cheating on me."

Akila looked at her younger sister for a moment. She wanted to put this just the right way so that Kyra would open up, not retreat and deny. Maybe if Akila could get Kyra to be honest with herself about a few things, she might have a chance at having a better relationship with Jason. That is, if Kyra could get Jason back.

"Kyra," Akila began. "Why were you so quick to believe that Jason had cheated on you?"

"I don't know."

"I mean, you hadn't even spoken to him, and he'd told you that he'd never cheated on a girlfriend before."

"Yeah, I know."

"Did you believe him when he said that?"

"Yes. I did. He didn't even want to pursue things with me while he was still with Lisa. He broke up with her the day after we kissed because he wanted to be honest with her."

"Well, does that sound like someone who would cheat on someone he loved as much he loves you?"

Kyra just sat silently looking first at her hands in her lap, then at her sister.

"Does it?" Akila pressed gently.

"No," Kyra whispered.

"Then why were you so quick to believe that he'd cheated on you?"

"I don't know."

"Come on, Ky. Just tell me what you think, what you feel. We could always talk, remember?"

"Yes, I do. But it's been a long time since we really talked. Most of your senior year you were so busy, and then you left for college . . . I don't know, it hasn't been the same."

"I know," Akila moved from her chair to sit beside Kyra on the twin bed. "I know. I'm sorry for that, too, Kyra. I'll do better, I promise. But let me help you here, okay? Tell me why you think you were so ready to believe that Jason had slept with Lisa."

Kyra considered her sister for a long moment and then told her the truth. "Because I figured that deep down inside he couldn't possibly be willing to really give up sex just to be with me." Kyra felt like a huge weight had been lifted off her chest once she'd spoken the words aloud. She'd thought them before, many times, but she'd never said it aloud. It was the nagging fear that she carried around in this relationship with Jason.

"Why?" Akila wanted to know.

"Because sex is supposed to mean so much to guys, to men. And Jason has been having sex for two years now. He told me how much he loved it. He's told me how much he wants to have sex with me. And there is Lisa, his girlfriend, who he had sex with for a year, always around, always available. We messed around pretty seriously. We touched just about everywhere. I figured that might be frustrating him to the point where he felt, at least sometimes, like he just had to have it."

"Have you talked to Jason about this?"

"Yes."

"Have you told him what you told me?"

"Pretty much."

"Well, maybe you shouldn't just tell him pretty much; maybe you'd better tell him everything," Akila advised.

"Everything?" Kyra asked. She was embarrassed just thinking about telling Jason all of these things about sex.

"Everything. Then he'll know what you're feeling and thinking and he can respond to that."

"Maybe you're right."

"I'm right."

"Okay, I'll talk to him. I'll tell him everything."

"Good. Then let me know what happens."

Kyra nodded. Akila stood up and stretched.

"You hungry? Let's go to Uno's and get some pizza," Akila said.

"Okay. Seafood pizza."

"You can get an individual seafood pizza, I can't stand that stuff."

"Thanks, Akila," Kyra said as she stood up and gave her sister a hug.

"You're welcome, baby sister, anytime."

35

After the state regional victory, Jason surprised all of his friends and teammates by telling them to go on to The Biz without him; he'd show up later. Lieutenant Simpson, the owner, had offered to throw a victory party if the basketball team won; everything would be half off for Cross students with their student ID cards, and free for the basketball team members and their dates. Everybody would be going. Well just about everybody, Jason thought. Kyra probably wouldn't be there.

"You all right, man?" Greg asked. He'd pulled Jason over to the side so that he could have a private word with his friend.

"Yeah. I just need a few minutes to myself, you know."

"You going to see Kyra or something?"

"No, it's not like that. I just need to be by myself for a little bit before I get with everybody else."

"All right. Don't be too long, okay?"

"Okay." Jason had been fingering the letter that Kyra sent him the entire time that he'd been talking to Greg. He held it in his varsity jacket pocket. The paper was smooth and cool beneath his fingers. He literally itched to read it. His fingers tingled. This girl was driving him crazy. Literally. He still couldn't believe that he'd shown up at her house after midnight, snuck in, and seen her. He could still see the way that she looked in her nightgown as she stood before the lamp. He swallowed and fingered the letter again. She was definitely driving him crazy.

He drove to the Big Boy restaurant near Belle Isle, not far from Kyra's house, and got a booth to himself. He ordered a strawberry milk shake and pulled the letter from his pocket. *To Jason*, the envelope read simply. He lay it down and ran his hand across it, pressing it to the table. He sighed deeply, picked up the letter, and opened it. It smelled of vanilla. He shook his head. Hold on, old boy, he told himself, hold on. She had written the letter in her neat, open script, in black ink on fine, bone-colored stationery. It was good paper, he noted distractedly— heavy, with a good feel to it. He allowed himself to begin reading it.

Dearest Jason,

I don't know where to start. Do I start by saying how much I miss you? Or with how sorry I am? Do I start by asking how you've been? Or do I begin with where my feelings are deepest, do I begin by saying that I love you? Are you even reading this? Did you throw this letter away or burn it?

I'll start anyway.

I love you, Jason. I love you so very much. And I've missed you more than I could imagine. I think of you nearly all the time and you are in my dreams. People are constantly writing songs about us: the good times, the bad times, these times now when we're apart. The songs are on the radio, on every station I turn to. Have you heard them?

I'm sorry, baby. I'm sorry that I didn't trust you. I never should have believed someone who couldn't stand me in the second place and who wanted you in the first place. I apologize for not talking to you about my worries. I should have told you before what I'm going to tell you now. I could hardly believe it when you wanted me in the beginning. You, who were (and still are) so popular, so cool, so fine, wanted me. You could have anyone, and you wanted me. Even when I got over that, I couldn't truly and deeply believe that you could give up sex for me. Everybody I talk to says that sex is the best thing since before the wheel. I heard something on a nightly news program that said that typical teenage boys and men think about sex more than two hundred times a day. Two hundred times!

I knew that you and Lisa had been lovers. What I overheard her say sounded entirely possible . . . if you couldn't give up sex.

You have never been dishonest with me. You told me honestly how much you liked sex, you told me how much you wanted to make love to me. But you also told me that I was worth waiting on and that you loved me. I should have believed you. I'm sorry that I didn't.

I know that it will be difficult for you to trust me now. Will you try, though? I can promise you that if I'm ever doubtful or worried again, about anything, I'll talk to you. I will trust you enough to talk to you. Give me a chance.

Jason, I want us to be together again. I want to hold you and kiss you, to talk to you and to be yours again.

Do you remember that first time we kissed? I do. I remember everything. Everything.

Call me, or come to me.

I love you,

Kyra

P.S. My parents ask about you. They miss you, too.

"Damn," Jason said aloud softly. This girl is killing me, he thought. Then he read the letter again.

36

The second-hour announcements blared through every classroom as they did each morning. As usual, second hour found Jason in his honors French class on the second floor and Kyra in AP physics on the fifth floor. An additional ten minutes were tacked on to the second hour in order to accommodate the daily school announcements. Lessons stopped and many students used the time to veg out. The student announcer informed the school of an upcoming skating party, parent–teacher conferences next Thursday, the Drama Department's production of *Sarafina!*, which would begin that Friday, and the chess team's latest victory.

"We're proud to give an extra shout-out to the Cross boys' basketball team," the announcer continued. "As you know they recently won the city championship for the second year in a row!" Kyra stopped looking over her notes for her sixth-hour government quiz and gave the announcements her undivided attention. "Every member of the team made the Cross family proud this weekend when they won the State Regional Title. Jason Vincent, the star point guard, led the team in points and assists, with Greg Hoover right behind him in stats. Congratulations to the entire team." Kyra was proud of Jason and wished that she could tell him. But she knew that it would be best if she backed off and allowed Jason to make the next move.

"Here's one last announcement," the announcer said. "The Hamilton Science Scholarship is a prestigious statewide competition that pits some of the brightest high school science minds against one another. What's at stake? $250,000 in scholarships, with $50,000 going to the winner. For the first time ever, Cross has a *junior* in the semifinals—our very own Kyra Evans. She'll be presenting her science project to the judges this weekend at East Lansing's elegant Doubletree Hotel and Conference Center. You go, girl! Good luck at the semifinals!"

Kyra smiled and said thanks as kids in her class congratulated her. She hadn't been expecting the school to announce it.

Three floors down Jason listened attentively to the announcement of Kyra's accomplishment. He hadn't heard that she'd made the semifinals, but he had expected that she would.

Way to go, Ky, he thought. Way to go.

37

"Do you have the camera?" Ms. Evans asked her husband.

"Yes, yes, for the twentieth time, yes," Mr. Evans said impatiently.

Ms. Evans, Mr. Evans, Akila, and Renee bustled busily around Mr. and Ms. Evans's hotel room. Mr. Hillard, her science teacher, was three doors down in his room. They were in East Lansing for the final portion of the Hamilton Science Scholarship Competition. Friday had been a long day, eight hours of interviews and presentations for Kyra, during which she had to dazzle the prestigious group of scientists, college professors, high school teachers, and editors of various science journals with the validity of her project.

Her family, best friend, and teacher had been there for moral support and to help her cart her materials around. They gave Kyra words of encouragement, refreshments, and carried her display boards for her. All of the members of the panel had copies of her report, and Kyra carried her own copy in a small leather attaché case.

Friday had been stressful for everyone, but especially Kyra, of course. But on Saturday morning they had awakened to find out that it had gone exceptionally well. Kyra had been selected from the twenty-five semifinalists as one of the five finalists. They'd all driven down together at eight o'clock, before breakfast, to read the list that was supposed to be posted by 7:55 A.M. They cheered right there, hugging and congratulating Kyra. Then they hurried off as another family pulled up. They didn't want to celebrate in front of them in case that student had to find out that she or he was not a finalist.

At one o'clock today the five finalists would present their work before an audience in the Grand Auditorium on stage. Their work would be displayed on a huge overhead screen so that everyone in the auditorium could see their efforts. Each finalist would be given fifteen minutes to explain the highlights of their research. After each student had presented, a winner would be announced fifteen minutes later. Every judge had already seen every project and studied them carefully in advance. The auditorium show was just an opportunity to showcase the finalists before family, friends, fellow competitors, and interested onlookers.

Her family, Renee, and Mr. Hillard were already proud enough to burst. Kyra was the only junior who had been selected as a finalist, to start. Then there was the fact that all five of the finalists were guaranteed a $25,000 scholarship, while the first-place winner would walk away with $50,000. So there was immense excitement in the room as everyone prepared to go. Everyone was well dressed and looking fine. Her brother, Sadi, had called to congratulate Kyra on making it to the finals and a bouquet of roses had arrived at eleven o'clock from him, special delivery from a local florist.

Today Kyra was dressed smartly in a charcoal-gray pants suit, matching leather shoes, and a silk blouse with a rich yet subtle pattern of red, ivory, black, and gray. Her mother had lent her some of her heavier gold jewelry. She'd blown out her hair, and placed only a few thin braids around the crown of her head. Then she'd tied it all back into a ponytail, and coiled it into a smart, simple twist. She looked elegant, intelligent, and poised.

Kyra was excited, too, she really was. But while everyone moved about her getting themselves and her ready, she sat perfectly still, thinking. She thought of all the hard work that she'd put in, nearly a year of hard work, to get this far. She thought of the support she'd received from Mr. Hillard, her parents, Renee, Akila, and yes, Jason. She thought of yesterday's competition and the nervousness, excitement, and sometimes downright anxiety of the other competitors. She thought of the wave of joy and relief that had washed over her when she read her name on that very short list of finalists this morning. The Hamilton Science Scholarship Competition had been all that she'd looked forward to and more. She was loving it, even if she did sometimes feel nervous enough to pass out. She loved the challenge and the competition. She had her presentation down pat—that had been the case for two weeks. She was ready for today. She was excited about today.

But a part of her, a very important part of her, was feeling something else. She missed Jason. She wished that he were here. She wanted him to see her do her best. She wanted to be able to hold him if she won, and hold on to him if she lost.

And so, try as she might, deserve it as she might, she couldn't feel completely happy.

Jason checked his watch, again. Then his dashboard clock, again. 12:27 P.M. He was still more than thirty minutes away at this rate. He punched the gas and sped ahead. He was going to be on time. He'd already missed Friday; he wasn't going to miss any part of today.

38

Kyra sat and waited for her turn. The stage was beautiful, with professional lighting, a podium in polished oak, potted plants, and huge floral arrangements. A high school student dressed in black and white would quietly wheel out all of the items needed for each person's presentation when it was their turn. Kyra was the third presenter. The woman who introduced her made a big deal of the fact that she was the only junior to make it to the finals this year, one of only six juniors to make it this far in the history of the competition. Everyone applauded.

The hotel's auditorium was a nice size; it seated four hundred. Just about every seat was filled, too. A bunch of folks looked like college students, probably from Michigan State University, which was in East Lansing, and from some neighboring junior colleges. There were a few groups of high school students, most likely a field trip arranged by their science teachers. Many of the other competitors were there with their teachers and families. And of course there were the families, teachers, and loved ones of the finalists. All of the various competition judges sat in the front rows. Kyra scanned the audience fruitlessly. She couldn't make out her family, though she knew where they sat, or much of anybody else, once they'd dimmed the lights. She had hoped that Jason might still show up, that she would see him, and then they dimmed the lights.

Kyra started with a joke. It was a good one, short and gracefully delivered. The audience laughed, and not out of kindness either. She spoke clearly and pleasantly and looked out into the audience with a confidence devoid of any arrogance. She walked over to the table that held the overhead projector and explained the displayed material in a simple yet intelligent manner. The audience was both charmed and impressed.

When she finished, she did what none of the earlier presenters had done and what, it turned out, the last two were too nervous to do too. "I want to take this opportunity to thank my mother and father who have given me so much love and support. I want to thank my sister, Akila; my brother, Sadi; and my girl Renee, who has always believed in me; and my science teacher, Mr. Hillard, for guiding me and allowing me to make my own way when I was ready. I want to say a special thank-you to someone who means a lot to me. He's not here, but I want to thank him anyway. He was there supporting me for most of it. Thank you, Jason. And I want to thank the judges, and you, the audience. I know that hearing all of these science projects can't be the most exciting way to spend a Saturday"—the audience chuckled—"but it's been the way that I've spent a lot of my Saturdays over the past year. You've been great," she said. "Thank you." The audience erupted into warm, generous applause.

Of course, they were loudest in the middle section, fourth row, where her family, teacher and Renee sat. But the applause was pretty loud in the left-hand rear section, two rows from the back, where a young man stood on his feet, alone, and clapped.

"Well, here we are, at the point we've all been waiting for," the announcer began. The lights had been lifted on the audience, not fully, but enough. Kyra could see her family, friends, and teacher, but she was too nervous to scan the audience for Jason. "I guess no one has been more anxiously awaiting this moment than these five fine young people here on the stage, huh?" the announcer asked no one in particular. "Would all of the semifinalists in the audience please stand? Let's begin by giving them a big round of applause." The audience clapped loudly and soundly. "They've all worked very hard, very hard. We're going to be calling each them up to award them with this certificate of achievement, this medal, and these scholarships for five thousand dollars."

The audience clapped again as the young people lined up at the stairs to the stage. Each student's name was called along with the title of their science project, and both pieces of information were displayed on the huge overhead projector screen. The crowd clapped again as each student received their award: camera flashes went off, and some family members even cheered.

Kyra sat nervously waiting for them to finish and to announce the winner. All five of the finalists had presented impressive projects. Although, Kyra admitted to herself, her actual presentation of her project was the best, she wasn't sure that her project itself was. She thought so, but wasn't sure. And then they were finished, and all of the attention turned once again to the announcer and the five finalists on the stage.

"Let's give all of our finalists a big round of applause," the announcer urged. The audience clapped. But much to Kyra's surprise, they also stood for an ovation. She was so touched she feared she might actually cry. When the applause quieted, a high school student walked out on stage with five envelopes in hand and gave them to the announcer. "In fifth place, for his development of case studies on 'The Excessive Use of Diuretics and the Side Effects of Magnesium Accumulation in the Bloodstream,' Mr. Michael Chin," the announcer said. Michael got up with an obvious mixture of disappointment and pride. "In fourth place, for her 'Investigation of How the Alteration of Environmental Factors in Middle Schools Leads to a Reduction in the Number of Students Recommended for Ritalin Treatment,' Ms. Sarah Henderson.

"In third place," he continued, "for his study of 'The Evidence that Premature Wrinkling in Women Correlates Directly with Low Fat Intake,' Mr. Kyle Weatherspoon. In second place, for his research on 'The Treatment of Arthritic Pain Using Magnetic Ice Packs,' Mr. Bryan Lott." Kyra actually heard her mother give a small scream. "And in first place, for the first time in the history of the Hamilton Science Scholarship Competition, a junior, from Detroit's Cross High School, Ms. Kyra Evans, for her outstanding research into 'The Isolation and Molecular Structure Determination of a Hormone Involved in the Mechanism of Fat Breakdown and Its Potential for Reversing the Adverse Effects of Diabetes'!"

The audience erupted into applause, and Kyra saw her family and Renee hugging one another. Her father was up front snapping pictures. Kyra heard the announcer speak and she wore the look of stunned happiness that would be expected of the winner. However, she was looking at the first person who'd stood up, before the ovation, and begun walking toward the front of the auditorium as the third-place winner was being announced. She kept her eyes pinned to him as the second-place winner was announced and he neared the stage. She stared at him even as she heard her mother's small scream, and she was looking only at him as she was announced as the first junior to win the Hamilton Science Scholarship Competition.

She walked up to receive her award, happier than she had ever been in her life. She had won; she had done her best and won, and it felt totally and absolutely wonderful. And Jason had come to be here with her, so now it felt perfect. She stood at the front of the stage where the announcer told her to stay, while many cameras flashed as she posed with her certificate, medal, and scholarship.

Then she walked over to the edge of the stage where Jason stood and stooped down to receive his outstretched hand. In front of everybody, he kissed her hand. Then she really did cry, and laughed out loud. Her father got a picture of that, too.

39

Late March found Detroit still cold and the trees leafless. The grass was a dismal yellow, and in places, sadly matted by mud from last night's rain. No flowers had bloomed yet, and the sky overhead was a discouraging steel gray. It would rain again soon.

"It really is a beautiful day," Jason said with a grin.

"Just beautiful," Kyra said as she inspected the world around her. Everything seemed perfect.

They walked together through Kyra's neighborhood, hand in hand.

"I mean, I don't think I've seen a better day," Jason said, looking at Kyra.

"You know, I might just have to agree."

"Are you still wearing your medal?"

"No silly, only at bedtime. What about you? Are you still wearing your gold medal from the state championships?"

"Yeah, it's underneath my sweater. Don't tell anybody," Jason said in a stage whisper.

"Your secret is safe with me." She stopped walking and turned to him, still holding his hand.

"Can I tell you another secret?"

"Please."

"I love you."

"I love you, too. But that's not a secret."

"How much is."

"How much?"

"More than anything or anyone else in my life."

"That's too much, Jay," Kyra said, deeply moved.

"I can't help how I feel."

"You're right." They kissed then, slowly and sweetly.

"You want to know another secret?" he asked.

"Mmm-hmmm," she said with her eyes still closed.

"I'm ready for your daddy's chili."

Kyra opened her eyes to see Jason's beautiful smile. "You're so silly, Jason. Is that all you're hungry for?"

"Give me another one of those kisses."

"Coming right up."

acknowledgments

At first I was going to write of those ultracool, suavely brief acknowledgments I see so often. I was worried that the one below would seem pretentious, you know, like I'm full of myself. But the truth is, I'm not ultracool or suave, and I'm not stuck on me; I'm stuck on the people who have encouraged me along the way. Some of them are listed below. Besides, how many chances like this do you get? So here goes:

I'll begin by thanking God, the Creator, from whom all blessings flow.

Thank you to Janell Agyeman, my agent at Marie Brown and Associates, who read my book, believed in it, and found my book a home. A great big thank-you goes out to Alessandra Balzer, who has proven to be a fantastic editor, who can guide and encourage without overwhelming. Thank you to Arianne Lewin, Ms. Balzer's assistant, who got her share of questions along the way and volleyed her way through each one with humor and warmth. Sharon Draper, whose books my students love; thank you for letting me bend your ear. May your successes continue to grow; you're good people.

Thank you to all of my great teachers. I want to thank all of the young people who attended or attend Cass Tech, who gave me their support: Aretha Steele, who read it first; Dianna Foster; Ashley Bradford; Kelley Femster; and Jason Collins Baker—and to all of the young people who read my story and encouraged me; best wishes in all that you do. Thank you, too, to every student that I've ever had at Farwell Middle School and Cass Tech; you have each touched my heart and spirit and I am grateful to have served as your teacher. I'm also grateful to the staff at Cass Tech; you all have always been so supportive, thank you. I'm especaially grateful to Mr. George Cohen, my principal at Cass, and one of my biggest cheerleaders. A special thank-you to Dr. Cynthia Salhi, who gave me all of the science project information in the book. Thank you, Kia Williamson, who gave me my first fan letter after reading my manuscript—that was so great.

Thank you to my best friend, Yolanda Bullock; I love ya. To the Davidson clan and Harrington relations; thanks for the love and support. Love to my little sister, Rachel McKeithen; there are no limits for you. Sherral, Ivan, and

Richard McKeithen, my sister and brothers; I love you. Marsha "Cuz" Robinson: when you read and liked it I knew I was on to something. To my uncle, Chris Embry, who keeps telling me I can do it: thanks for the encouragement. Much love to my amazing Embry family, whose love and support help keep me going. Much love to my Pittsburgh clan, whose humor, strength, and feistiness make the journey more than worthwhile each year. Grandma Pauline Embry, I am blessed beyond measure to have you as a grandmother: your love and faith in me are beautiful—*you* are the story-teller. Grandma Peaches Washington; thank you with all my heart for not allowing the miles and the years to keep your love from me; it warms and lifts my heart, always. Thank you, Mae Frances McKeithen, my mama, my heart, my first hero, cheerleader, story giver, and protector; I would be nothing without you. Omar Bryan, my son; you are already a gifted writer, and Aaliya Marie, my daughter; your art can leave me speechless. I am still in awe at how much I love you two.

Finally, to my husband, Omar, the best man that I have ever known. My heart belongs to you.

Check out:

by DANA DAVIDSON

Chapter 6

Tuesday evening Kylie stood at the kitchen window, gently biting her lower lip. She lived in one of the small but proudly maintained homes in the Ralph Bunche co-ops. They'd been on a wait list for three years to get into the pretty community. The kitchen window faced the parking lot. Ian was supposed to come in ten minutes and Kylie had already made up her mind that he probably wouldn't show.

Her mama's old black Honda Accord sat parked directly in front of their place as it usually did. The two spots adjacent to the Accord were empty. Empty and waiting, it seemed. "It's early," Kylie whispered to the worried parking spaces. He was due to arrive at five P.M. and already the sun was well into its descent. The sky, bleak all day, pitiless as a sheet of steel, pulled its cloak of shadow about itself. A cold wind bit across the landscape, and the parking lot was still. No one seemed willing to brave the cold and comfortless vista. Kylie worried that Ian would feel that a date with her wasn't worth coming out into such an evening.

She went to the mirror in the dining room and checked herself again. She wore faded jeans and an oversized blue sweater with a white T-shirt showing at its V-neck. She thought that she looked okay but her hair, again, betrayed her. She'd shampooed and blow-dried it and curled it under. But it had too many split ends and the whole cut was uneven and lifeless-looking. Kylie sighed and turned away from the mirror.

The girls that she saw Ian with at school had the latest haircuts, the sweetest designer clothes and shoes, gold jewelry, and a perfect sense of style. They carried small leather purses that held money and cell phones, and, she thought glumly, the secrets to being popular and noticed. Those girls drew boys like Ian to them like the moon pulled the tides of the sea.

Kylie had already spent an hour helping Nae Nae with her third-grade language arts assignment. Now the kids were coloring at the table and Jillian was curled up on the couch reading a murder mystery. The aroma of her mother's baked chicken, mashed potatoes, gravy, and sweet peas still hung in the air an hour after dinner.

Everything seemed calm and pleasant, a sharp contrast to the tension building up inside of Kylie. Despite the cool conversation that she had had with Ian yesterday she could see all sorts of ways this evening could go wrong. While she didn't know why Ian was interested in seeing her, she knew why she wanted to see him: he made her insides flutter. She liked the look of him and the way his voice sounded. When he danced with her Friday night she'd enjoyed his nearness, and wanted more of it. But what did he see in her?

She was so caught up in these thoughts that for a moment she hardly noticed the dark blue Capri pull into one of the parking spaces next to her mother's car. She jumped slightly when she woke to the reality before her.

"He's here. Now just say hello and then let him be," Kylie reminded her brother and sister.

"All right," Nae Nae said.

"Kylie has a lover boy," Stevie whispered with a grin.

"He is not my lover boy, and for God's sake, don't say anything like that when he gets in here. He's not my boyfriend, okay?"

"Okay," he said. Stevie was a little alarmed by the urgency in his sister's voice. Kylie was usually so calm and collected. Stevie stopped grinning and got a little nervous himself. Then Nae Nae leaned over and nudged him playfully and he relaxed a little. "I'm sorry," he said to Kylie.

"Oh, no, it's all right, sweetie. I'm sorry I snapped at you." She stooped to give him a quick hug, and the doorbell rang just as she released him. Jillian uncurled her legs and slipped her feet into her fuzzy, pale-blue house shoes. She marked her page with a bookmark.

"All right," Kylie said looking at her mother.

"All right," Jillian said, offering Kylie what she hoped was a reassuring smile.

Kylie opened the door to find Ian standing there with his hands inside the pockets of his brown leather coat and his hazel eyes gazing directly into hers.

"What's up?" Ian said. And then he smiled, and Kylie thought surely he must hear this singing inside of her. Everyone must hear it.

"Hi," she said, smiling back. "Come on in."

Ian stepped inside and Kylie closed the door behind him, shutting out the cold.

"Hello," Jillian said from the couch, "I'm Ms. Winship."

"How are you today?" Ian asked.

"Oh, I'm well enough," Jillian said. "How about yourself?"

"I'm pretty good, thank you," Ian said politely. He said "Hi," to Nae Nae and Stevie.

"So what are your plans for this evening, Ian?" Jillian asked. Kylie put on her coat while they talked.

"I thought that we'd drive out to Sheldon and get something to eat, then hang out at the laser tag place out there for a while. You know, if that's all right with you and Kylie."

"That sounds fine," Jillian said.

Ian looked over at Kylie to see what she thought, and she nodded yes.

"Well, you all better get going then. Be back by nine o'clock, Kylie, you two have school tomorrow," Jillian said.

"Okay." Kylie said. Then she gave both her sister and brother a quick kiss on the cheek. Jillian stood, ready to see the two of them out the door.

"You ready?" Ian asked her.

"Yes. Bye, Mama," Kylie said.

"Bye, Kylie." Ian and Kylie stepped into the evening and Jillian shut the door behind them.

Ian headed to his side of the car and Kylie to the passenger side. After unlocking his door, Ian hit the power locks and Kylie climbed in. Ian got in and started the car, and the heaters flooded the small car with warmth. A popular rapper filled the air with his rhythmic sound. Without a word, Ian backed out of the parking space and they were off.

Kylie sat beside him nervously, liking the music but too self-conscious to even nod her head to the beat. Ian gripped the steering wheel with one hand and allowed his head to bob up and down, up and down as they sped along the street. Kylie wanted to look at him, but she didn't want him to see her do it, so she sat stiffly, looking straight ahead, barely seeing what they were passing. They were soon out of her east-side Detroit neighborhood, and on the expressway, one of thousands of darkened vessels bejeweled by red, yellow, and white lights. She wished that he'd say something.

Less than twenty minutes later they were in the nearby town of Sheldon, cruising down its quiet streets where the shops, restaurants, and cafés were warmly lit and inviting. She'd filled the time in the car imagining all of the things she *would* say. In her imagination she was incredibly witty and smooth.

When he spoke she was startled back into her anxiety. "We're here."

She looked more carefully out of the window. They were parked in front of a row of stores, a café, and a Coney

Island restaurant flooded with bright lights at the end of the block.

When they got out of the car the cold air hit Kylie hard. She pulled her hood over her head and pressed her hands into her pockets. Ian was waiting for her when she rounded the front of the car and they walked side by side. When they got to the café they were both drawn by the jazz notes filtering out on the night air, and they looked in to see the pleasant glow of the lights, the cozy tables, the busy waitstaff.

"You want to check this out?" Ian asked.

"Sure," she said and he opened the door for her. Inside it was warm and deliciously aromatic. The scent of smoked sausages, chili, French fries, hamburgers, and rich coffees floated in the air. Nearly every table was occupied, and a small jazz band was in full swing on a slightly raised platform. Kylie liked the place immediately. "It's nice," she said.

"Yeah."

"Hi," a redheaded young woman said. She smiled cheerfully, and Kylie couldn't help but smile back. "Two?"

They followed her to a tiny table that had a clear view of the band and most of the café. Kylie eased out of her coat, all the while looking around her and avoiding eye contact with Ian. The walls held framed posters of city and countryside scenes of Italy, France, Germany, Switzerland, Brazil, Egypt, Canada, and the United States. There was a bar that served coffee and a kitchen not far from their table.

"You're quiet," Ian observed.

"You too."

He smiled. "Yeah. So how are you?"

"I'm fine. How are you?"

"I'm tight. Are you hungry?"

"Not really. I ate dinner already."

"Oh. I'm starving." Ian picked up one of the menus that sat on the table and began looking it over. After about a minute he set it aside.

"So, what are you getting?" Come on, Kylie urged herself, try.

"A smoked sausage and fries."

"That sounds good."

"If you want something, just let me know." Kylie noticed that he was looking around the restaurant as he made the offer. His disinterest irritated her, even as she told herself that she shouldn't let it.

"Well, I'll have a peach cobbler and a hot cocoa, then."

Ian looked at her and nodded. When the waitress came they placed their orders then settled back to listen to the music and look around.

"The music's good," Ian said.

"Yeah. Do you play any instruments?"

"The piano a little. I always wanted to play really well, but I've never had lessons."

"You should take a class at Cross."

"My schedule is always too full. Do you play an instrument?"

"Yeah, the thigh."

"What?" Ian leaned in closer to hear her better.

Kylie smiled. "The thigh." She slapped her thigh to the jazz band's beat. "You know."

"I like to play the thigh, too," he said, his eyes holding hers. They both laughed, Kylie's giggle a little nervous.

After that they relaxed some and talked. The time clipped away and the air between them became easy and pleasant, like the music and the food. The warmth and flavor of the room seeped inside of them and came out in their words and laughter.

Kylie felt good. This is how she had hoped things would go. She was glad that they'd ended up at the café, it was more intimate, grown-up, and romantic than the Coney Island restaurant and laser tag would have been. After a while she checked her watch and it was 8 P.M.

"You ready to get out of here? We could drive around for a little while before I take you back," Ian said as he paid the bill.

"Yeah, okay," Kylie said. They got back into their coats and pulled on their hats and gloves. Outside the temperature had dropped a few degrees and the clouds had been blown away to reveal a sky enchantingly dark and wide, pierced by the occasional sharp, bright star. Kylie paused outside the door and breathed deeply.

Ian looked up where Kylie looked, then looked at her. "Pretty," he said softly.

"Yes," Kylie said, gazing into his eyes by the light that shone from the café window. After the sweet rhythm of the evening she felt like kissing him under the lovely night sky.

"Let's get you out of the cold," Ian said. They hurried to the car and got in, greeted by the chill interior. Ian started up the car and they sat silently as it warmed up. "God, it's cold," he said. Kylie nodded. It wasn't long, though, before the car had warmed up some and Ian pulled out into traffic.

R&B music played as the air warmed around them and Ian cruised easily down the road, headed nowhere in particular. Kylie felt comfortable and languid. She didn't feel any pressure to talk, nothing like the nervous silence at the beginning of their date. She had carefully tucked away any concerns about why Ian might have invited her out. Right now she had what she wanted, the warm attentions of a boy she liked and an evening when she got to be a sixteen-year-old, hanging out and free of care.

After a while they were back in Detroit, and Ian pulled onto Belle Isle. The island was about six square miles, surrounded by the Detroit River and approached by a quarter-mile-long, beautiful white bridge. The island was composed of patches of woods, grass, ponds, picnic areas, and winding roads that made a pleasant place for families, couples, and friends to hang out. They watched the Canadian skyline across the Detroit River as they cruised around the island. Tonight the river was a dark ribbon, still along the edges where the water had frozen over, and laboriously in motion through the middle where the cold, cold water marked a slow path. On the interior of the path, trees crowded together for warmth and created dark smudges against the blue-black sky. It wasn't long before Ian had parked the car facing the water and the Canadian skyline.

The car hummed quietly beneath them as they bobbed their heads gently to the music.

"Are you going to be in the talent contest this year?"

Kylie asked Ian. The winter talent show was in six weeks.

"Yeah. One of my boys is going to play the keyboard while I sing lead and two of my boys sing backup." He sat facing forward, tapping the steering wheel with his fingertips as he spoke. "It should be tight. He can really play."

"Who's that?"

"Marcus Shipp. You know him?"

"No."

"Oh. Well, he's been playing the piano since he was five and he started playing the keyboard when he was around nine or something. He's bad."

"Sounds like he would be. A prodigy or something."

"Yeah, he is. Are you coming to the show?"

"Yes. I know some people who are gonna be in it."

"Like me," he said smiling at her.

"Yeah, like you now."

"Do you want to get out and look at the sky again?"

"Sure. That would be nice."

Outside the wind held itself still as Ian circled around his car and stood beside Kylie. They gazed at the sky and Kylie felt the solidity of the earth beneath her feet, and the chill against her cheek, comforting reminders that she was really there and that this night with Ian was real.

"I've had a really good time with you tonight," Ian said. "I'm glad we never made it to laser tag." He stood before her now, near and enticing. Kylie already knew that she would not satisfy her urge to kiss him. That would be too ridiculous. It would ruin everything to step out on such a limb and feel it crack and break beneath her feet. Better to stay here on the ground, where she was safe.

"Me, too," she answered softly. His eyes looked thoughtful and confused. And then he was drawing his face close to hers and her breath caught in her throat as she realized that he was going to kiss her. Her mouth went instantly and dramatically dry, and she was flooded by the fear that she was about to deliver a kiss as dry as the Sahara to a boy as fine as Ian. But before she completed that train of thought his lips were against hers. To her surprise, they were warm and tender. Somehow, fleetingly, she had thought that his lips would be cold from the night air. She heard the gentle *whoosh* of the sleeves of his coat as he moved his hands from his pockets to her arms. She felt his mouth open over hers, unhurried and sure, and without thinking she was French-kissing him back. She felt the gentle languidness inside of her give way to a thrilling hum and she thought, Ian is the sweetest kisser I have ever known.

When they pulled apart it took her awhile to feel the earth beneath her feet and the chill air upon her cheek. At first she could only feel the pull of the earth spinning. And it was several moments longer before she realized that it was not the world's spinning that she felt, but the spinning of a new world inside of her.

She was even less prepared for his second kiss. But it came, as sweet, and then sweeter than the first.

As they drove toward her home Kylie thought that as much as she had enjoyed the night so far, she had wondered where they could meet together comfortably, with something in common. She was neither a performer like him, nor was she popular. He knew nothing about taking care of younger siblings, preparing meals, or being a part-time "mother." They had no friends in common; they didn't hang out at the same places.

It was here, she realized. Here in these kisses they were perfectly matched. The other things, she thought, would come.

Less than fifteen minutes after kissing her Ian pulled out of Kylie's parking lot and into the little traffic that moved down her street toward the freeway. He tried to empty his mind, but instead, Kylie remained in his thoughts. When he'd picked her up he'd felt stiff and kind of uncomfortable. He'd been in her home, meeting her mother, sister, and brother, and he was basically planning to play her to the left. As he was at other times with other girls, he was polite, but his motives were all messed up. The thought of it irritated him so much that he had barely been able to open his mouth during the ride to Sheldon.

Then there was that whole Sheldon thing, he thought with a grimace. He had driven all the way out there because he didn't want anyone to see him with Kylie. She wasn't cute or cool enough for him to go out with. It wasn't fair, and it might not be right, in some people's eyes. And while he could admit this to himself, still there it was, a fact of life.

But, he'd liked her! Ian thought in frustration. She was easy to talk to, and she could be funny. And that kiss . . .

He had kissed her because it was part of the plan. He couldn't very well get her to sleep with him in just a few weeks without getting her to think that he liked her. So, he knew he had to kiss her tonight. At the café as they'd talked and laughed together, he had begun to warm up to her. At that point he still wasn't all that attracted to her. But the way that she'd looked at him before he kissed her made him pause. He could see right there in her face that she liked him, and that did something to him. And the way that she had kissed him back . . . he had to stop to relish the thought. The kiss was so good, it was like she was handing him something precious. "Damn," he whispered aloud. The second kiss he gave without even thinking. He had *wanted* to kiss her.

"Just do this and be done with it," he mumbled. He would never have Kylie for a girlfriend. Never. She would never fit in with FBI, and he would never give up FBI for a girl.